Fiction Priz...
2007, and ...ernationa...
the prest...ous Italian Viareggi...
been tra...lated into thirty-five languages.

'Ammaniti sets a new standard in post-apocalyptic fiction . . . This story of children running wild in Sicily brilliantly manipulates the usual models even as it transcends their limits . . . In the midst of wonderfully detailed disorder, one girl named Anna struggles to survive, fighting off feral dogs and crazed children and enduring one of recent literature's most nightmarish visions of hell on earth'
Guardian

'One of Italy's foremost literary talents . . . *Anna* combines the wayword fantasy of J.G. Ballard with comic-strip adventure"
Times Literary Supplement

'Brave and uncompromising . . . A brutal but moving post-apocalyptic tale set in a world where adults have all been wiped out . . . written with such heart and compassion for the plight of the characters that you can't help but get sucked in and root for them'
Big Issue

'Ammaniti won the Italian Strega Prize for *I'm Not Scared*, and *Anna* has the same taut narrative, with straight-from-the-bow suspense, but its mark is philosophical . . . concerned not only with the will to live but also what makes us alive'
Irish Times

'*Anna* has pretty much everything you could hope for from a post-apocalyptic picaresque adventure story'
London Review of Books

'Ammaniti has an enviable ability to keep readers thoroughly absorbed'
The Herald

ANNA

NICCOLÒ AMMANITI

CANONGATE

This paperback edition published in 2018 by Canongate Books

Published in Great Britain in 2017 by Canongate Books Ltd,
14 High Street, Edinburgh EH1 1TE

canongate.co.uk

1

Copyright © Niccolò Ammaniti, 2015
English translation © Jonathan Hunt, 2017

The moral right of the author has been asserted

First published in Italy by Giulio Einaudi editore

British Library Cataloguing-in-Publication Data
A catalogue record for this book is available on
request from the British Library

ISBN 978 1 78211 836 7

Typeset in Bembo by Palimpsest Book Production Ltd,
Falkirk, Stirlingshire

Printed and bound in Great Britain by Clays Ltd, St Ives plc.

MIX
Paper from
responsible sources
FSC® C018072

He was three, maybe four years old. He sat quietly on a small synthetic leather armchair, chin bent over his green T-shirt, jeans turned up over his trainers. In one hand he held a wooden train which hung down between his legs like a rosary.

On the other side of the room the woman lying on the bed might have been anywhere between thirty and forty. Her arm, covered with red blotches and dark scabs, was attached to an empty drip. The virus had reduced her to a panting skeleton covered with lumpy dry skin, but it hadn't succeeded in robbing her of all her beauty, which showed in the form of her cheekbones and her turned-up nose.

The little boy raised his head and looked at her, grasped one arm of the chair, climbed down and walked over to the bed with the train in his hand.

She didn't notice him. Her eyes, sunken in two dark wells, stared at the ceiling.

He toyed with a button on the dirty pillow. His fair hair covered his forehead; in the sunlight that filtered through the white curtains it looked like nylon thread.

Suddenly the woman rose up on her elbows, arching her back as if her soul was being torn from her body, clutched the sheets in her fists and then fell back, coughing convulsively. She tried to swallow air, stretching her arms and legs. Then her face relaxed, her lips parted and she died with her eyes open.

Gently the little boy took hold of her hand and tugged at her forefinger. He whispered: 'Mama? Mama?' He put the train on her chest and ran it over the folds in the sheet. He touched the blood-caked plaster which hid the needle of the drip. Finally he went out of the room.

The corridor was dimly lit. The *beep beep* of a medical device came from somewhere or other.

He passed the corpse of a fat man crumpled up on the floor beside a wheeled stretcher. Forehead against the floor, one leg bent in an unnatural position. The light blue edges of his smock had pulled apart, revealing a greyish-purple back.

The little boy staggered on uncertainly, as if he couldn't control his legs. On another stretcher, near a poster about breast cancer screening, and a photograph of Liège featuring St Paul's Cathedral, lay the body of an old woman.

He walked under a crackling neon light. A boy in a night-gown and foam-rubber slippers had died in the doorway of a long ward, one arm forward, the fingers contracted into a claw, as if he were trying to stop himself being sucked down into a whirlpool.

At the end of the corridor the darkness struggled with gleams of sunlight that entered through the doors at the hospital entrance.

The little boy stopped. To his left were the stairs, the lifts and reception. Behind the steel counter were PC monitors overturned on desks and a glass screen shattered into thousands of little cubes.

He dropped the train and ran towards the exit. He closed his eyes, stretched out his arms and pushed the big doors, disappearing into the light.

Outside, beyond the steps, beyond the red and white plastic ribbons, were the outlines of police cars, ambulances, fire engines.

Somebody shouted: 'A kid. There's a kid . . .'

The little boy covered his face with his hands. An ungainly figure ran towards him, blotting out the sun.

The little boy just had time to see that the man was encased in a thick yellow plastic suit. Then he was snatched up and carried away.

Four years later . . .

Part One

Mulberry Farm

1

Anna ran along the autostrada, holding the straps of the rucksack that was bouncing on her back. Now and then she turned her head to look back.

The dogs were still there. One behind the other, in single file. Six or seven of them. A couple, in worse shape than the others, had dropped out, but the big black one in front was getting closer.

She'd spotted them two hours before at the bottom of a burnt field, appearing and disappearing among dark rocks and blackened trunks of olive trees, but hadn't thought anything of them.

This wasn't the first time she'd been followed by a pack of wild dogs. They usually kept up the chase for a while, then tired and wandered off.

She liked to count as she walked. How many steps it took to cover a kilometre, the number of blue cars and red cars, the number of flyovers.

Then the dogs had reappeared.

Desperate creatures, adrift in a sea of ash. She'd come across dozens like them, with mangy coats, clumps of ticks hanging from their ears, protruding ribs. They'd fight savagely over the remains of a rabbit. The summer fires had burnt the lowlands and there was virtually nothing left to eat.

She passed a queue of cars with smashed windows. Weeds and wheat grew around their ash-covered carcasses.

The sirocco had driven the flames right down to the sea,

leaving a desert behind it. The asphalt strip of the A29, which linked Palermo to Mazara del Vallo, cut across a dead expanse out of which rose blackened stumps of palm trees and a few plumes of smoke. To the left, beyond what was left of Castellammare del Golfo, a segment of grey sea merged with the sky. To the right, a line of low dark hills floated on the plain like distant islands.

The road was blocked by an overturned lorry. Its trailer had smashed into the central reservation, scattering basins, bidets, toilet bowls and shards of white ceramic over dozens of metres. She ran straight through the debris.

Her right ankle was hurting. In Alcamo she'd kicked open the door of a grocery shop.

★

To think that, until the dogs' appearance, everything had been going fine.

She'd left home when it was still dark. From time to time she was forced to go further afield in search of food. Previously it had been easy: you only had to go to Castellammare and you found what you wanted. But the fires had complicated everything. She'd been walking for three hours under the sun as it rose in a pale cloudless sky. The summer was long past, but the heat wouldn't let up. The wind, after starting the fire, had vanished, as if this part of creation no longer held any interest for it.

In a garden centre, next to a crater left by the explosion of a petrol pump, she'd found a crate full of food under some dusty tarpaulins.

In her rucksack she had six cans of Cirio beans, four cans of Graziella tomatoes, a bottle of Amaro Lucano, a large tube of Nestlé condensed milk, a bag of rusks, which were broken, but would still make a good meal soaked in water, and a half-kilo vacuum pack of pancetta. She hadn't been able to resist that; she'd eaten the pancetta immediately, in silence, sitting on some bags of compost heaped up on the floor, which was covered with mouse droppings. It was as tough as leather, and so salty it had burnt her mouth.

★

The black dog was gaining ground.

Anna speeded up, her heart pumping in time with her steps. She couldn't keep this up much longer. She was going to have to stop and face her pursuers. Oh for a knife. As a rule she always carried one with her, but she'd forgotten to pack one that morning, and had gone out with an empty rucksack and a bottle of water.

The sun was only four inches above the horizon – an orange ball trapped in purple drool. Soon to be swallowed up by the plain. On the other side, the moon, as thin as a fingernail.

She looked back.

He was still there. The other dogs had gradually dropped away. Not him. He hadn't closed on her over the last kilometre. But she was running flat out; he was just loping along.

Waiting for darkness before he attacked? Surely not. Dogs didn't plan so rationally, did they? Whatever: she wouldn't be able to keep this up until nightfall. The pain in her ankle had now increased and spread to her calf.

She passed a green sign. Five kilometres to Castellammare. The white line between the lanes provided a sure guide to concentrate on. The only sounds were her breathing and her feet hitting the asphalt. No wind, no birdsong, no chirping of crickets or cicadas.

Passing another car, she was tempted to get in and rest, but thought better of it. What about dropping the rusks on the road for the dog to eat? Or climbing over the fence at the side of the road? No, the mesh was too tight, and there didn't seem to be any breaks in it she could slip through.

Or the central reservation on the other side? Here some oleanders had survived the fire. Their branches hung down, heavy with pink flowers, their pungent scent mingling with the smell of burnt wood.

The partition was high.

But you're the kangaroo.

That was the nickname Signorina Pini, her old gym teacher, had given her, because she could jump higher than the boys. Anna didn't like it; kangaroos have long floppy ears. She'd have preferred to be associated with the leopard, a far more elegant jumper.

Hurling the rucksack over the bushes, she took a short run-up, used the concrete kerb as a springboard and jumped through the branches onto the other side.

She retrieved the rucksack and counted up to ten, panting. Then she punched the air, flashing her teeth in a full smile, a rare event for her.

She limped on. If only she could find some way of getting over the fence on this side of the road, she'd be safe.

Beyond the fence was a steep slope down to a narrow road which ran parallel to the autostrada. Not the best place to climb over with a swollen ankle. She slipped off the rucksack and looked back.

She saw the dog leap through the oleanders and come galloping down the road.

He wasn't black at all; he was white, his coat covered with ash. The tip of one of his ears was missing. And he was huge: the biggest dog she'd ever seen.

And if you don't get moving he's going to eat you.

She grabbed the mesh of the fence to climb up, but was paralysed by fear. She turned round and slid down onto the road.

The dog raced down the last few metres of the autostrada

and jumped over the guardrail and ditch. Then he jumped on her — all forty stinking kilos of him.

Anna stuck out her elbow, aiming at the dog's ribs. He collapsed in a heap. She stood up.

He lay there, an almost human astonishment in his eyes.

She picked up the rucksack and hit him on the head, on the neck, then on the head again. He yelped, struggling to get to his feet. Anna swung round full circle like a hammer-thrower, but the strap of the rucksack broke, she lost her balance and put out her foot to steady herself, but her sore ankle couldn't take the weight and she fell to the ground.

They lay there for a moment, looking at each other, then the dog sprang at her, snarling.

Raising her good foot, Anna rammed it into his chest, throwing him back against the guardrail.

He fell down on his side, panting, his long tongue curled under his nose, his eyes narrowed.

As he tried to get up, she looked around for a stone or a stick to hit him with, but saw nothing but burnt paper, plastic bags and crushed cans.

★

'Why don't you leave me alone?' she shouted, getting to her feet. 'What have I done to you?'

The dog stared at her, baring his teeth and growling.

She stumbled away in a daze, vaguely aware of oleanders, a dark sky and the blackened roofless shell of a farmhouse. After a while she stopped and looked back.

He was following her.

She came to a blue estate car. Its front was crushed, the rear window had lost its glass and the driver's door was open. She slipped inside and tried to close the door, but it wouldn't move. She pulled with both hands. The door creaked shut, but bounced back off the rusty lock. She pulled again, but it still wouldn't close, so she wrapped the safety belt around the handle to hold it. Laying her head against the steering wheel, she sat there with her eyes closed, breathing in the smell of bird droppings.

On the passenger's seat beside her was a skeleton covered in white guano. The shrivelled remains of a Moncler quilted jacket had fused with the covering of the seat. Feathers and yellow ribs showed through splits in the fabric. The skull hung down on the chest, held up by withered tendons. A pair of high-heeled suede boots covered the feet.

Anna slipped through onto the back seat, climbed into the boot and crawled up to the rear window, hardly daring to look out. There was no sign of the dog.

She curled up beside two suitcases that had been stripped of their contents, crossing her arms over her chest, with her hands under her sweaty armpits. The adrenaline rush had passed and she could barely keep her eyes open. She tried to jam the suitcases into the window frame. One was too small, but she managed to wedge the other one into the gap by pushing it with her feet.

She ran her fingers over her lips. Her eyes fell on a dirty page torn out of a notebook. The first line read, in capital letters: HELP ME, FOR THE LOVE OF GOD!

Written by the woman on the front seat, no doubt.

The note said her name was Giovanna Improta and she was dying. She had two children, Ettore and Francesca. They lived on the top floor of Via Re Federico 36, in Palermo. They were only four and five years old and they'd starve to death if they didn't get help. There were 500 euros in the hall cupboard.

Anna tossed the piece of paper aside, leaned her head against the side window and closed her eyes.

★

She woke up abruptly, surrounded by darkness and silence. It was a few seconds before she could remember where she was. She badly needed a pee, but didn't dare leave the car. She'd be defenceless – and blind: there was no moon.

Better to do it in the boot and move over onto the back seat. She unbuttoned her shorts. As she pulled them down, a sudden noise took her breath away. The sound of dogs sniffing. She put her hand over her mouth, trying not to breathe, shake, or even move her tongue.

Dogs' claws scratched on the bodywork, and the car lurched.

Her bladder relaxed and warm liquid slid between her thighs, soaking the carpet under her buttocks.

She started silently praying for help, to no one in particular.

The dogs were fighting among themselves, circling the car, their claws clicking on the asphalt.

She imagined thousands of them surrounding the car, a carpet of fur stretching as far as the sea and the mountains, enveloping the whole planet.

She clamped her hands over her ears. *Think about gelato.* Like big, sweet, multicoloured hailstones. You used to choose the flavours you wanted and they'd scoop them out into a cone for you. She remembered one visit to the ice-cream stall in the private beach area, 'The Mermaids'. Peering through the glass top of the refrigerator, she'd decided on 'chocolate and lemon'.

Her mother had grimaced. 'Ugh!'

'What's the matter?'

'Those flavours don't go together.'

'Can I have them anyway?'

'Oh, all right, then. You'd better eat them, though!'

So she'd gone to the beach with her gelato and sat by the water's edge, while the seagulls strutted along, one behind the other.

Until the fire came, it had still been possible to find other

sweet things. Mars bars, flapjacks, Bountys, boxes of chocolates. Usually dry, mouldy or nibbled by mice, though
sometimes, if you were lucky, you'd find them in good
condition. But it wasn't the same as ice cream. Cold things
had disappeared with the Grown-ups.

She took her hands away from her ears. The dogs had
gone.

★

It was that phase of dawn when night and day have equal
weight and things seem larger than they really are. A milk-
white band lay across the horizon. The wind rustled between
ears of wheat spared by the fire.

Anna climbed out of the car and stretched. Her ankle was
numb, but less painful after the rest.

The road unreeled in front of her like a strip of liquorice.
The asphalt around the car was spattered with pawprints.
Fifty metres away, something lay on the white line between
the lanes.

At first it looked like her rucksack, then a tyre, then a
heap of rags. Then the rags rose up and turned into a dog.

★

THE DOG WITH THREE NAMES

He'd been born in a scrapyard on the outskirts of Trapani,
under an old Alfa Romeo. His mother, a Maremma sheepdog
called Lisa, had suckled him and his five siblings for a couple
of months. In the desperate fight for her nipples, the frailest
one hadn't survived. The others, as soon as they were weaned,
had been sold for a few euros, and only he, the greediest
and most intelligent, had been allowed to stay.

Daniele Oddo, the scrap-dealer, was a parsimonious man.

· 16 ·

And since the 13th October was his wife's birthday, he had an idea: why not give her the puppy, with a nice red ribbon round its neck?

Signora Rosita, who had been expecting the latest Ariston tumble dryer, wasn't too enthusiastic about this bundle of white fluff. He was a holy terror, who crapped and peed on the carpets and gnawed the feet of the sideboard in the sitting room.

Without making a great effort, she found him a name: Dopey.

But there was someone else in the house who was even more put out by the new arrival. Colonel, an old, bad-tempered, snappy wire-haired dachshund, whose natural habitats were the bed, onto which he would climb thanks to a stairway made specially for him, and a Louis Vuitton handbag, where he'd sit and snarl at any other four-legged creature.

Colonel may have had his virtues, but they didn't include mercy. He'd bite the puppy whenever it strayed from the corner to which he had banished it.

Signora Rosita decided to shut Dopey out on the kitchen balcony. But he was a determined little guy; he whimpered and scratched at the door, and the neighbours started complaining. His precarious status as a household pet ended the day he succeeded in slipping inside and, pursued by his mistress, skidded on the polished parquet floor and got tangled up in the wire of a lamp, which crashed down on top of the row of china pandas arrayed on the cocktail cabinet.

Dopey was sent straight back to the scrapyard and, still with his milk teeth and a zest for playing, had a chain put round his neck. Lisa, his mother, on the other side of the yard, beyond two walls of junk, would bark at any car that came in through the gate.

The puppy's diet changed from canned venison nuggets to Chinese cuisine. Spring rolls, bamboo chicken and sweet and sour pork, the leftovers from the China Garden, a foul-smelling restaurant on the other side of the road.

Christian, Signor Oddo's son, worked in the scrapyard. Or maybe 'worked' isn't exactly the right word for it: he sat in front of a computer watching pornographic videos in a container that had been turned into an office. He was a slim, nervy boy, with bushy hair and a pointed chin which he highlighted by wearing a goatee beard. He also had a second job – selling expired pills outside the local high schools. His dream, however, was to become a rapper. He loved the way rappers dressed, the gestures they made, the women they had and the killer dogs they owned. Though it wasn't easy to rap with a lisp.

Observing Dopey through sunglasses as big as TV screens, he felt that the puppy, which was growing into a quick, strong dog, had potential.

One evening, sitting in his car outside a shopping mall, he told Samuel, his best friend, that he was going to turn Dopey into 'a ferocious killing machine'.

'That name, though, Dopey . . .' Samuel, who was training to be a fashion designer, didn't think it suited a killing machine.

'What should I call him, then?'

'I don't know . . . How about Bob?' ventured his friend.

'Bob? What kind of a name is that? Manson is more like it.'

'You mean as in Marilyn?'

'No, you fool! Charles Manson. The greatest murderer of all time!'

Christian dreamed of some illegal immigrant or gypsy breaking into the scrapyard at night to steal something and being confronted by Manson. 'Just imagine some poor guy trying to get away by climbing over the fence with his guts hanging out and Manson snapping at his arse,' he guffawed, slapping Samuel on the back.

To make Manson more aggressive, Christian studied websites about fighting dogs. He bought a Taser and, using it and a broomstick wrapped in foam rubber, started a training course of electric shocks and beatings designed to turn the dog into a killing machine. In the winter he doused him with buckets of icy water to harden him against the weather.

Before a year had passed, Manson was so aggressive the only way of feeding him was to throw him food from a distance and fire a jet of water into his bowl from a hose. They couldn't even let him off the leash at night for fear of losing a hand.

Like thousands of other dogs, Manson seemed destined to spend his whole life chained up.

The virus changed everything.

The epidemic wiped out the Oddo family in the space of a few months, and the dog was left alone on his chain. He survived by drinking the rainwater that collected in the metal remains of cars and by licking up dry scraps of food from the ground. Now and then someone would pass by in the street, but nobody stopped to feed him and he'd howl in despair, his nose to the sky. His mother answered his calls for a while, then she fell silent, and Manson, exhausted by hunger, lost his voice too. He could smell the stench of the corpses in the common graves of Trapani.

Eventually instinct told him his owners weren't going to bring him any more food and he was going to die there.

The chain round his neck, about ten metres long, ended at a stake fixed in the ground. He started pulling, using his back legs for leverage and his front legs for support. His collar, now that he'd lost weight, was loose, and in the end he managed to wriggle out of it.

He was weak, covered in sores, riddled with fleas and unsteady on his feet. He passed his mother's body, gave her a perfunctory sniff and staggered out of the gate.

He knew nothing of the world and didn't stop to wonder why some human beings had become food while other, smaller ones were still alive, but whenever the live ones crossed his path he ran away.

It didn't take him long to get back into shape. He fed on street litter, entered houses to devour whatever he found there, and chased off crows feasting on corpses. During his wanderings, he met up with a pack of strays and joined them.

The first time he started eating a dead sheep, the others snarled at him. He learned by experience that there was a hierarchy in the group – that he must keep away from females on heat and wait his turn before eating.

One day, on a piece of waste land behind a warehouse full of tyres, a hare crossed his path.

The hare is a difficult animal to catch; it's quick and its sudden changes of direction can disorientate the pursuer. It has only one weakness: it soon gets tired. Manson's body, by contrast, was a mass of hardened muscles. After a long chase he caught it, shook it to break its backbone, and started devouring it.

A shambling hound slightly higher in rank in the pack than him, with pendulous ears and a mushroom-like nose, appeared in front of him. Manson retreated with his tail between his legs, but, as soon as the other started to eat, Manson jumped on him and ripped off one of his ears. Surprised and terrified, the other dog turned round, dripping with blood, and sank his teeth into the Maremma's thick coat. Manson backed away, then jumped forward and with one twist of his neck tore out the other dog's jugular, windpipe and oesophagus, leaving him writhing in a pool of blood.

Fights among dogs and wolves are seldom lethal; they serve to clarify the hierarchy, to distinguish the lower ranks from the leaders. But Manson wasn't in the habit of playing by the rules; he didn't stop till his adversary was dead. Christian Oddo's intuition had been right. Manson was a killing machine, and all the pain and torture he'd undergone had made him indifferent to wounds and merciless in victory.

Blood excited him, gave him energy, won him the respect of other dogs and the favour of bitches on heat. He liked this world: there were no chains, no cruel humans, and all you had to do to gain others' respect was use your fangs. In a few weeks, without even having to fight the chief, who rolled over on the ground with his legs apart, he became the alpha male, the one who had first choice of the food and impregnated the females.

Three years later, when the explosion of a natural gas tank surprised the pack as they surrounded a horse in the car park of the Sunflowers shopping mall, he still hadn't lost his rank. What a horse was doing in the car park was a mystery of interest to none of them. Emaciated and covered in sores, it had got one of its legs stuck in a shopping trolley and was standing there in a cloud of flies, near the cashpoints, its big brown head hanging between its legs. The horse was in that state of dumb resignation that can sometimes come over herbivores when they realise that death has caught up with them and that all they can do is wait. The dogs were closing in slowly, almost casually, certain that they were soon going to eat some fresh meat.

Manson, as leader of the pack, was the first to attack the horse, which barely even kicked out when it felt his teeth sink into its hind leg. But a wall of fire, fanned by the wind, suddenly enveloped the scene in a blanket of acrid, scorching smoke. Surrounded by flames and terrified by exploding petrol pumps, the dogs sheltered behind a household appliance store. They stayed there for several days, nearly asphyxiated, under a vault of fire, and when everything had been burnt and they came out, the world was an expanse of ash devoid of food and water.

★

Anna pulled back her hair.

The Maremma crept forward and stopped, ear cocked, eyes fixed on his prey.

She looked at the fence. It was too high. And there was no sense in going back to the car: he'd tear her to pieces in there.

She opened her arms: 'Come on then! What are you waiting for?'

The dog seemed uncertain.

'Come on!' She sprang up and down on her toes. 'Let's get it over with.'

The dog flattened down on the asphalt. A crow passed overhead, cawing.

'What's the matter? Are you scared?'

The dog sprang forward.

She sprinted towards the car and reached it so fast she hit her hip against the side. Groaning, she slipped in through the door and shut it behind her.

There was a thud, and the car swayed.

Anna grabbed the seat belt, wound it round the door handle and tied it to the spokes of the steering wheel. Through the misty glass of the side window she saw the dark shape of the dog jump up.

She climbed into the back and crouched down in the boot, but almost at once the suitcase she'd jammed in the rear window came crashing down on top of her, followed by the enormous dog. She fended him off, using the case as a shield, and searched for some kind of weapon. There was an umbrella under the seat. She grabbed it with both hands and held it out like a spear.

The dog jumped into the back seat, snarling.

She jabbed the tip of the umbrella into his neck, and blood spattered her face.

The dog yelped, but didn't retreat. He advanced along the seat, rubbing his filthy back against the ceiling.

'I'm stronger than you!' She stabbed him in the side. When she tried to pull the umbrella out, the handle came off in her hand.

The dog lunged at her, the umbrella sticking out of his ribs. His teeth snapped shut a few centimetres from her nose. She smelled his warm putrid breath. Pushing him away with her elbows, she climbed over onto the front seat, falling among the woman's bones.

The dog didn't follow. His coat plastered with blood and ash, his mouth dripping with red foam, he looked at her, turning his head as if trying to understand her, then swayed and collapsed.

★

Anna was singing a jingle she'd made up: 'Here comes Nello, funny-looking fellow; his trainers are pink and his whiskers yellow.'

Nello was a friend of her father's; he drove over from Palermo now and then in a white van to bring her mother the books she needed. Though Anna had only seen him a few times, she remembered him well; he was a nice guy. She often thought about those whiskers.

The sun had risen among streaky white clouds, shedding welcome warmth on her skin.

She shifted the rucksack on her back. The dogs had torn at it, but hadn't succeeded in getting it open. The bottle of Amaro Lucano hadn't been broken.

Before leaving, she'd taken one last look at the big dog from the door. He was still breathing hoarsely, his dirty coat rising and falling. She'd wondered whether she should put him out of his misery, but didn't dare go any nearer. Better to leave him to die.

She started down a road which ran alongside the A29 for a while before curving away towards the sea through a retail park. All that was left of the discount store where they used to buy food were the vertical supports and the iron frame of the roof. The Furniture House, where they'd bought the sofa and bunk bed, paying by instalments, had been burnt down. The white stone steps at the front were now covered with a thick layer of ash. The handsome flowerpots decorated with Moors' heads had gone. Inside there were only the skeletons of a few sofas and a piano.

Anna crossed the forecourt of a Ford salesroom lined with neat rows of burnt-out cars and walked out onto the fields. All that remained of the vineyards were some vine supports, stumps of olive trees and dry stone walls. A combine harvester near the ruins of a farmhouse looked like an insect, but with a full set of teeth. A plough seemed to be rooting in the earth like an anteater. Here and there shoots of fig trees appeared among black clods of soil, and light green buds could be seen on charred trunks.

*

The low modern structure of the De Roberto Elementary School floated on a black sea among waves of heat which seemed to bend the horizon. The basketball court behind the building was overgrown with grass. Fire had melted the backboards behind the hoops. The windows had lost their glass; inside, the desks, chairs and lino were covered with earth. A drawing of a giraffe and a lion by Daniela Sperno still hung on the wall of Anna's classroom, 3C. The teacher's desk was on the dais by the whiteboard. Some time ago Anna had opened the drawer and found the register, the little mirror with which Signorina Rigoni used to check the hairs on her chin, and her lipstick. Anna usually went in and sat at her old desk for a while. But this time she walked on by.

*

The ruins of the residential village Torre Normanna appeared in the distance. Two long straight roads like landing strips, lined with small terraced houses, formed a cross in the middle of the lowland area behind Castellammare.

There was a sports club with two tennis courts and a swimming pool, plus a restaurant and a small supermarket. Most of her schoolmates had lived in this village.

Now, after the looting and the fires, the pretty little Mediterranean-style houses were reduced to shells of concrete columns, heaps of roof tiles, rubble and rusty gates. In those that had escaped the fire, doors had been ripped off hinges, windows smashed, walls covered with graffiti. The roads were littered with glass from smashed car windows. The asphalt of Piazzetta dei Venti had melted and thickened, forming humps and bubbles, but the swings and slide of the children's playground, and the big sign of the restaurant, 'A Taste of Aphrodite', featuring a purple lobster, were intact.

She walked quickly through the village. She didn't like the place. Her mother had always said it was inhabited by nouveau-riche bastards who polluted the soil with their illegal sewers. She'd written to a newspaper to complain about it. Now the nouveau-riche bastards were no longer there, but their ghosts peered out at her from the windows, whispering: 'Look! Look! It's the daughter of that woman who called us nouveau-riche bastards.'

Outside the village she took a road which followed the bed of a dried-up stream at the foot of some round, bare hills that looked like pin-cushions, pierced as they were by vineyard props. Reeds grew thickly on both sides of the road, their plumes rising up against the blue sky.

A hundred metres further on, she entered the cool shade of an oak wood. Anna thought this wood must be magical; the fire hadn't succeeded in burning it, but had merely licked at its edges before giving up. Between the thick trunks the sun painted golden patches on the covering of ivy and on the dog roses that swamped a rickety fence. A gate opened onto a path overgrown by long-untrimmed box hedges.

Just visible on a concrete post was a sign: 'Mulberry Farm'.

2

Anna Salemi had been born in Palermo on 12 March 2007, the daughter of Maria Grazia Zanchetta and Franco Salemi.

The couple had met in the summer of 2005. He was twenty-one and worked as a driver for Elite Cars, his father's private taxi firm. She was twenty-three and studying Italian literature at the University of Palermo.

They noticed each other on the ferry to the Aeolian Islands, exchanging glances among the crowd of tourists crammed on the deck. They disembarked on Lipari, with their separate groups.

The next day they met again on Papisca beach.

Maria Grazia's friends rolled joints, read books and discussed politics.

Franco's friends, all male, played football, challenged each other to games of beach tennis and showed off the muscles they'd built up in the gym during the winter.

Franco's approach was pretty clumsy. He kept pretending to miskick the ball, moving it closer and closer to the beautiful girl sunbathing naked.

Finally Maria Grazia said: 'Stop kicking that ball around me. You want to talk to me? Come over here and introduce yourself, then.'

He asked her out for a pizza. She got drunk and pushed him into the pizzeria toilets, where they made love.

'I know we're very different. But it's through their differences that people complete each other,' Maria Grazia confessed to a friend who was amazed she liked such a vulgar lout.

Back in Palermo they continued to see each other and the next year she got pregnant.

Franco was still living with his parents. Maria Grazia shared a room in a student flat and had an evening job at a wine bar in Piazza Sant'Oliva.

The Zanchetta family lived in Bassano del Grappa, in northern Italy. Her father had a small business that manufactured hi-fi equipment and her mother taught in a primary school. Their daughter loved warm weather, the seaside, Sicily and the character of its inhabitants. After finishing school she decided to move to the island, against her parents' wishes.

Maria Grazia didn't even consider abortion. She explained to Franco that he was free to choose: either he could recognise the child, or she'd become a single mother, and that would be fine with her.

Franco asked her to marry him, feeling that it was his duty.

Six months later the wedding took place in the village hall of Castellammare, the Salemi family's place of origin. The Zanchettas thought their daughter deserved better than this southern taxi driver and didn't attend the ceremony.

There was no honeymoon. The couple moved to the centre of Palermo, where they lived in a flat on the third floor of an old palazzo near the Politeama Theatre.

Signor Salemi discovered that he had heart problems and retired, leaving the running of Elite Cars to his son.

Two months later, in an inflatable birthing pool full of warm water, Anna was born, dark-skinned like her father, with her mother's features.

'I brought Anna into the world by accepting pain. Because women can give birth in the peace of their own homes.' So Maria Grazia would say to anyone who asked her about her unusual choice.

The Salemi family couldn't stand their daughter-in-law. They called her 'the madwoman'. What other word was there for a woman who gave birth like a monkey and smoked pot?

Over the next two years Maria Grazia, as well as looking after the baby, graduated and got a temporary job teaching Italian and Latin at a high school. Franco, meanwhile, had expanded Elite Cars, buying more taxis and hiring new drivers.

They didn't see much of each other. He would come home exhausted in the evening, bringing boxes of food from the takeaway, and collapse on the bed. She taught during the day, and in the evening, in her book-filled study, cuddled the baby and read about psychology, the environment and women's liberation. And she started writing stories, which she hoped to publish.

Sometimes they quarrelled, but on the whole they respected each other's interests, even if they didn't understand them.

And gradually the same differences that had brought them together became a source of division which drove them further and further apart. Without ever saying as much, they allowed the gap to widen, in the awareness that neither of them would be able to close it.

When Franco's old grandmother died, she left him a cottage in the countryside near Castellammare. He wanted to sell it, but Maria Grazia was tired of living in the city, with all the pollution and noise. Anna would have a healthier upbringing in the countryside. Franco, however, couldn't move; his work was in Palermo.

'What's the problem? You can come over at weekends, and I promise you I'll learn to cook better than your mother,' she said.

They took out a bank loan and renovated the cottage, putting in double glazing, a new central heating system and an attractive new roof. Maria Grazia sowed a large organic vegetable garden, declaring that her daughter needed to eat vegetables free of any chemical pollutants. She started teaching at a high school in Castellamare.

After a year of shuttling back and forth between the city and the country, Franco fell in love with the woman who owned the tobacconist's shop opposite Elite Cars' garage. One evening, finding courage in wine, he confessed everything to his wife.

Maria Grazia gave him a big hug. 'I'm happy for you. The important thing is that you continue to be a good father and come to see your daughter every weekend as you've always done in the past.'

From that moment on, their relationship bloomed like the zucchini in the vegetable garden. She persuaded him to read *Women Who Run With the Wolves* and he took her to see an air display by the Italian Air Force aerobatic team in Marsala.

After an isolated drunken fit of passion, Maria Grazia became pregnant again. A baby boy was born. They called him Astor, after the great Argentinian tango musician, Astor Piazzolla. Franco continued to go back and forth from Palermo and to see the tobacconist.

Who knows? Maybe with time they'd have got back together. But the virus arrived from Belgium, and this family, like millions of others, was swept away.

When Franco and Maria Grazia died, Anna was nine years old and Astor was five.

*

The roof of the farmhouse was covered with dry leaves and branches. The porch, supported by white pillars, concealed the front door. On the upper floor two windows with faded shutters each opened onto a small balcony. In the middle of the façade, in a whitewashed niche, was a small statue of the

Madonna overgrown by a caper bush. The pink plaster had flaked away and what little remained of the gutter had leaked onto the walls, streaking them with green. The Virginia creeper, in only four years, had taken over one side of the house, and the big gnarled mulberry tree had spread its branches over the roof as if to protect it.

Anna opened the gate, closed it behind her and went down the path, which ended in a clearing of bare earth. To the left was the former vegetable garden, now a field of nettles. On the other side a long wooden bench stood among weeds in front of the wreck of an old black Mercedes and a row of rusty barrels where Anna collected rainwater. A dirty, naked little boy was crouching beside the car, hacking at the hard earth with a rake. Tufts of black hair emerged from under the cycling helmet on his head.

As soon as she saw her brother, the weight lifted from her heart. 'Astor!'

The little boy turned round and smiled, displaying a row of irregular teeth, then went on digging.

Anna sat down beside him, exhausted.

He stared at her torn knees and scratched legs. 'Did a smoke monster do that?'

'Yes.'

'What was he like?'

'Nasty.'

'Did you beat him?'

'Yes.'

Astor spread his arms. 'Was he big?'

'As big as a mountain.'

He pointed at the hole he'd dug. 'It's a trap. To catch rhinoceroses and rats.'

'That's great. Are you hungry?'

Her brother stretched his back. He was thin, with long legs and a prominent belly. The nipples on his flat chest looked like lentils and his pointed face was dominated by huge blue eyes which homed in on things as quickly as bees on nectar. 'Not very.' He took hold of his penis and pulled it like an elastic band.

His sister gave him a shove. 'Stop that!'

'What?'

'You know.'

Astor was obsessed with his penis. Once he'd covered it with sticky tape, and it had been a terrible business getting it off.

Anna took off her rucksack. 'How come you're not hungry?'

'Did you find anything good?'

Anna nodded, putting her hand on his back, as they walked towards the house.

★

The fine barrel-vaulted sitting room, fitted with rustic furniture and Persian carpets by Maria Grazia Zanchetta, was awash with rubbish. The windows were stopped up with cardboard, and the half-light revealed mountains of bottles, jars, books, toys, printers, newspapers, bicycles, mobile phones, envelopes, clothes, radios, pieces of wood, teddy bears and mattresses.

In the kitchen, light filtered in from the windows, painting bright strips on swarms of flies feasting on remnants left in tins of tuna and meat. Cockroaches and ants scuttled across greasy floor tiles. The marble table was covered with count-less bottles of water, Coca-Cola and Fanta.

Anna took a long drink. 'I was dying for that.'

Astor peered into the rucksack. 'Any batteries?'

'No.'

Batteries were precious and hard to find; they were almost always flat nowadays. She had a secret stock of them for the torch. If Astor got his hands on them he'd use them all up listening to music.

Anna produced a jar of beans. 'Like some?'

A sideways wag of his forefinger said no.

She raised a suspicious eyebrow. 'What have you been eating?'

'Nothing. I've got the shakes.'

She put her hand on his forehead. 'You're boiling hot.' It couldn't be Red Fever – he was too young – but she was still worried. 'Put some clothes on.'

'I don't want to.'

'Go and get dressed.' She took a big white tube out of the rucksack. 'Otherwise, no present.'

'What is it?'

'Off you go.'

He kept jumping up, trying to grab the tube.

'Off you go!' Anna went outside, sat down on the bench and opened the jar of beans with a knife.

Two minutes later Astor turned up in a dirty jacket that reached down to his knees. 'Where's my present?'

She handed it over. 'I think you'll like it.'

He eyed her curiously, unscrewed the top and started sucking.

Anna snatched it out of his hand and pushed him down onto the ground. 'What have I told you a thousand times?' He tried to get up, but she put her foot on his chest, pinning him down. 'What have I told you?'

'Always read and smell before putting things in your mouth.'

'So?'

Astor grabbed hold of her foot, trying to free himself. 'You said I'd like it. So it must be all right.'

'It doesn't matter. You must always read.' She gave him the tube again. 'Come on.'

He puffed out his cheeks in exasperation and rubbed his eye. 'Ne . . . Nes . . . Nest—' He broke off and pointed to a letter: 'What's this?'

'An accent.'

'What's it for?'

'It's not important.'

'Nestle. Co . . . con . . . den . . . condensed mil . . . milk.'

He went on sucking in silence, holding his ear with his hand.

*

Anna spent the afternoon sleeping on the bench in the yard. The knocks she'd taken in the fight with the dog were beginning to hurt. A bruise had formed on the hip she'd hit against the car and her knuckles were swollen.

Astor lay beside her, under a blanket. She touched his forehead; it was very warm.

She went back into the house, fetched the torch, climbed the stairs and walked along the corridor until she came to a closed door. Taking her shoes off and switching on the torch, she took a key out of her trouser pocket and turned it in the lock.

The beam of the torch lit up a carpet with a coloured check pattern and a dusty writing desk with a laptop in the middle. The walls were covered with childish drawings – of houses, animals, flowers, mountains, rivers and a huge red sun. The beam fell on a bedside table made of dark wood, a pile of books, a radio alarm and a bedside lamp, then on a double bed with a brass headboard. On the red and blue bedspread there was a skeleton with its arms crossed. All the two hundred and six bones that made it up, from the phalanges of the feet to the skull, were decorated with intricate geometrical patterns traced by a black felt-tip pen. The forehead and cheekbones were adorned with rings and earrings, the eye sockets covered by birds' nests full of speckled eggs. The vertebrae of the neck and the ribs were twined around with strings of pearls, thin golden chains, amethyst necklaces and coloured stones. Curled up beside the feet lay the skeleton of a cat.

Anna sat down at the desk, rested the torch on it and opened a well-worn exercise book. The hard brown cover bore the words: THE IMPORTANT THINGS.

Silently moving her lips, she read the rounded, careful handwriting that filled the first page.

My dearest children, I love you so much. Soon your mama won't be here any more and you'll have to fend for yourselves. Be good and intelligent and I'm sure you'll manage.

I'm leaving you in this exercise book some instructions that will help you to cope with life and avoid danger. Look after it carefully and whenever you have a doubt open it and read. Anna, you must teach Astor to read, so that he can consult it too. You'll find that some of the advice won't be useful in the world you're living in. The rules will change and I can only imagine them. You'll have to correct them and learn from your mistakes. The important thing is that you always use your heads.

Mama is going away because of a virus that has spread all over the world.

These are the things I know about the virus. I'll tell you them as they are, without any lies. Because it wouldn't be fair to deceive you.

THE VIRUS

1) Everybody has the virus. Males and females. Little children and grown-ups. But in children it sleeps and has no effect.

2) The virus will wake up only when you reach maturity. Anna, you'll reach maturity when dark blood comes out of your vagina. Astor, you'll reach maturity when your willy goes hard, and sperm, a white liquid, comes out of it.

3) If a person has the virus, they can't have children.

4) When you reach maturity, red blotches start to appear on your skin. Sometimes they appear straight away, sometimes it takes longer. When the virus grows in your body you start to cough, you find it hard to breathe, all your muscles ache, and scabs form in your nostrils and on your hands. Then you die.

5) This point is very important and you must never forget it. Somewhere in the world there are grown-ups who have survived and they're preparing a medicine that will save all children. They'll reach you soon and cure you. You must be certain of that, you must believe it.

Mama will always love you, even though she isn't with you. Wherever she is, she'll love you. So will Papa. You must love each other too, and never part. You're brother and sister.

She knew this part off by heart, but always re-read it. She turned to another page in the middle of the book.

HAVING A TEMPERATURE

The normal temperature of the human body is 36.5. If it's higher than that, you have a fever. If it's 37 or 38 it's not serious. If it's higher than that you must take medicine. To measure your temperature, use a thermometer. There's one in the second drawer in the kitchen. It's made of glass, so mind you don't drop it or it'll break. (There's a plastic one too, but that one has a battery and I don't know how long it will go on working.) You have to put it under your arm and wait for five minutes. If you don't have a clock, count very slowly up to 500 and see where the silver strip stops. If it's more than 38 you must take medicines called antibiotics. You must take them for at least a week, twice a day. There are lots of antibiotics. Augmentin, Aziclav, Cefepime. I've put them with the other medicines in the green cupboard. When you run out of them, you'll have to go and look for them in chemists' shops or houses. If you can't find these ones, look

at the leaflet inside the box; it will tell you the active ingre-
dient; if it's a word that ends in 'ina' it's all right. Amoxicillina,
cefazolina, things like that. And you must drink a lot.

Anna tucked her hair behind her ears and closed the book.

The glass thermometer had been broken. The plastic one
had stopped working. The antibiotics Mama had left in the
cupboard had been eaten by mice. Minerva, the chemist's
shop in Castellammare, had burnt down along with the rest
of the village.

A thermometer wasn't essential in this case. Astor was
boiling hot; there was no doubt his temperature was over
38 degrees. But it was too late to go looking for medicines;
that would have to wait till the next day.

She put the exercise book back in its place and went out
of the room, locking the door behind her.

★

Outside, the sun had gone down behind the wood and the
air was still.

'Come on, Astor, bedtime.'

He followed her sleepily upstairs.

Their bedroom wasn't much tidier than the rest of the
house. No remnants of food, but heaps of clothes, toys, bottles
of all shapes and sizes. Two chests of drawers were covered
by streams of melted wax from hundreds of candles. The
wall behind had been blackened by their smoke.

Anna covered her brother up and gave him a drink of
water, but he was promptly sick.

She went back downstairs. In the green cupboard, she
remembered, there was nothing left but mouse droppings.
She imagined rows of mice with temperatures, gnawing pills
and feeling better.

In the sitting room she found a box of Crescina. The name

ended in '-ina', but she wasn't sure it was an antibiotic. The leaflet said it was a food supplement suitable for men and women of all ages and recommended for hair loss. Her brother wasn't losing hair, but it wouldn't do him any harm. She also found some Dafalgan suppositories. Good for high temperatures and headaches.

She made Astor swallow the Crescina and took out a suppository. 'This goes up your bum.'

He eyed her dubiously. 'I put a felt-tip pen up my bum once, and I didn't like it. Can I eat it instead?'

Anna shrugged. 'Well, I suppose it won't make much difference.'

He chewed the suppository with a grimace, then turned on his side, shivering.

His sister lit a candle, lay down beside her brother and put her arms round him, trying to warm him up. 'Would you like me to tell you a story?'

'Okay.'

'Which one?'

'Any one, as long as it's good.'

Anna remembered the book of fairy tales her mother had given her. Her favourite was the one about poor Cola the Fish. 'This story's about the time when there was a king and the Outside didn't exist and there were still Grown-ups. In those days there was a boy in Sicily called Cola who could swim underwater, just like a fish.'

Astor squeezed her hand. 'Is the sea made of nothing but water?'

'Yes, salt water – you can't drink it. Cola the Fish was such a good swimmer he could go right down to the sea bed, where it's dark and you can't see a thing. And while he was down there, he would take treasure out of sunken ships and bring it up to the surface. He had become so famous that the king decided to set him a challenge.'

'Why?'

'Because that's what kings do: decide things. He threw a gold cup into the water and Cola the Fish brought it straight back up again. Then the king ordered his men to sail further out to sea, then he took off his crown and threw it into the water. "Let's see if you can do it out here," he said. Cola dived in and stayed underwater a very long time. Just when everyone on board had started drinking a toast . . .'

'What does that mean, drinking a toast?' mumbled Astor, with his thumb in his mouth.

'Clinking bottles together. While the people on the ship were drinking a toast, the boy came back up with the crown. But still the king wasn't satisfied. He took off the precious ring he wore on his finger and threw it into the sea where it was so deep anchors ran out of rope before they could touch the bottom. "Have you got the courage, Nicola?" the king asked, with a sneer. "Certainly, Your Majesty," said Cola the Fish. He took a deep breath and jumped in. Everyone on the ship stared at the dark blue sea. They didn't know their ship was floating like a cork over a ditch so deep that if you threw a stone in it wouldn't reach the bottom till the next day. There were creatures living in that eternal darkness that no human being had ever seen or imagined. Long transparent snakes, luminous soles as wide as pumpkin fields, octopuses so huge they could crush a house with their tentacles. They stayed there two days waiting for him. Then the king yawned and ordered his sailors: "Back to the palace. He's dead." Just at that moment Cola the Fish emerged from the sea, looking very pale and holding the king's ring. "Your Majesty, I have something important to tell you. I went right down to the bottom and saw that Sicily is supported by three columns. But one of them is badly damaged and on the point of collapsing . . ."'

Anna glanced at her brother, who was breathing deeply, still sucking his thumb. '"Sicily will sink into the sea." The king thought for a moment. "In that case, do you know what my orders for you are, Nicola? Go back down there at once and hold up our island." The boy looked at the sun, the sky, the coast of the land that he would never see again and said: "Yes, Your Majesty." He took a breath so deep it sucked in the air, the clouds and the dry seaweed on the beach, and dived down. Since that day he has never come up again. There. That's the end of the story.'

Astor was sleeping with his head bent over on one side.

Anna thought of that poor boy standing there all alone at the bottom of the sea, holding up the island. She imagined swimming down to him like a deep-sea diver and telling him that his king and all his court were dead, and that Sicily was entirely inhabited by children.

She ate some beans, then picked up the bottle of Amaro she'd found in the garden centre and held it close to the candle's flame. The label showed an angry peasant woman standing with one hand on her waist and the other holding a basket full of herbs.

Looks just like Signorina Rigoni. She used to stand like that when the class was being too noisy.

Anna took a swig of Amaro. It was so sweet it made her curl up her toes.

There were some things about Grown-ups she just couldn't understand. Why did they call it 'Amaro' – bitter – if it was sweet?

After a few more swigs, her eyelids grew heavy. Outside the window millions of stars dotted the sky like a sprinkling of white paint, and cicadas were singing. When the cold weather came they would disappear. She'd never seen any cicadas, but they must be really big creatures to make all that noise.

★

When Anna woke up, her arms were wrapped round her brother, and the mattress was soaked in sweat. Turning on the torch, she played it over Astor. His face was buried in the pillow, and he was grinding his teeth.

She picked up the bottle of water from the floor and drank her fill. Outside, everything was quiet, the silence broken only by the hoots of an owl and Astor's heavy breathing.

Getting out of bed, she went out onto the balcony and sat down to enjoy the cool air. Beyond the rusty railing and the black shapes of the trees lay the burnt, noiseless expanse of the plain.

The bird was hooting from the fig tree behind the tool shed. The tree had always been small, but in the last two years it had grown so much its branches reached down to the ground.

She remembered Mama once tying the ropes of the swing to it, and Papa objecting that the fig was a treacherous tree, likely to break.

But thinking about it again, she wasn't so sure. Perhaps she'd read about the treacherous fig tree in some book, or dreamed of it. Memories often mingled with written stories and dreams, and in time even the clearest ones faded, like watercolours in a glass of water.

She remembered Palermo. Their flat, from where you could see an office full of people sitting in front of monitors. She recalled trivial things. The black and white chessboard of the floor tiles in the sitting room. The kitchen table with a slot for a roller that was used for making pasta. The clothes drying rack with its rusty corners. But she could no longer summon up the faces of Grandpa Vito and Grandma Mena. In fact, all the Grown-ups' faces were disappearing, suppressed by the passing days. The old people had white hair, some men grew beards, the women dyed their hair, painted their skin and put on perfume. In the evenings they sat in bars and drank wine in glasses. There were lots of waiters. In the restaurants of Palermo they brought you *parmigiana di melanzane* and spaghetti.

Mama had come to hate Palermo, because the people wouldn't stay in quarantine. Anna remembered that even before the Red Fever reached Castellammare she'd stopped sending her to school. They'd barricaded themselves in the house with stocks of food piled up in the kitchen and the sitting room.

One evening Papa had come over in his Mercedes. The car had skidded in the drive and crashed into the benches, the horn blaring. Papa had climbed out, more dead than alive. He was barely recognisable, his face drained by the virus, his eyeballs bulging, his skin covered in blotches. He dragged himself to the door, but Mama wouldn't let him in. 'Go away! You're infected!' she shouted.

He hammered on the door with both fists. 'I want to see the children. Just for a moment. Let me see them, just for a moment.'

'Go away. Are you trying to kill us?'

'Open the door, Maria Grazia, please . . .'

'Go away, for God's sake. If you love your children, go away.' Mama sank down onto the floor in tears. He staggered back to the car, got in and sat there, slumped forward, head against the windscreen, mouth open.

Anna climbed up onto the back of the sofa and looked at him through the window. Mama drew the curtains, picked her up and took her and Astor into bed with her. Anna thought she was going to say something, but they all just lay there in silence.

The next day, Papa died. Mama made a phone call and the authorities came to take him away.

Anna could have said goodbye to him, gone up to him, but at that time her mother didn't know that children couldn't catch the disease.

Not long afterwards Mama caught it.

Anna's memories of that time were confused. Mama writing all day, half naked, her elbow on the table. Mama filling the exercise book with Important Things. Her long blonde hair falling in greasy tufts over her face. Her thin ankles. Her long calves. Her toes pressed down against the floor. The hollow curve of her stomach, revealed by her unfastened dressing gown. The red blotches on her neck and legs. The scabs on her hands and lips. Her constant coughing.

All so long ago, yet when she thought about it, she missed her so much she felt as though she'd fallen down a hole she'd never get out of.

★

The day released a flock of small white clouds into the blue sky.

Astor's temperature seemed to have dropped, but he was still far from well. He gazed at Anna with big, bewildered eyes. When she tried to get him to drink, he brought up yellow bile.

Exhausted, he rubbed his stomach. 'It hurts here.'

'Look, I'm going out to find some medicine. I won't be long.'

'Okay, I'll come with you.'

'You know that's not possible. Do you want to get caught by the smoke monsters?'

He shook his head. 'Don't you go either, then.'

'I'll bring you a present.'

'Don't want a present.'

She sighed. 'I don't believe this.'

He turned away, pouting sulkily.

'What if we have Christmas first?'

He turned back to face her, excited. 'Christmas? Can we? Really?'

'Yes, really.'

'Have you already got my present?'

'Yes.'

'Shall I hide, then?'

'Yes, go on.'

Astor hid under the blanket. Anna went into Mama's room, took the CD-player from one of the drawers in the desk, then put on a Father Christmas hat and some red Moon Boots. Reluctantly, she pulled down a hedgehog soft toy which lay on top of a cupboard, out of Astor's reach. A birthday present to her from Grandma Mena. Astor had always coveted it, but she'd never given in. She wrapped it in a sheet of newspaper.

'Are you coming? I'm ready,' Astor shouted.

Anna pressed 'Play' and a song started up at full volume. Her choice for Christmas was always George Benson's 'The Ghetto'. She didn't know why. Maybe because of its driving rhythm, maybe because she'd found the CD under a Christmas tree in a service area on the autostrada.

She instantly started dancing. A dance that consisted of swaying her bottom, hands on hips, and jutting her chin out, like a pigeon pecking at birdseed. Her brother was a round hillock quivering with excitement under the blanket. She passed by him, singing all the time, jumped up onto a chair and counted, pointing her finger: 'One . . . Two . . . And three. Go, Ghetto! Your turn.'

The blanket flew off and Astor started jiving about, rotating his wrists and occasionally slapping himself on the head. That was his Christmas dance.

Anna was relieved. If he was dancing, he couldn't be too ill. Maybe it was all an act to keep her at home. But he *had* thrown up.

'The present! Give me the present.'

Anna took out the parcel and handed it to her brother. 'Merry Christmas.'

Astor tore off the wrapping and gazed at the toy. 'Is it mine? Really?'

'Yes, it's yours.'

Brother and sister started dancing again, just as George Benson struck up anew with 'Yes, this is the ghetto'.

★

Anna packed the rucksack: a bottle of water, a can of peas, a kitchen knife, some batteries that still worked, and a double CD of Massimo Ranieri.

Ready.

She said goodbye to Astor, who'd gone back to bed with his new cuddly toy, and set off.

3

The first few times Anna had left Astor alone at home, she'd gone no further than the Manninos' farm – Mama's supplies seemed inexhaustible. But after a year all that remained were a few tins of sweetcorn, which gave Astor indigestion.

The farm was at the edge of the wood. A long low building, with a red-tiled roof. Opposite, cattle sheds and paddocks with metal fences. To one side a barn, full of bales of hay.

The parents had been carried off by the Red Fever and their children, too small to fend for themselves, had died in their bunk beds. The Manninos were small-scale farmers, far-sighted people, and the big larder behind the kitchen was full of jars of marinated aubergines and artichokes, preserves, jam, bottles of wine, legs of ham. Anna went there regularly to stock up, but one day she found it stripped clean. Someone had come by and carried off everything they could. The rest was strewn across the floor.

She was forced to search further afield. In the first group of buildings she came across, among corpses, flies and mice, she raided the kitchen cabinets. At first she went through the apartments with her hands over her face, singing and peering between her fingers at the bodies, but before long she grew used to them and saw them as constant, intriguing presences. They were all different, each with its own pose and expression, and later, depending on the degree of humidity, exposure to light, ventilation, insects and other necrophagous creatures, they turned into fillets of *baccalà* or revolting masses of pulp.

To prevent Astor from following her or hurting himself, in these early days, before going out, she would lock him up with his soft toys and a bottle of water in the cupboard under the stairs. The first few times he cried, screamed and banged on the door, but after a while, being intelligent, he understood that this imprisonment had its advantages: every time his sister reopened the door she brought food and presents.

Astor said that while he sat there in the dark, little creatures that lived underground would pop out. 'They're like lizards, but they have blond hair and they talk to me.'

Anna was pleased with her solution. It left her free to move around, and her brother didn't see the destruction and the dead bodies, didn't smell that sickly sweet odour that stuck in your nose and you couldn't get rid of even by inhaling perfume.

After a while, however, Astor started throwing tantrums again. First he wanted light, and Anna certainly couldn't give him a candle in the cupboard. Then he started saying the long-haired lizards didn't want him there any more and said nasty things to him.

Then the questions started. What's out there, beyond the wood? Why can't I come into the Outside with you? What kind of animals live there?

To persuade her brother to let her lock him up, every evening Anna would tell him stories about the Outside. He'd listen quietly until his breathing became regular and his thumb slipped out of his mouth.

The Outside, beyond the magic wood, was a waste land. No one had survived the wrath of the god Danone (Anna had called him that in honour of the chocolate puddings of which she had fond memories): no adults, no animals, no children. The two of them had the good fortune to live in that wood, which was so hidden away and dense that the god couldn't see into it. The few animals that had survived had taken refuge there. Beyond the trees there were only craters and haunted ruins. Food and other things grew at the bottom of ditches. Sometimes tins of tuna sprouted there, sometimes cereal bars, sometimes toys and clothes. The smoke monsters, the god Danone's servants, roamed that world. They were giants made of black gas who killed anyone who crossed their path. Some evenings, in Anna's stories, the smoke monsters would turn into prehistoric monsters like those in the *Big Book of Dinosaurs*. If Astor took one step outside the farm, they'd eat him alive.

'Couldn't I escape? I'm a fast runner.'

Anna was categorical. 'Impossible. And even if the smoke monsters weren't around, the air's poisonous and would kill you. If you went outside the fence, you'd be dead before you'd walked a few metres.'

Astor would chew his lips, unconvinced. 'Why don't you die, then?'

'Because when you were small, Mama gave me a special medicine, and the monsters can't hurt me. You were too small to be given it.' But at other times she replied: 'I'm magic. I was born like that. When I die the magic will pass onto you and you'll be able to go out and find food yourself.'

'Wow! I can't wait for you to die. I want to see the smoke monsters.'

Anna had to explain to her brother what death was. They were surrounded by corpses, yet she was at a loss. So she'd catch rats and lizards and kill them in front of him.

'You see? Now it's dead. All that's left is the body; there's no life in it. You can do what you like, but it'll never move again. It's gone. If I hit you on the head with a hammer, it'll happen to you too: you'll go straight into the other world.'

'Where is the other world?'

Anna would grow impatient. 'I don't know. Beyond the wood. But it's always dark and cold, though the ground is fiery and burns your feet. And you're alone. There's nobody there.'

'Not even Mama?'

'No.'

But Astor still wasn't satisfied. 'And how long do people stay in the other world?'

'For ever.'

These long tortuous ontological discussions wore her out. Sometimes Astor would accept her arguments; at other times, as if sensing that his sister wasn't telling him the truth, he'd look for contradictions. 'What about the birds that fly overhead, in the sky? How do they do that? I see them. Why don't they die? They haven't taken the medicine.'

Anna would improvise. 'Birds can fly above the poisonous air, but they can't stop.'

'I could do that too. Never stopping. Jumping from tree to tree.'

'No, you'd die.'

'Can I try?'

'No.'

Anna had an idea. Between the wood and the fields, about a hundred metres from the boundary of Mulberry Farm, were the Manninos' cattlesheds. The cows had died of thirst and their carcasses were crawling with worms. When you went near them, the smell of decay was overpowering.

Anna took her brother to the fence. 'Listen to me carefully. Since you're so set on it, I'm going to take you outside. But remember, I'm magic and I don't notice the smell of death. You'll have to be more careful. If a foul, sickening smell reaches you, it means you're about to die. Run back as fast as you can, don't stop, climb over the fence and you'll be safe.'

The little boy was no longer so keen on the idea. 'I'd rather not.'

Smiling to herself, Anna grabbed his wrist. 'You're going. I'm fed up with your questions.'

Astor burst into tears, dug in his heels and clung onto a branch. Anna had to drag him along.

'Come on!'

'No, please . . . I don't want to go into the burning land.'

She lifted him up and dumped him over the fence, then climbed over herself and, holding him by the neck, pushed him between the ivy-covered trunks and the holly. Astor, his eyes brimming with tears, held his hand over his mouth. But still the stench of rotting flesh penetrated into his nostrils. He eyed her in despair, gesturing that he could smell it.

'Go! Run home!'

With a cat-like leap, the little boy re-entered the farm.

From that day on, there was no need to lock Astor under the stairs.

*

The air was cool: ideal walking weather.

Leaving the wood behind her, Anna walked round Torre Normanna and onto the provincial road.

Some crows perched on electricity cables croaked at her like pious churchgoers in mourning clothes.

She speeded up. There was still some way to go to the Michelini twins' convenience store.

*

Paolo and Mario Michelini were identical twins. A year older than Anna, they'd been in the fourth year when she was in the third. Big, bulky, indistinguishable. Same expressionless little eyes, same carrot-coloured hair. Dotted with freckles, as if someone had left them next to a saucepan of boiling ragout at birth. They were no geniuses at school and never did their homework, but they frightened everyone, including the teachers, with their sheer size. If there was a football around, they'd take it, and if you wanted it back you had to pay.

Their mother dressed them alike: blue tracksuit, red T-shirt and trainers. Their father ran a Despar supermarket in Buseto Palizzolo.

Before the virus, Anna used to meet them on the school bus, but they ignored her. They'd sit at the back, playing Nintendo in silence; communication between them was almost telepathic. As far as they were concerned, the world was something to be looked at with four eyes, touched with twenty fingers, walked through with four feet and peed on with two dicks.

After the epidemic, Anna had gone past the Despar from time to time. The shutter was up and the chewing-gum and liquorice machines stood by the door, near a neat row of trolleys. Dirt and destruction surrounded the shop, but inside it everything was tidy. And at a particular time the shutter came down, as if the Red Fever had never existed. The only difference was that the shop sign didn't light up.

Anna had wondered if the twins' father had returned from the afterlife. Every time she felt an almost irresistible desire to discover the truth, but was scared. She hung around nearby, gazing at the door with its notice: a dog behind a cross, and the words 'We stay outside'.

One day, after walking backwards and forwards, she'd pushed the glass door open. A bell had rung. Inside, it was just like when she used to shop there with her mother on the way back from the beach. The food on the shelves, the panettone on special offer, the display case with the radios and razors for card-holders. Only the cheese and cold meat counter was empty and there were no crates of vegetables.

Anna had wandered around the shop as if in a dream. If she'd reached out her hand, the jars, boxes of cereal and bottles of balsamic vinegar would surely have vanished.

'Can we help you?'

The twins were standing side by side, in their tracksuits and white shoes. One was holding a shotgun.

'Would you like a trolley?'

Anna gestured that she wouldn't.

'We've got everything, including Easter eggs with a surprise, and Nutella,' the one with the shotgun had explained.

Nutella was very hard to find. It had been one of the first things to disappear after the epidemic.

Anna had looked around. 'Ferrero Rocher, too?'

'Certainly.'

'How do I pay you? With money?' But she knew the world was full of money and nobody cared about it.

'We swap things. Have you got anything to swap?'

She'd searched in her trouser pockets. 'I've got a Swiss knife.'

The two teddy bears had shaken their heads in unison. 'We're interested in batteries, but only if they have some charge left – we check them. We're also interested in medicines and Massimo Ranieri CDs.'

Anna had raised an eyebrow. 'Who's Massimo Ranieri?'

'A famous singer. Our father used to like him,' the one with the shotgun had replied. 'In exchange for him we can give you three large jars of Nutella or six small Toblerones. Everything you see in here can be swapped. It's a mini-market.'

Anna had never heard the twins utter so many words in succession.

Over the next few months, wherever she went, she looked for Massimo Ranieri CDs. There was plenty of Vasco Rossi and Lucio Battisti, but no Ranieri. Then one day, in an autostrada service area, she'd found, among mobile phone cases, deodorants and sodden books, a triple album titled *Naples and My Songs*.

That would buy her the antibiotics.

★

She'd gone the wrong way. There was a shorter route to the twins' shop and yet, as if her feet had made their own decision, she'd found herself on the autostrada.

The car with the dog in it was there.

Anna stared at the open door, biting her thumbnail. She wanted to see him before the crows left nothing but bones.

She drew the knife from her rucksack, went up to the car and peered inside. A patch of dirty hair. She screamed; there was no reaction. Leaning further in, she saw the dog through the gap between the front seats. In the same position as when she'd left him. The blood had dried below the neck and the back seat was soaked in it. Big metallic grey flies settling. Tongue hanging out of the open mouth, over dark gums covered in drool. One visible eye, as big as a biscuit and as black as diesel, wide open, staring into the void. Breathing so faint it was barely audible. Tail limp between the back legs, twitching slightly.

Anna touched him on the side with the tip of the knife. No movement of the body, but the pupil shifted, focusing on her for a moment.

As if he was looking forward to death. It happened to all dying creatures, human beings and animals.

In the past four years Anna had seen many children become covered with blotches and fade away. Slumped in a dark recess under the stairs, in a car like this dog, under a tree or in a bed. They would put up a fight, but eventually they would all, without exception, realise it was over, as if death itself had whispered it in their ear. Some kept going for a little while longer with that awareness; others discovered it only a second before they died.

· 53 ·

Anna's hand, almost of its own accord, reached out and stroked the dog's head.

Still motionless and indifferent, but for a moment the tail lifted and fell back down in what might almost have been a feeble wag.

Anna shook her head. 'Aren't you dead yet, you ugly brute?'

Among the rubbish in the gutter beside the guardrail she found a deflated plastic football. She cut it in two and got back into the car with one half. Taking the bottle out of her rucksack, she poured half its contents into the improvised dish. She held it near the dog's mouth. At first he ignored it, then he lifted his muzzle slightly and, almost reluctantly, dipped his tongue in the water.

She pushed the dish closer. 'Drink! Go on, drink.'

The animal gave a few more licks, then flopped down again.

Anna took a tin of peas, opened it and poured the contents out beside his mouth.

She'd done what she could.

★

Buseto Palizzolo, a small village of modern houses clustered under a hill, had also felt the effects of the fire. But the flames had only caressed the Michelinis' Despar, blackening the walls of the building and melting the green plastic blinds on the upper floors.

Anna knocked on the shutter. 'Open up, I want to do a swap.' She waited a few moments. 'Is anybody there? Can you hear me? It's Anna Salemi, from 3C. I want to do a swap. Open up.' Growing impatient, she walked round the building.

The tradesman's entrance at the back was barred, and through the small grilled windows she couldn't see a thing. Going back round to the front, she tried to lift the shutter, but it was locked. She kicked it. All those months spent searching for that stupid CD! She'd come all that way for nothing. Where was she going to find antibiotics now?

'All right, then, I'm going. I had a Massimo Ranieri CD. It's a really good one and I don't think you've got it.' She put her ear to the shutter.

Somebody moved inside.

'I know you're in there.'

'Go away. We don't swap things any more,' replied a sleepy voice.

'Not even Massimo Ranieri?'

The shutter clanked up. Out of the darkness of the shop emerged the silhouette of one of the twins. He was holding the shotgun.

Anna couldn't tell whether he was Mario or Paolo, but one look was enough to tell her that he had Red Fever. His lips were covered with scabs and sores, his nostrils swollen and inflamed, his eyes ringed. A reddish blotch covered his neck. He might live a few more weeks. A couple of months if he was tough.

She took the CD out of her rucksack. 'Well? Do you want it?'

The twin screwed up his eyes. 'Let me see.' He examined it and gave it back. 'We've already got it. Anyway, I'm fed up with Massimo Ranieri. I prefer Domenico Modugno.'

Anna craned her neck to peer into the shop. 'Are you on your own?'

The fat boy coughed, spattering a yellowish sludge on the floor. 'My brother's dead.' He raised his eyes and counted silently. 'It's been five days now.'

Anna waited only a couple of seconds. 'Listen, I need some medicine.'

'I told you we don't swap things any more.' The twin turned round and shuffled back into the shop. She followed him.

It took her eyes a minute or two to get used to the gloom. Everything was on the floor – jars of honey and orange marmalade, dry dog food, tins of ragout, tubes of anchovy paste. A can of oil had been knocked over and shards of a broken bottle were immersed in a pool of wine.

It horrified her to see all that good food wasted. The day before she'd almost been torn apart for a few tins of beans. 'What on earth happened?'

'I stopped tidying up.'

'Look, will you give me these medicines? It's important, they're for my brother. If you want, I've got some charged batteries too.'

The twin went behind the counter, rested the shotgun against the wall, flopped down on a small wicker chair, legs stretched out in front of him, arms hanging by his sides, and started coughing again. The Red Fever hadn't succeeded in slimming him down yet. Two sausage-like legs, white skin dotted with freckles and fair hairs, protruded from the track-suit trousers. A spherical head sitting on rounded shoulders, without the interval of a neck.

'I don't need your batteries. I've got loads of them.' He opened a drawer full of packets of cigarettes. 'Would you like one?'

'Yes, thanks.'

'What brand do you like?'

'Any one.'

He passed her a packet of Marlboro, together with a lighter. 'How old's your brother?'

Anna lit the cigarette. 'Seven, maybe eight.'

'It can't be Red Fever, then.'

'He must have eaten something rotten. He's got a temperature and he keeps being sick. I need some antibiotics.'

The fat boy rubbed his neck. 'Do you want to see him?'

Anna realised he meant his twin brother. 'All right. But which one are you?'

'Mario. Paolo was my brother.' He led her into the area at the back of the shop, a storeroom full of cardboard boxes and crates, and a white van with the word 'Despar' on the side. 'I put him here.'

Paolo lay in a big open freezer, the kind that used to be used for storing pizzas and bags of prawns. Heaped up around him were jars of tuna preserved in oil, of various makes. He was starting to swell up. The eyes had gone, sucked down inside two purple blobs. Hands like blown-up gloves. He smelled really bad.

Anna took a drag on her cigarette. 'I bet tuna was his favourite food.'

'And how old are you?' Mario asked her.

'I've lost count.'

He smiled, displaying small yellow teeth. 'I remember you at school.' He examined her. 'Have you got the blotches?'

Anna shook her head.

'Why do you think my brother died first? I can't understand it – we're twins. We were born together, we should have died together.'

'The Red Fever comes to everyone differently. You can even catch it at fourteen.'

He nodded, pursing his lips. 'How long do you reckon I've got?'

Anna stubbed the cigarette out under her sole and went up to him. She scrutinised his neck, made him lift up his T-shirt so she could see the other blotches on his back, and checked his hands. 'I don't know . . . Maybe a couple of months.'

'That's what I think.' He rubbed his eye. 'But have you heard the rumour? They say a Grown-up has survived.'

How many times had she heard such stories? Everyone she met said there were Grown-ups who'd survived somewhere or other. It was all bullshit. The virus had exterminated the Grown-ups, and as soon as children reached puberty, it killed them too. That was the truth of the matter. And after all these years she no longer believed the rumours about a vaccine. But she kept quiet, still hoping to get the antibiotics for Astor.

'I know you don't believe it. I didn't either, at first. But it's true.' Mario put his hand on his heart.

'What makes you so sure?'

'The guy who told me must have been at least sixteen. Had a beard, and not a blotch on him. Said a big woman had saved him. Not a normal Grown-up, bigger. They call her "the Little Lady". She's three metres tall. Caught the Red Fever, but recovered.' Mario's face, until then about as expressive as that of a grazing cow, came to life. 'It cost me five bottles of wine to find out where she lives.'

'And where does she live?' asked Anna.

'In a place in the mountains. The Spa Hotel, he said. Do you know it?'

Anna thought for a moment. 'Yes, I do. It's not far away.'

'Have you been there?'

'Not to the hotel itself, but very close. Anyway, it's easy to find on a map.'

'This Little Lady can cure you.'

Anna couldn't suppress a sceptical smile. 'How does she do that?'

'You have to kiss her, on the mouth. Her saliva is magic.'

Anna burst out laughing. 'Kiss her using your tongue, you mean?'

'That's right.'

'What if she won't let you? If she doesn't like you?'

'She will, she will. As long as you take her some presents.' He started coughing again, nearly choking. Then he went on in a feeble voice: 'Especially bars of chocolate.'

'Chocolate's no good nowadays. It's all white and tasteless.'

Mario smiled like a grocer displaying his mortadella. 'We have a special way of preserving it. We keep it cool, down in the cellar. Sealed up in plastic containers. Five bars get you a kiss, and six . . .'

Anna interrupted him. 'Do you want me to take you there?'

'Where?'

'To the Little Lady. I'll show you the way, if you like.'

The twin fell silent for a moment, scratching the scabs on his lips with his fingernail. He pointed to the storeroom door. 'Let's go back in there.' They returned to the shop. 'What am I going to do with Paolo?'

'He's dead. Leave him here.'

Mario picked up a cereal bar, took off the wrapper and scoffed it without offering her a bite. 'The trouble is, I've never been anywhere without my brother. We used to like being in the shop. Swapping things with customers, collecting batteries, medicines . . . Since the fires, nobody's come any more. Only gangs trying to raid the shop.'

'We wouldn't be gone long.'

'How long?'

'A couple of days.'

'I don't know . . . I suppose I could give you some chocolate so she'd let you kiss her too.'

Anna smiled. 'Yes, but that's not enough. If you want me to take you there, you'll have to give me the medicines I need for my brother.'

He opened three drawers. 'Take as many as you want.'

She immediately found two boxes of antibiotics and put them in the rucksack. 'And you'll have to give me all the food we can carry. I'll choose it, though. And some live batteries.'

'Okay.'

'This is what I suggest: we drop by at my house to give my brother the medicines, then we leave tomorrow morning.'

Mario had perked up. 'All right, I'm tired of being on my own. What's your brother's name?'

'Astor.'

'Funny name.' Mario extended a plump hand. 'It's a deal.'

Anna's plan was simple. At Torre Normanna she'd run off with the stuff, and to hell with Mario and the Little Lady.

★

They advanced along a country road which passed through a suburb consisting of a few houses, a small church and a roundabout, in the middle of which was a monument to servicemen killed in the First World War. Fire had consumed the public gardens around the local tourist office, and the trunks of the eucalyptuses looked like black pencils stuck in the earth. All that remained of the newsagent's kiosk was its iron frame. The nose of a fire engine was rammed into the barber's shop.

Anna was carrying a bag full of jars. Michelini, wearing a red cap with 'Nutella' on the peak, the shotgun slung over his shoulder, was pushing a wheelbarrow full of boxes. The load was covered by a piece of tarpaulin held down with bungee cords.

They were sweating and only found respite from the heat when the sun went behind the clouds.

Anna couldn't make up her mind whether she liked Mario or not. He'd fallen silent soon after leaving the shop and started to slow down after a couple of kilometres. It might have been the effects of Red Fever, but she suspected he was just lazy. At this rate it'd be dark before they got home. 'Do you want to switch jobs? Shall I push?'

Michelini shook his head.

'Is the gun loaded?'

'I've got four bullets.' Bullets were hard to come by. He'd fired all the others in the early months of the epidemic, during the looting and riots.

They started down a narrow road flanked by dry stone walls.

The twin stopped for a breather. 'It's strange for me without Paolo.' He looked at Anna. 'Have you got any hairs yet?'

'Yes.'

'Show me.'

Anna undid her shorts and pulled them down to her knees. Without taking his hands off the wheelbarrow, Michelini bent down to look at the little strip of black hair.

'What about breasts?'

Anna pulled up her T-shirt. On her chest were two hillocks surmounted by pink nipples.

They set off again, moving away from the village. Anna was seething with impatience, but was forced to fall in with the snail's pace of Michelini. To take her mind off it, she suggested they play a game.

He was dripping with sweat. 'What game?'

'Think of an animal.'

'All right. A walrus.'

'You're not meant to say it; you just think of it and I ask you questions till I find out what it is. Got it?'

'Yes.'

'All right, then. Does it fly, walk or swim?'

Michelini gave a crafty smile. 'It flies, walks and swims.'

'What animal could that be?'

'A duck.'

'You're not meant to tell me straight out.'

'You asked what kind of animal it was.'

'I was thinking out loud. Think of another one.'

'All right. A rabbit.'

'Maybe we'd better just walk.'

They passed a billboard on which there was an advert showing a car with a man dressed in jacket and tie, saying: 'Choose your future today.'

★

Nine wraith-like figures were coming across a field of burnt olive trees. The two oldest ones were out in front: a fat male and a skinny female, both painted white. The others were about Astor's age, naked and painted blue, their hair falling on their shoulders in tangled masses. Some of them had sticks.

Anna and Michelini watched them from behind a wooden fence. The twin scratched his chin. 'What shall we do?'

'Speak quietly,' whispered Anna. 'If they spot us they'll steal everything we've got.'

Not far away, on the other side of the road, was a small block of flats with an underground garage over which was the sign: 'Pieri's Car Repair Workshop'.

Anna grasped the handles of the wheelbarrow and started moving forward, with her head down, hiding behind the fence. 'Keep down and follow me without making a noise.' But she'd only gone a few metres when a shot rang out behind her.

Michelini was standing in the middle of the road. A plume of white smoke was coming out of the barrel of the shotgun.

She gaped at him. 'What have you done?'

'That'll scare them off.'

'You fool.' Anna started pushing again, but the wheelbarrow swerved to the right and left. She ditched it and ran towards the building, without looking back. Going down the concrete ramp, she was confronted with three lowered shutters. The one on the left was raised about twenty centimetres. Leaves and earth carried by rainwater had accumulated in the gutter. By scrabbling like a dog, she opened a gap, then she took off the rucksack, and squeezed underneath, holding her breath to make herself thinner. Her legs went through, and so did her thorax, but her head wouldn't. Pressing her cheek on the floor she made it inside, her face grazed on both cheeks. She reached out to retrieve the rucksack.

The workshop was in darkness. She tried to lower the shutter, but it wouldn't budge. Holding her hands out in front of her, she advanced towards the end of the room. Her knee banged against a car and her shin hit some shelves full of metal objects, which fell down onto the floor with a crash. She swallowed the pain and with her fingers followed the shelves, touched the rough wall, found a door and opened it. Beyond, the darkness was even blacker, if that were possible. She ventured forward on her hands and knees until she felt the edge of a step.

Outside, some shots rang out.

She sat down, nursing her knee, and prayed they hadn't seen her.

*

The first shot had made the small group turn round.

A fat boy was standing in the middle of the road holding a shotgun, and a figure was bent over, running towards a small block of flats, pushing a wheelbarrow.

The older girl had blown a whistle, pointing them out to the blue children. They had picked up some stones and charged at him, screaming.

Michelini, holding the weapon at hip level, had fired his three remaining shots into the group. The last shot had hit one of them, who'd collapsed in a cloud of ash. 'Yes!' Throwing the gun aside, he'd started galloping towards the block of flats, but the fever and all the kilos he was carrying made breathing difficult. He turned round to check where his pursuers were and a stone hit him on the head. He let out a yell and, as he was putting his hand to his temple, tripped over. He took three disjointed steps, wheeling his arms in an attempt to regain his balance, but crashed like a bulldozer into the fence at the side of the road and fell on his face, with his arms outspread, in a field. He didn't even try to get up again. He clutched the grass in his fists, pushed his face into the warm earth and thought of his brother.

★

The children's shouts echoed in the garage.

Anna stumbled up the last flight of stairs and slammed into a closed door. Opening it, she found herself in the entrance hall of the block of flats. Daylight came in through the frosted glass of the big front doors. To one side were the mailboxes, covered with dust, next to them a yellowed notice announcing the date of a residents' meeting and another one decreeing that bicycles and pushchairs must not be left unattended.

She tried to open the small wicket door, but it wouldn't move. Not knowing what else to do, she ran up the stairs. On the first floor all the flats were locked. Same thing on the second. On the top floor, too, everything was bolted shut.

The children were in the entrance hall.

She opened the landing window. Down below was the concrete ramp of the workshop; fifty metres further off, Michelini's body. To the left, a metre away, a balcony jutted out from the wall.

They were on the stairs.

She climbed up to stand with both feet on the window-sill, looked behind her, flexed her legs and jumped, arms outstretched. Her chest hit the railing, but she managed to grab hold of the bars. Putting one foot on the edge of the balcony, she climbed over.

Gulping down air, she limped along the balcony, which ran along two sides of the building in an L-shape. Round the corner were some air conditioners, a boiler and a French window, which was ajar. She slipped inside, closed it and sat down on the floor, panting and gazing at a dishwasher and a chrome-plated rubbish bin.

They were on the landing. Banging on the door.

Anna stood up and searched the kitchen drawers till she found a long serrated knife. She grabbed it and sat down in a corner, waiting. 'If you come in, I'll kill you. I'll kill you all.'

But she heard them go back down the stairs, and before long it was quiet again.

She crouched down against the fridge, still holding the knife, while the adrenalin drained out of her. She had to make sure they'd gone. Opening the French window, she wriggled on her stomach as far as the railing.

They were walking in single file along the shadowy road towards the sunset. The white-painted girl, with Michelini's cap on her head, was pushing the wheelbarrow.

Anna went back indoors and collapsed on the floor exhausted, her arms round the rucksack.

★

She decided to spend the night there.

A quick check confirmed that the door onto the landing could be opened from the inside.

The flat was in good condition. It had suffered no intruders, apart from ants and cockroaches. It was agreeably tidy. In the study, which was full of books, a framed certificate stated that Gabriele Mezzopane had taken a degree in general medicine at the University of Messina.

The doctor was in the living room, in front of the television, on a big beige velvet armchair, whose backrest was tipped forward. His bottom was still on the cushion, but his upper body was slumped over a low table, his forehead on the glass. He was well preserved. The skin still attached to the skull looked like cardboard which had been soaked and then dried in the sun. Dry yellow flax-like hair formed a crown around the scaly skull. The golden arms of his glasses rested on shrivelled ears. He wore a moth-eaten striped dressing gown, pyjamas and felt slippers. A walking stick leaned against the arm of the chair, from where an electric wire ran to a grey control pad with red buttons, clasped in the corpse's stiff hand. On the table, next to the head, was a plasticky sheet of paper with some numbers and names on it, and a telephone with large keys.

When she entered the bathroom, a swirl of bats was sucked out of the small window, leaving the green tiled floor scattered with droppings like grains of black rice.

She found a gas-fired camping lantern in the broom cupboard. Before turning it on, she checked that the blinds were all lowered. In the kitchen units there remained some tea bags and moth-infested packets of pasta. In the fridge, next to some black sludge that had dripped down from shelf to shelf, there was a jar with some meat sauce in it.

'Goveđi gulaš', the label said. She unscrewed the lid. A green and black mould formed a layer an inch thick. She skimmed it off and held the jar to her nose. She wasn't sure the stuff was still edible, but she ate it anyway. The meat was tasteless, but relieved her hunger a little.

On a shelf, next to some jars of coffee, she found a bottle of Nonino grappa. Carrying it into the bedroom, she put the lamp on the bedside table, took off her shoes and lay down with a couple of pillows behind her back. She took two sips of grappa, which ran down warm and dry into her throat.

She stroked the bedclothes, which were pulled tight across the mattress. 'As snug as a bug in a rug.' How she remembered those words!

Whenever her father had come over from Palermo to see them, he'd brought some cassata, potato croquettes and arancini from the Mastrangelo takeaway. They called it their wild supper, and you had to eat it with your fingers out of the paper tray, sitting around the coffee table. Afterwards her father would put her to bed and tuck in the bedclothes.

'Tighter, tighter, pull harder!'

'But you'll suffocate.'

'More, more. Till I can't move.'

Papa would put his hands under the mattress. 'Like that?' He'd give her a kiss. 'Now you're as snug as a bug in a rug. Go to sleep now, there's a good girl.' And he'd turn off the light, leaving the door ajar.

The flame of the lantern burned with a hissing sound and its white light caught a silver frame on the bedside table. She picked it up and inspected it.

In the photograph Dr Mezzopane was smartly dressed, with a polka-dot tie, and was holding the hand of a lady in a straw hat.

She put the photograph back and started spinning round with her eyes closed, banging against the walls, her feet rubbing on the carpet until they burned.

She opened the wardrobe. On the inside of one door was a mirror.

The alcohol had planted a foolish smile on her face. She took her T-shirt off and sorted through the clothes that were hanging there. Many were women's garments. Belonging to the lady in the straw hat, no doubt. She pulled them out and dumped them on a chair. They didn't appeal to her; an old woman's clothes. Except for one shorter, purple dress which left her back exposed; only it hung down on her like a sack. She tried on a red stretch T-shirt and a light-blue skirt that came down to her ankles. On a lower shelf, neatly arranged, were some shoes. She put on a pair made of black satin with high heels and glitter on the toes. She watched herself as she turned a pirouette. In that dim light she could hardly see herself, but didn't think she looked at all bad.

You look perfect for a party.

She lay back on the bed. A memory burst in her mind like a soap bubble.

'Anna, how vain you are!'

She was a little girl, standing in front of the mirror, arms straight, legs apart, wearing a pink flowery dress she'd been given by her grandmother. Her short hair held in place by a velvet band. Mama was sitting on the bed next to the ironed clothes, shaking her head and smiling.

She could smell the hot iron on the ironing board and the sweetish scent of the spray. Getting off the bed, she picked up the lantern and staggered into the study, her eyes only half-open. Among the books on the desk was a large green volume, an Italian dictionary. She was so drunk she could hardly read the minuscule print.

It took her quite a while, but eventually she found what she was looking for. Slurring her words, she read out loud: 'Vain. Full of vanity, said especially of a person who, believing him- or herself to possess physical and intellectual gifts, shows them off in order to receive praise and admiration from others.'

'It's true, I am vain.'

Returning to the bedroom, she got undressed and slipped between the sheets. She turned the little wheel of the lantern, which dimmed and went out with a puff.

*

Bang. Bang. Bang.

What was it? A gate? A Persian blind blown by the wind?

Anna's heart beat faster. The noise was so loud the bed and the floor were shaking.

Bang. Bang. Bang.

The blows were rhythmic, mechanical.

The blue children. They're trying to get in.

She sat up, got out of bed and walked towards the bedroom

door, which was quivering in its frame. After a moment's hesitation she gripped the handle and opened it a little.

A bluish glare lit up the opposite wall and the floor. Now the noise was so deafening she couldn't even think.

Her legs were stiff with fear. As she approached the living room she was blinded by sabre-thrusts of light which slashed across the ceiling and glittered on the glass of a display case full of cups and medals, on the pictures on the wall, and on the gilded case of the barometer. Beneath the banging a voice could be heard.

She leaned against the wall, unable to go on. Her body seemed to be crawling with ants.

The voice was inside the television.

'Some are laughing, others crying. Many are lying on the ground. Many are trying to board the ship by climbing up the sides,' said a man.

Anna was in the centre of the room. The lights of the chandelier flickered in time with the shade of the standard lamp, and the red zeros of a clock pulsed like the eyes of a predator lurking in the shadows. A black and white picture showed on the screen. Thousands of people, massed on the quay of a harbour. Behind them, columns of smoke, enveloping cranes and containers.

Bang. Bang. Bang.

In front of the television the armchair opened and closed, roaring and vibrating like the jaws of a mechanical monster. Dr Mezzopane's withered corpse was being pushed back and forth on the table, his head, on one side, sliding across the glass, dragging the jawbone with it, staring at Anna with white bulbous eyes like hard-boiled eggs.

She screamed, and went on screaming as she opened her eyes, sucking in the warm, musty air of the flat with a sound like whooping cough.

The sun filtered through the blinds, sprinkling bright dots on the walls, carpet and bed. Sparrows were twittering.

Lying there in bed, she realised that she was covered in sweat. She felt as if she'd been pulled out from under a heap of warm damp sand. Gradually she started to fill her lungs and breathe more freely.

This wasn't the first time she'd dreamed of a sudden return of electricity. The nightmare was truly alarming, even worse than those in which Grown-ups came back to eat her.

She got up from the bed. Her mouth was thick with the aftertaste of grappa. In the broom cupboard, behind the washing machine, she found two small plastic tanks full of water as flavourless as rain. Donning her shorts and a white T-shirt adorned with the slogan PARIS, JE T'AIME, she picked up her rucksack and left the flat.

★

Michelini's body was not far from the road, his round head deep in nettles, his hands dug into the earth. His T-shirt was rolled up to his shoulders, revealing a pale back covered with blotches. They'd taken his shoes.

Further off, in the middle of the field, the small body of a blue kid lay among the stubble.

She wondered whether to go back to the convenience store to stock up again. No, the important thing was to take the medicine to Astor. The shop could wait till another day when there was more time.

She set off for home.

A light autumn breeze was blowing; soon the weather would change. Anna was happy. She had the antibiotics. All the food in the Michelinis' shop would keep them going for at least a year. And once it started raining again, they'd have water too.

Now there could be no more excuses; she must teach Astor to read properly.

4

Maria Grazia Zanchetta had fallen ill three days after Christmas, and died at the beginning of June, still repeating to her daughter that she must teach her brother to read.

In the last weeks of her life, exhausted by fever and dehydration, she'd slipped into a stupor from which she'd occasionally re-emerge, muttering deliriously. They mustn't miss the last chairlift, there were too many jellyfish in the sea and the flowers growing in her bed were too prickly. But sometimes, especially in the morning, there were flashes of lucidity; then she'd seek out her daughter's hand and keep mumbling the same things, which even the virus couldn't erase from her mind.

Anna must be good, must look after Astor, must teach him to read, must not lose the book of Important Things.

'Promise!' she'd gasp, dripping with sweat.

The little girl was sitting beside her. 'I promise, Mama.'

Maria Grazia would shake her head, closing her bloodshot eyes. 'Again!'

'I promise, Mama.'

'Louder!'

'I promise, Mama.'

'Swear to me that you'll do it.'

'I swear I will.'

But she still wasn't satisfied. 'No you won't . . . You . . .'

Anna would hug her, inhaling a pungent odour of sweat

and sickness, quite different from the pleasant soapy smell her mother had always had. 'I will, Mama. I swear I will.'

In the last week she completely lost consciousness and her daughter understood that there was not long to go.

One afternoon, while the children were playing in her room, Maria Grazia opened her mouth and eyes and stretched out her limbs, as if a mountain had been placed on top of her. Then the grimace that had twisted her face went away and her own features reappeared.

Anna shook her, squeezed her hand, put her ear to her nostrils. Not a single breath. She picked up the book of Important Things from the table and delicately leafed through it. It was full of chapters: water, batteries, personal hygiene, fire, friendships. On the last page was the following chapter:

WHAT TO DO WHEN MAMA DIES

When I die I'll be too heavy for you to carry me outside. Open the windows, Anna, take everything you need and lock the door. You must wait a hundred days. On the page next to this one I've drawn a hundred bars. Every morning cross one of them out. You can only open the door again when they're finished. Until then, don't open it, on any account. If it gets too smelly in the house, take your brother and go to live in the toolshed. Only return to the house to get what you need. When the hundred days are up, come back into my room. Don't look at my face. Tie me up with a rope and pull me outside. It'll be easy for you, because I won't be very heavy. Take me into the wood, as far away as you can, to some spot that you like, and cover me with stones. Clean my room thoroughly with bleach. Throw the mattress away. Then you can come back into the house.

Anna opened the windows, took the exercise book, the toys and the fairy tales and, just as she'd been ordered, locked the door.

Over the next few days, she and Astor spent most of the time outside. Her brother kept her very busy, but as soon as he went to sleep she'd run upstairs, stand by the door and look through the keyhole. All she could see was the opposite wall.

What if she'd made a mistake? What if Mama wasn't dead?

She seemed to hear her imploring in a feeble voice: 'Annina, Annina . . . I'm sick . . . Open the door. I'm thirsty. Please . . .' Then she'd take out the key, turn it over and over in her hands, rest her forehead against the doorpost. 'Mama! I'm here. If you're alive, call to me. I'm out here, by the door. I'll come in. Don't worry, you don't disgust me. I'll come in for a second and take a look, and if you're dead I'll close the door again straight away. I promise.'

Some time later, while she and Astor were in the farmyard, three crows landed on the balcony outside their mother's bedroom. Perched in a row on the railing, they croaked like self-satisfied gravediggers.

Anna picked up a stone from the ground and threw it at them. 'Go away, you bastards.' The three ugly birds hopped down and went haughtily into the house.

She ran upstairs, fetched the key and opened the door. A sickly stench hit her. She clasped her hand over her mouth, but the smell had entered her throat. The three crows were hopping over the corpse, tearing strips of skin off the legs with their beaks. She shooed them away, but they took their time before flying off, looking rather resentful.

It was impossible not to look at her.

Mama was dead, there was no doubt about it. Her skin was mainly yellow, like washing soap, or dark red in the parts where the body touched the mattress. Her features had disappeared into a rubbery mask, the mouth a yellow doughnut, the nose sunken between the eyelids. Her neck, rippling with green veins, had engulfed her mouth.

Anna left the room sobbing, and swearing she'd never open the door again until the hundred days had gone by.

As predicted in the exercise book, the smell became unbearable. Anna moved into the toolshed annex with her little brother, only returning to the house, with a cloth over her face, to replenish their stock of food.

The days passed slowly in an interminable summer, and the shed's corrugated iron roof became scalding hot. They took to sleeping in the porch or on the back seat of the Mercedes. Every morning Anna would open the exercise book, cross out one bar and have a fleeting glance at the bedroom window. The wind billowed the curtains, white like sails.

She knew there was only a corpse in there, yet she would dream she saw her mother come out onto the balcony, stretch, then rest her elbows on the railing. 'Morning, children. Up already?'

'Yes, Mama.'

'What are you doing?'

'Playing.'

Sometimes she'd manage for weeks on end to put crosses in the exercise book, prepare meals, dig holes to put shit in and gaze at the stars through the rear window of the Mercedes, without thinking about her too much. Then something nice would happen and she'd blurt out: 'Mama, look . . .' And a white-hot blade would go straight through her heart.

When the ninety-ninth day came, she decided to spend it in the car.

Throughout the day an autumn breeze had been shaking the treetops. She and her brother had huddled under a blanket. Anna was just longing for the moment when she could open that door. Everything would be so much better once Mama had been buried.

Sleep came suddenly and, overcome by the tension, she

collapsed beside her brother. Some time later she opened her eyes. The wind had dropped and the moon was a perfect ring in the black sky. No haze blurred its outline. Not a sound came from the woods, not even the hooting of owls. All at once she seemed to hear something – a faint noise, an icy shudder, perhaps a sigh. She sat up, digging her fingers into the seat cushion. Through the side window she thought she saw a shadow come down the porch steps and pass by her, as light as a feather. It moved on down the drive and faded into the trees, as though the wood had been waiting for it.

The next morning Anna marked the last cross in the exercise book and said to Astor: 'Now stay here, keep quiet and don't be a nuisance.' She entered the house, fetched the long rope she'd set aside for this occasion and went upstairs. The smell of decay had gone, or perhaps was now such an integral part of the house it no longer bothered her. Walking hesitantly along the dark corridor, she took a deep breath and went in.

The floor was covered with leaves, but nothing else had changed. The desk with the computer on it, the bookcase crammed with books, the poster of the ballerina, the bedside tables crowded with medicines, the radio alarm – they were all still there. On the bed lay a shrivelled corpse. The swelling had gone down, the skin had retracted onto the bones and was now covered with blackish mould. The head had shrunk and tapered.

Anna felt neither fear nor disgust. That thing there wasn't her mother. At the sight of those remains, she sensed that life is just a long succession of periods of waiting – sometimes so short you're not even aware of them, sometimes so long they seem endless. But with or without patience they all have an end.

Mama had died at the end of her illness, and now, a hundred days later, her body was light and could be buried.

Astor, who now drove her crazy with his tantrums, would stop doing so when he grew older. It was just a question of waiting.

She tied the rope round her mother's ankle and pulled hard. The corpse, being stuck to the sheets, put up some resistance, then fell on the floor. Without another backward glance she dragged it along the corridor, down the stairs and across the sitting room. The body swung from side to side, and finally latched onto the jamb of the front door, as though not wanting to leave the house, but with another tug found itself ploughing across the yard. The little girl pulled it through the dust, then through the leaves of the wood. Behind the bramble-covered ruins of the pigsty rose the green dome of a fig tree. Under its vault there was a small quiet world. Mama would be happy here; it was shady in summer, and in winter you could see the sky. The stones were there, ready. She arranged the corpse beside the trunk. Fallen fruit formed a brown layer on the ground, where wasps and ants were feasting.

Anna picked up a stone and put it on her mother's chest. Then she stopped. Even if she covered her with stones the insects would soon strip the flesh off, and in a few weeks there'd be nothing left but bones.

Why not let the ants deal with Mama? Bones can be kept indoors; they don't smell. Mama would be able to go back to her bedroom and lie on her bed, with her things and her children around her. Anna would put her back together again with the help of the illustrations in the encyclopaedia.

She brought some jam from the boxes in the larder and spread it over the body, saying: 'There you are, ants. That'll make it tastier for you. Come on . . . tuck in . . . it's delicious. Clean it up . . . every single crumb . . .'

★

Within a month the insects had done their job. There were still a few scraps of dried flesh on the bones, but Anna didn't let that discourage her. Carrying them all to the bedroom, she sat down cross-legged and scraped them clean with the tip of a screwdriver. After that, she thought it would be a nice idea to draw lines, rings and other tiny geometrical figures on them with a black felt-tip pen. Then she laid them out on the bed and reassembled the skeleton.

Astor would do the same with her when her time came.

*

Anna had fallen into an unthinking stupor. She felt as if she was walking along a road that flowed in the opposite direction. The pursuit, then the nightmare, and finally lack of sleep had left her drained, and now, like a beast of burden, she was enjoying the cool breeze, the silence and the warm rays of the sun, pulsing in the clear sky. So she was a little slow in noticing the bell, and it was only when she heard a voice behind her shouting: 'Out of the way! Out of the way! Look out!' that she awoke from her reverie. Turning round, she saw a bicycle coming straight at her.

She jumped up onto a low wall just in time to avoid being flattened by a boy in a cowboy hat riding an orange mountain bike.

The cyclist went past her, squeezing the brakes, which screeched, but the bike didn't slow down, so he jammed his feet on the ground just in time to avoid crashing into a lamp post. He dropped the bike on the road. 'These brakes are useless.' He shook his head and turned round. 'Are you deaf?'

Anna didn't reply.

The boy came towards her. 'I nearly ran you over.'

He seemed about the same age as Anna, but stood some ten centimetres taller than her, and that funny hat made him look like a mushroom. He was tall and thin, with a suntanned face and two mischievous hazel eyes.

What was going on? For the past year the plain had been deserted, but in the last two days she'd come across the blue and white children and now this boy.

Anna stepped down off the wall and walked on.

The cyclist followed. 'Wait a minute.'

Anna continued to walk, feeling the boy's eyes on her. She turned round and snapped: 'What do you want?'

'Look, there's no need to be scared of me.'

Anna saw the adult features emerging from the childish face and thought he might grow into a handsome man.

'I'm not scared; I'm in a hurry.'

He overtook her and barred her way. 'If you're on your way to the party, you're wasting your time. It's all bullshit.'

Anna put her hands on her hips. 'What party?'

'At the Grand Spa Hotel. People from all over Sicily are going there. They're going to burn the Little Lady.'

'Why are they going to do that?'

'So they can eat the ashes. It's said to cure the Red Fever.'

Anna smiled. Michelini's story had been that you had to French-kiss her.

'I've been there and I've never seen the Little Lady,' the boy went on. He doffed his hat in a chivalrous gesture and introduced himself. 'My name's Pietro Serra. What's yours?'

'Anna.'

Smoothie. She remembered the word her mother used to use when she went to the newsagent's kiosk and the owner eyed her like she was a chocolate just waiting to be unwrapped.

Better cut across the fields to get rid of him. 'Well, I'm off.' She'd only gone a few metres when she heard the bell ringing and the brakes screeching again.

He stopped alongside her. 'Would you give me some water, please, Anna?'

Sticking out of a bag strapped to the bicycle's luggage rack was the neck of a bottle. 'What about that?'

'That . . .' Pietro improvised, 'isn't as good as yours.'

Anna burst out laughing. 'How do you know that?'

'I just do.' He reached for the rucksack. 'Go on, just one swig . . .'

She stepped aside. 'No! I said no!'

'If you let me have some of your water, I'll give you a ride.'

This cocky boy was unnerving. He had a way of looking at her that made her feel ill at ease. 'Two people can't ride on one bike.'

'Who says they can't? You can sit here, on the crossbar.'

Anna hesitated for a moment before replying: 'I don't like bikes. Anyway, I don't want to ride on one with you.'

'See? You *are* scared!'

Anna clenched her fists in irritation. 'I'm not scared, it's just that . . .'

'. . . you're in a hurry,' Pietro finished her sentence for her.

The two of them looked at each other, without finding anything else to add.

The girl broke the silence. 'Well, goodbye, then.'

'Goodbye, Anna.'

★

Anna, with the cowboy hat on her head, screamed as she clung onto the bicycle's handlebars. The wind streamed over her face, and her eyes were watering, as they used to do when she stuck her head out of her father's Mercedes.

Pietro was pedalling flat out. 'Well? Do you like it?'

They were racing along, squeezed against each other, on a narrow road that cut across the fields as straight as a ruler. Lamp posts and prickly pears flashed by on either side.

'Yes,' said Anna, though the crossbar was cutting into her buttocks and she was terrified of falling off. Every time Pietro's arms touched her, she flinched and wanted to move away, but didn't.

Pietro went into a bend without slowing down. Anna screamed and shut her eyes. When she opened them again, she was safe. 'Go slowly round the bends. Faster on the straight bits, though.'

'Faster than this?' panted the boy, his forehead glistening with sweat. 'Where do you want me to take you?'

'Torre Normanna. Do you know where it is?'

'Yes, but can I go a bit slower? This is killing me. I thought you didn't like cycling.'

'I like the wind in my face.'

'Have you ever been on a motorbike? You really do feel the wind then. If you open your mouth, it blows out your cheeks.'

'I rode on a Vespa with Salvo, the boy who used to deliver our shopping.'

'My father used to have a Laverda Jota.' Pietro gazed into the distance, shaking his head. 'It was orange, like this bike. Some day I'll find one that works. And I'll ride on it.'

'Oh yeah . . .' Anna burst out into one of her deep-throated laughs.

But he was sure of it. 'I will, you know.'

They went the rest of the way in silence. The ruins of Torre Normanna grew bigger with each turn of the pedals. They raced past wrecks of crashed cars, melted rubbish bins, the remains of a bar with a sign that said: 'Takeaway hot arancini.'

Anna had the impression that he was pressing too close against her, but she didn't actually dislike it. In the end she kept still, with his chest brushing against her back.

Pietro stopped by the village sign. 'Is this a good place to drop you?'

'Yes.' Anna jumped off the bike, rubbing her sore behind. She untied the rucksack from the luggage rack and gave him back his hat. 'Thanks. Well . . . goodbye, then.'

Pietro smiled and raised his hand. 'Goodbye.'

They said 'goodbye' twenty more times, but when she'd taken a dozen steps he called after her: 'Anna!'

He wants a kiss.

She turned round. 'Yes?'

Pietro had taken out of his jacket pocket a crumpled page from a magazine, folded in four. 'Have you ever seen these?'

In the middle of the page, circled by a red felt-tip pen, was a faded photograph of a pair of yellow suede trainers with three black stripes: 'Adidas Hamburg, 95 euros'. Next to it were some smaller photographs. The headline of the article was 'The Great Vintage Sportswear Revival'.

She looked up. 'The ones with the ring round them?'

'Yes. Have you ever seen them? Think carefully.'

'I don't think so.' She looked at her own filthy trainers.

'Are you quite sure?'

Anna didn't see the point of all this. He must have a thing about shoes. Strange – the walking boots he was wearing were battered and shapeless. 'Are you really keen on them?'

Pietro hesitated for a moment, as if reluctant to admit it, then said: 'Yes. I've been searching for them for ages.'

Anna looked at him dubiously, then said: 'Well, good luck then.'

Pietro kicked a stone. 'Listen . . . have you got the Red Fever yet?'

'No. Goodbye.' And she went off.

Pietro watched her walk away. 'Neither have I,' he shouted.

★

'All the people I meet are crazy.' Anna was talking to herself as she hurried along the path towards home. 'A boy who spends his time searching for a pair of shoes . . . and ugly ones at that.'

She thought about the party again. Did the Little Lady really exist? There were lots of stupid stories about how to be cured of the Red Fever. Many kids were convinced that a certain number of Grown-ups had survived the epidemic, that there were still some alive across the sea, in Calabria. They were hiding in underground shelters; all you had to do was find them and you'd be cured. Others believed you had to dive underwater with a hen and stay down till it died; you recovered because you transferred the virus to the hen. Some thought the thing to do was to mix food with sand, or go up onto a mountain near Catania which sprouted clouds. There were lots of stories of that kind. All Anna knew was that she'd seen thousands of Grown-ups reduced to heaps of bones and had never met any living person older than fourteen.

★

She went straight into the kitchen, took a jar of peeled tomatoes off the table, opened it with the knife, hooked out a dripping tomato with two fingers and popped it into her mouth, shouting: 'Astor, I'm back. Everything okay?'

She ate some old biscuits, which tasted of mould, then poured the oily remains of a can of tuna into the jar of tomatoes and drank the sauce, beginning to sweat. Outside the day was cool, but indoors the old stone walls retained the heat. She drank half a bottle of water. 'I found the anti-biotics!' Taking another tomato from the jar, she crossed the living room.

There was a white chair by the stairs, with a broken leg.

'Oh no! You've broken Mama's chair.' She went upstairs, her face red with sauce, and walked along the landing. 'Hey! Did you hear me say I'm back?'

Everything was on the floor. The book of fairy tales lay in a pool of water. Shaking her head, she picked it up and put it on the bedside table.

Every time she left him alone, Astor did something stupid. But this time he'd gone too far; he was going to catch it. He seemed to do it on purpose, to punish her.

She looked down from the balcony, called him twice, then went back inside. If he'd gone outside, it meant he was feeling better.

Her hunger still wasn't sated. A jar of peas wouldn't be bad. She started down the stairs, musing about the boy on the bike. Where would he have gone? Perhaps he'd stayed in Torre Normanna.

A beam of sunlight shone between the pieces of cardboard stuck to a window, painting a strip of light on the steps, a ball of blankets and a red cap. She picked the cap up. On the peak was the word 'Nutella'. She turned it over in her hands and held it up to her nose.

She remembered Michelini's body sprawled by the roadside. The hands clutching weeds, the straddled legs, the back of his head . . .

She had a flashback to the blues walking off down the road, the tall girl with the red cap on her head . . .

Her heart started thumping. She walked on down the stairs, the blood throbbing in her eardrums. It was as if she'd never had to cope with a stairway before. It seemed to be swaying.

She went out into the porch. With one hand she screened the sun, which was expanding and shrinking in the centre of the cloudy sky. 'Ast— Ast— Astor.' She tried to call her brother, but her lungs were empty. The acid taste of tomato returned to her mouth. She restrained the impulse to throw up and found enough breath to say: 'Astor . . . Astor . . . Astor . . .'

He wasn't in the Mercedes, nor behind the rubbish bins. *Maybe he's in the wood.*

A brown falcon hung motionless in mid-air, intent on something hidden among the trees.

She plunged into the undergrowth, tripping on stones and dry branches. Holly scratched her legs, but she hardly noticed.

A purple patch stood out in the greenery. She went towards it. It was a piece of cloth; she snatched it free of the thorns.

Mama's dress. The nice one.

What was it doing there? Anna knew Astor had a hidden key and went into the room when she was out. But why had he thrown the dress into the brambles?

She staggered, and had to lean against a tree trunk. Breathing in, she screwed up her eyelids and called Astor's name louder, at the top of her voice, but the only answer came from the birds in the trees.

She reached the edge of the grounds, passing under a great oak tree which her brother loved to climb. She walked on round the fence, but couldn't focus on anything. She kept seeing the blue children running along like mad dogs.

She came to the old pigsty overgrown by brambles. He wasn't there either. Nor was he under the fig tree.

She checked the rubbish heap behind the house, where her brother sometimes liked to rummage.

She fell on her knees, panting. 'Calm . . . you must keep calm . . .'

He might be anywhere, the fool – sleeping in some animal's lair, on a branch at the top of a tree, on the roof of the house.

Maybe he managed to get out.

No, he'd never have gone outside the fence.

She sat down on a tree trunk, rubbing her face with her hands, her mind entangled in anxious thoughts. Hot sweat poured from her armpits.

The wood – her magic wood – surrounded her, but gave no answers.

'Where are you? Come here,' she shouted. Then she started running again: 'Astor! Astor! Where are you? I'll kill you when I find you!' She went back towards the house. It was possible that she had a cap like that herself. She'd brought all kinds of things home over the years; maybe they included a Nutella cap and she'd forgotten about it.

How stupid she was – she'd panicked needlessly. Her brother was asleep somewhere. She hadn't checked the toolshed or Mama's bedroom; she'd rushed outside without looking carefully.

She pushed through the box hedge and came out onto the drive. She passed something white and round among the weeds. She stopped, turned back, picked it up and nearly collapsed.

She was holding her mother's skull.

Her mind empty of thought, she walked into the house. Her eyes noted that the crockery, instead of being on the dresser, was on the floor. Astor's pedal car was upside down, the mandolin smashed. She laid the skull on a box and went upstairs.

The door of Mama's bedroom was open, the metal lock sticking out among jagged strips of wood.

★

Gradually Anna re-emerged from a shroud of misery, swaying backwards and forwards between wakefulness and sleep. The morning sun warmed her forehead and hurt her eyes. Her cheek lay in a pool of dry vomit, and there was an empty gin bottle next to her nose. Her tongue was so swollen it seemed too big for her mouth, and a piercing pain ran through her head from one temple to the other. She couldn't remember how she'd ended up on the back seat of the Mercedes.

Only faint traces – fragments, moments of pain – remained of the hours that had passed since she'd found the door of Mama's bedroom smashed open. Everything was enveloped in a shadowy haze, with occasional flashes, which lit up two Annas, one fighting desperately, the other looking on in silence. The thread that connected the images of that night had been broken; beads of memory floated in a sea of slimy black oil.

Mama's bedroom ransacked. Bones scattered everywhere. Jewels stolen. Drawers pulled out. The bookcase toppled. Astor's toy giraffe: she'd bitten its head off; the synthetic taste of its stuffing still lingered in her mouth. She'd punched the bathroom mirror, cutting her knuckles, and wrapped herself, bleeding, in a curtain, her open lips sucking the thin cloth. The bottle of gin. Tearless crying and desperate sobs. An earthy smell of moss. Leaves rustling in time with her breathing. Her mother's purple dress.

And an overwhelming despair.

She sat in the driver's seat, head against the window, staring at her wounded hand.

She had a feeling that during the night a living presence, hidden in the darkness, had been watching her from the wood.

The dog from the autostrada.

She must have dreamed it, yet this memory was more vivid than all the others. The dog beside her. Sitting there quietly, his thick tail sweeping the ground. Speaking to her: 'Do you remember the nursery rhyme, Anna? Clap hands, little children, and come to the window: the bogeyman's beaten and laid in his bed. All fear has been banished, new life is beginning. Rejoice little children, the bogeyman's dead!'

He looked at her with his dark pupils. 'Shall I turn out the light?'

Now her father was there, tucking in the bedclothes. 'I'll leave the door open a little, don't worry.'

Part Two

The Grand Spa Hotel Elise

5

Anna Salemi decided to go looking for the blue children. If she found them, she'd find her brother too. The idea that he might be dead didn't even cross her mind.

She left Mulberry Farm on 30 October 2020, never to return. In her rucksack, in addition to some clothes, a bottle of water and the antibiotics for Astor, were a torch, a cigarette lighter, the book of Important Things wrapped in a green sweatshirt, a kitchen knife and her mother's right thighbone.

The trees quivered with twittering sparrows, foxes rustled among the bushes, crows cawed harshly. Outside the wood she found herself under a carpet of dense bluish clouds which pressed down like an inverted stormy sea. Gusts of warm air from the coast pushed her forward, ruffling her hair. At the end of the plain a thunderstorm gathered over the mountains in a glow of sandy light. A clap of thunder as loud as a cannonade gave the signal for the start of proceedings and rain poured down furiously on the thirsty fields, which absorbed it in silence, exhaling a damp aura of burnt earth.

Long before she arrived in Torre Normanna Anna was soaking wet, her feet sloshing in her walking boots, her hair plastered down on her forehead, the strip of cloth drooping from her wounded hand.

For months she'd been longing for rain, but it had chosen the worst possible moment to come, when it would only make things more difficult. But at least there was a chance it had stopped the blues. They might have taken shelter in Torre Normanna.

The village was engulfed in a cloud of water which overflowed from blocked gutters, flooding the streets. Piazzetta dei Venti had disappeared under a lake which rippled violently, lashed by the downpour.

The storm paused for a deep breath before unleashing hail.

Anna took refuge under the porch of A Taste of Aphrodite. The corrugated iron roof of the veranda shook under volleys of frozen pellets the size of cherries. She took the exercise book out of the rucksack. The sweatshirt had protected it, and only the corners of the cover had got wet.

The door of the restaurant had been broken open. Inside, in the large circular room, tables and chairs were heaped up in one corner as if they'd been pushed there by a bulldozer. On the wall there was still a blackboard with a handwritten notice: 'Today's speciality, tuna steak *alla Messinese*, 18 euros'. A brass lamp hung crookedly from the ceiling, as if someone had battered it with a stick.

Anna walked into the kitchen, sending mice scattering in all directions. Only a few tiles were left on the walls, the others strewn on the floor in heaps of white shards. The big fridge lay on its back, its doors wide open.

Anna knelt down, opened one of the salad drawers and put the thighbone and the book inside. Then she closed it and went out.

The hail had stopped and been replaced by a thin drizzle.

She was wasting time. There was nobody here. Perhaps they'd gone towards the autostrada. Or maybe to Castellammare. She kicked a white plastic chair.

Calm down.

Gripping the straps of her rucksack, she set out along

the road that led out of the village. After a few steps she stopped.

An orange bike was leaning against a cottage gate.

★

The front door was locked from the inside. A little way to the right, however, a French window was wide open, giving access to the sitting room. Here, too, everything had been wrecked. Smashed furniture, graffiti on the walls, ashes from a bonfire on which chairs had been burned.

She walked up the stairs, which were covered in debris. She entered the first room. On top of a mirrored wardrobe two little owls opened four bright golden eyes and flew away. Fast asleep on a double bed, wrapped in a dirty eiderdown, was Pietro. Tufts of ruffled hair, a section of forehead and one eyebrow stuck out at one end of the roll of rags.

Anna pushed at his backside with the sole of his foot. 'Wake up!'

The boy opened his mouth and gave a strangled groan. He tried to get up, but, straitjacketed in the bedclothes, slid off the mattress. 'What? What? Who is it?' He grabbed the knife that lay next to his bag and pointed it at his attacker.

'Have you seen some blue children?'

Pietro screwed up his eyes and recognised Anna. 'You're crazy.' He dropped the knife and put a hand to his chest. 'I nearly died of fright.'

'Have you seen some blue children?'

Pietro crawled over to the wall and put his back against it, rubbing one eye. 'The blue kids . . .'

Anna had to swallow a lump in her throat before she could speak: 'They've taken my brother.'

Pietro gaped at her as she stood in front of him, dripping wet. 'When?'

'Yesterday morning, I think.' She went over to the window. 'They can't be far away. Did you meet them?'

'No. But I know them,' he replied, yawning.

A glimmer of hope showed in Anna's face. 'Who are they?'

'They live at the hotel. The older kids catch them in the countryside and use them as slaves.'

'Why?'

Pietro stretched his back. He was wearing a pair of tattered yellow and green striped underpants and a vest that was too small for him. 'To prepare for the Fire Party. They've got lots of them up there.'

Anna shut her eyes and opened them again. The room around her seemed to crumble to pieces and reassemble itself quickly: the mattress, the wardrobe, the boy in his underpants. Her chest rose and she breathed again. Astor was alive. She swallowed. 'How do you get to the hotel?'

'Just a minute.' Pietro rubbed his cheek. 'I'm not very good at thinking in the morning.'

Anna waited three seconds. 'How do you get to the hotel?'

Pietro lowered his head. He squeezed the base of his nose. 'Go under the autostrada, and when you come to the round-about take the road to the mountains. Eventually you'll come to a big notice that says "Grand Spa Hotel Elise". Keep going straight on and you'll get there. It's a long walk, though, I'm warning you.'

Anna stepped forward, crouched down and gave him a hug.

Pietro sat there stiffly and, in embarrassment, picked up a jar of jam from the floor, dipped in his finger and put it into his mouth. 'And watch out, it's not a nice place.'

Anna shrugged her shoulders. 'I've got to get my brother back.'

Pietro took a sip from a half-empty bottle of water. 'Why?'

'What kind of a question's that? He's my brother!'

Outside it was still raining, but the blanket of clouds had parted over a patch of blue sky.

As she was going downstairs, Pietro called out to her. 'Wait! Put this on. It's dry.' He threw her a cardigan.

She caught it and said, 'Thanks.'

★

For a while Anna kept looking back, hoping to see the boy appear on his bike. She'd have liked to have someone alongside her to share her anxiety, which increased with every step she took.

The rain had cleared the mountains of the haze that had shrouded them throughout the summer. Now they were closer. Everything was sharply defined: the green patches of the trees, the bites taken out of the land by quarries and the gullies of white rock which split the mountains like ripe tomatoes.

Somewhere up there was Astor.

★

Anna walked at a regular pace, arms alternating with legs. Thoughts slowly detached themselves from a tangled skein and drifted away. She no longer resorted to pointless exercises like adding up numbers on car numberplates or guessing how many steps it would take to walk from one point to another.

The underpass below the autostrada was flooded. She walked through it, getting her shoes soaked, arrived at the roundabout and took the road to the mountains.

In this area the fires had been particularly violent, fuelled by a succession of industrial plants and coal depots. Anything not made of stone or metal had been reduced to ashes. Carcasses of cars like roasted cockroaches filled a parking lot in front of a low building. On its roof was the skeleton of a large sign.

'Pi . . . zza . . . rium,' she deciphered. 'Pizzarium'.

She was fainting with hunger and a blister had formed on her left heel.

On the other side of a long iron fence lay the remains of a factory. There was not much left of the buildings, but some huge white cisterns had survived. Twined around them was a network of rusty, moss-covered pipes. Water seeping out of the joins had flooded the asphalted yard, turning it into a swamp in which large pieces of polystyrene floated.

She found a gap between the bars and walked forward, threading her way through a tangle of marsh plants. Red dragonflies and long-legged mosquitoes swarmed around her and frogs hopped between her feet.

Lying down on the bonnet of a Cinquecento, she took off her rucksack and shoes.

Her toes were rubbery and white, as if she'd dipped them in bleach. She burst a blister with her thumbnail, then removed the bandage from her hand. The cut between the knuckles was deep, but no longer bleeding. She rubbed her calves and leaned back against the windscreen under the lukewarm sun.

One by one, the frogs started croaking again.

What a wonderful place the Pizzarium must have been. You went in with money and came out with a slice of warm pizza, wrapped in white paper, the melted mozzarella seeping out from below, the red juice of the tomatoes scorching your palate. And if you didn't like the Margherita you could have one with mushrooms, potatoes, zucchini or anchovies.

So lost was she in the world of pizza that it was some time before she noticed that the frogs had fallen silent. Opening her eyes, she saw in front of her, a few metres away, the dog from the autostrada.

He was standing motionless, paws in the water, neck

outstretched. Where Anna had wounded him the hair had formed crusty black balls from which a thick reddish liquid oozed out. The rest of his coat was white and ruffled. He seemed even bigger, if that were possible.

The girl held her breath; the Maremma panted, his tongue curling up in front of his black nose.

Anna laid one hand on the rucksack. Inside was the knife. She couldn't detach her gaze from those hypnotic eyes as black as lapilli.

How could he be here, in front of her, alive?

The animal lowered his head and took two laps of water, watching her all the time.

Anna breathed in, waiting for something, even she didn't know what – perhaps only for him to disappear. Then she stood up on the bonnet, raised her fist and growled at him: 'What do you want with me? Leave me alone! Wasn't that beating I gave you enough?'

The dog lay down in the mud and rolled over in it, arching his back and stretching out a paw as if in greeting. Then he lifted his thigh, showing his belly, pink with black patches, and gave a whine of pleasure.

Anna was taken aback.

That devil had trapped her in a car and damn near eaten her alive, and now he was behaving like those lapdogs that ladies took around with them on leads and which turned into floor cloths as soon as you stroked them.

She jumped off the car. 'Go away! Shoo!'

The dog sprang to his feet and, tail between his legs, vanished into the reeds.

★

How on earth had he found her? And why had he run away, instead of attacking her?

That was what Anna was thinking about as she trudged

up a steep road which snaked along between burnt strips of meadowland. Now and then she turned round, certain that he was behind her, but he wasn't.

With the effort, another worry occupied her mind. She hadn't reached the hotel signboard yet; had she taken the wrong road? The rucksack felt as heavy as if it were full of stones. 'Another thousand steps, and if I don't find it I'm turning back,' she said to herself.

Two bends later, as though her thoughts had summoned it up, a big sign appeared at the side of the road. Under a layer of soot she could just make out the words: 'Grand Spa Hotel Elise. Exclusive Holiday Accommodation and Golf Club'.

She clenched her fist. 'So it's true! Thanks, Pietro!'

The rucksack was light again and her pace fast.

The road grew narrower. There were no houses on either side now, and the blackened areas gave way to greenery. The eucalyptuses were in full leaf, oleanders extended branches laden with flowers, prickly pears formed barriers of thorns. A cow placidly crossed her path without so much as a sideways glance. The wind now carried a fresh smell of grass, instead of the pungent reek of burnt vegetation.

On one slope, rows of vines drooped under the weight of withered grapes on which bees settled. She ran over to try some; they were so sweet they sent a shiver down her spine. Putting two bunches in the rucksack, she walked on.

She was feeling better. For the first time that day she managed not to think about her brother, but just enjoy the scenery, the sun casting a silvery tinge on pine foliage stirred by the breeze.

At the top of the slope she found herself looking out over a rolling plateau covered with wheat and clumps of broom, and bristling with wind turbines, like so many pinwheels stuck into the land by some giant.

In the past she'd sometimes looked up at them from the

plain, from where they'd seemed tiny and out of reach. She'd never imagined they were so huge.

Maybe she'd be able to see the hotel from the top of one of them.

The first one didn't seem far away; she'd only have to cross a field which sloped down into a narrow cleft and rose up again to a ridge. She hesitated for a moment by the roadside, then stuck her thumbs under the straps of her rucksack and set off.

After a few steps she was chest-deep in ears of wheat which scratched her arms and legs. Crickets darted around her. A pheasant flew up from the golden carpet, uttering its hoarse cries, then dropped down again further off. It took longer than she'd expected, but eventually she came to a square podium which emerged from the yellow crops like a concrete island.

Viewed from below, the tower was so tall the top was out of sight. An aluminium walkway led up to a small door that had been wrenched off its hinges and was hanging askew. An uninviting smell came from inside.

Anna took out her torch and shone it into a narrow spiral staircase which wound its way up the inside of the structure. On the bottom step some ants were stripping the flesh off a dead fox.

She stepped over the carcass and started up the stairs, climbing quickly, keeping the torch on the steps, which rose steeply and continuously, in a sweltering spiral. Before long she was dripping with sweat and gasping for breath. She sat down and rested her head against the wall. The metal was warm from the sun's heat.

She'd never felt so tired, uncertain and anxious. And to make things worse, the grapes she'd eaten were fermenting in her stomach.

She switched off the torch and darkness closed in, bringing reassurance.

She had long since learned not to be scared of it.

The rule was simple. Two films a week: on Saturday she'd decide, on Sunday Mama would; the rest of the time the TV set was covered in a coloured cloth, as if they were ashamed to have it in the house. But when the virus moved like a radioactive cloud from Belgium to Holland, France and the rest of the world, it was always left on, tuned in to the news channel.

After Mama's death Anna would spend all day in front of it. The book of Important Things didn't say anything about the TV, and she'd taken that as permission. But one by one the channels had disappeared, leaving blue screens in their place. Rai 1 kept going, but only broadcast written messages. The messages said not to go outside, that martial law was in force and that the number to call in an emergency was the civil protection helpline. The only thing she could do was keep watching all the DVDs in the bookcase over and over again, in a continuous cycle.

When the hydroelectric power station at Guadalami, the last one still functioning on the island, stopped, leaving Mulberry Farm and the whole of northern Sicily permanently without electricity, Anna was lying on the sofa watching *An Officer and a Gentleman*, the only good film in her mother's collection. Astor was sleeping beside her like a doll.

It was her favourite scene, when the soldier wearing a hat and a white uniform went into the factory and carried his girlfriend out, to the applause of the female workers. The television went dead and the blue numbers on the media player disappeared. Anna continued to stare at the black screen, not particularly concerned. The electricity supply had failed quite often in recent weeks.

This time it didn't come back. The age of light, as it would later be known, ended at that precise moment, as Richard Gere carried Debra Winger in his arms.

The day ended, the sun went down and the flower-shaped table lamp beside the sofa did not emit its reassuring yellow light. The fruit juice in the fridge became warm. Anna, with Astor clinging to her neck, switched on the torch and searched through the book of Important Things for the solution to the problem. The book said:

ELECTRICITY

Soon the electricity will run out and there will be no more light, no more television, no more computer, no more music, no more telephone, no more fridge. But don't be afraid. You'll soon get used to it. Human beings lived for a long time without electricity. All they had to do was light a fire. You'll live during the day and go to sleep as soon as it gets dark, just like the animals in the wood. At dawn you'll greet the sun with the birds. It'll be great. When you have nothing else to do you'll read books. And you'll make music by singing. At night, lock yourselves in the house and never go outside, on any account. Use candles. Batteries only in an emergency. But if you can, try to live in the dark.

That was it.

Without electricity, time lengthened out. Hours merged with one another, in days that dragged along with excruciating slowness. All sounds had vanished. The punctual chime of the bells of the village church. The ringing of mobile phones. The drone of aircraft. The wheezing of the rubbish collection lorry. When Astor slept, the silence was so oppressive it almost stunned her.

Anna learned to listen to the wind that made the windows shake and the leaves rustle; to the rumblings of her stomach, the calls of birds. In that clinging silence even the woodworm burrowing through the beams of the ceiling kept her company.

Anna had always been a talkative child. Now her mouth filled with words she had no use for. While opening the boxes that contained the tins of lentils, she'd talk to herself. 'There we are. Ready to eat. A nice little lunch.'

Even Astor's tantrums, which used to exasperate her, now made her feel less alone.

And she came to know Darkness.

She'd grown up in the knowledge that the lights of the house kept him outside the windows until Mama switched them off and they went to bed, when he could extend his black fingers over everything.

Back then she'd find him in the kitchen if she crept downstairs to get biscuits, but the oven clock with its red numbers and the green pilot light of the coffee machine would tell her not to be frightened. He'd be sliced in two by the car's headlights when they went out in the evening for a pizza, and you could momentarily kill him with the flash of your mobile phone. You created him so that you could carry the cake with candles on it, but that was fun. He hid in the toolshed, and there he really was scary. In that darkness reeking of petrol and paint, the grass trimmer, the old vacuum cleaner, a chair with its seat stoved in and the coat-hanger all became monsters waiting to tear you to pieces. In that total blackness only the mice grew bolder.

But now Darkness stifled, pressed in and, in collusion with silence, stunned her. Dull and compact, he penetrated every corner, every crevice: your mouth, your nostrils, the pores of your skin. Sometimes he came down so quickly you didn't even have time to prepare for it; at other times he came slowly: he mingled with the light, bloodied the sun and condemned it to disappear at the end of the plain. Candles were of no avail. The flickering ball that they spread around wasn't enough to defeat the gloom; on the contrary, it made everything more sinister and menacing.

In time Anna learned not to be afraid of Darkness; she entered his realm in the certainty that she would come out again. She'd lie under a blanket with her arms wrapped round her brother. When she needed a pee, she'd do it in a bowl beside the mattress, and eventually sleep would carry her off and give her back to the day.

Clouds or rain, cold or warmth, Darkness sooner or later lost his daily battle with the light.

*

As if someone had poured a bucket of water over her, Anna re-emerged from sleep stretching her arms, banged her elbow against the wall and jumped to her feet. The torch slipped off her knees. She stopped it rolling with the sole of her shoe and switched it on, painting ovals of light on the inside of the cylinder.

How long had she been asleep?

She stroked her wounded hand, waiting for her heart to calm down. She decided to climb another hundred steps. If she hadn't reached the top by then, she'd give up.

At forty-six the light framed a small open door and a little room full of buttons. Someone must have spent the night there: empty wine bottles and a blanket lay on the floor. On one side a vertical ladder led up to a trapdoor sealed by a kind of metal steering wheel. It was stiff, but by forcing with both hands she managed to turn it. She pushed the trapdoor up with her head.

She was dazzled by sunlight. After waiting for her pupils to adapt, she crawled out on all fours. The wind ruffled her hair, whistled in her ears and entered her mouth. Exhilarated and frightened, she clung to the handrail that ran round the roof of the turbine and looked out.

Beyond the hills the charred remains of villages formed encrustations on the plain, which spread out like a black table as far as the coast. Cutting straight across it, like a line drawn with a grey pencil, was the autostrada. The sea resembled a sheet of tin foil with a dark round island like a Baci

Perugina chocolate sitting on it, and another, smaller one further away. Behind that she thought she could make out a more shadowy strip – if it wasn't a trick of the light or an optical illusion.

The mainland.

Perhaps on the other side of the Strait the world had gone back to the way it used to be: Grown-ups had children and drove cars, shops were open, nobody died at the age of fourteen. Maybe Sicily and its orphans had just been forgotten. Of all the legends and ridiculous theories she'd heard, this seemed the only plausible one, the only one it was possible to believe in, the only one it was worth going to investigate.

She raised her chin and closed her eyes, trying to swallow the sharp lump in her throat. She gripped the railing and whispered: 'I swear that if I succeed in getting Astor back, I'll go across the sea and find out if any Grown-ups are still alive.' And she banged her forehead on the steel plate she was lying on.

She turned round to look inland. Hills merged into each other, changing from blue to azure to indigo. A road followed the undulations of the land until it reached a big isolated building beside a yellow crane.

The hotel.

*

She ran down the turbine into the darkness, shouting and slapping her hands against the walls. When she reached the bottom, her head was spinning. She crossed the wheatfield, the sky swaying around her, and returned to the road. Taking out the sweatshirt and putting it on, she set off again at a brisk pace.

After a short downward slope, the road continued on the flat, unreeling like a ribbon.

The landscape changed abruptly, as if it had been painted by a different artist. The yellow of wheat merged with the grey of rocks. The road was covered with a layer of thin sand. The only plants were bushes, agaves and a few sparse patches of dry grass. Skinny donkeys grazed on a steep ridge, and in the sky kestrels hung over their prey with outspread wings, as still as kites. In the fading daylight the rocky hills were like the shells of dead tortoises.

With a sense of foreboding, Anna turned round.

The dog was there. Following her, keeping his distance.

They walked in this way for a while, until, in exasperation, she picked up a stone and threw it at him. 'Go away!'

The Maremma dodged it with an agile leap and stared at her, as if he had something important to tell her.

She ran towards him, stamping her feet and waving her arms. 'Leave me alone!'

The dog turned around, loped away unhurriedly, as if weighed down with ballast, and disappeared into the bushes.

She walked on, but a moment later he was behind her again. 'Look, okay, you can follow me if you like. But I've got nothing to give you.' And she strode on without looking round again.

*

In a dusty lay-by the wreck of a blue coach shimmered in the dim twilight. Its windows were smashed and it was daubed with graffiti. Inside, the seats had been slashed and the floor was strewn with litter.

Climbing up onto the roof, Anna sat down cross-legged on the steel plating.

The dog looked at her for a while, with his head on one side, then disappeared under the coach.

The grapes in the rucksack had been squashed, but Anna ate them anyway, staring at the sky which tinged the orange filaments of the sunset with pearly grey, darkening higher up into starry night.

As soon as the darkness fell, the wind dropped. Her hunger hadn't passed and she felt rather exposed up there. Using the rucksack as a pillow, she lay down on her side with her hands between her thighs.

She tried to imagine what it would be like when she reached the hotel.

Stop thinking.

She rocked herself to and fro, and her fears were gradually overcome by tiredness.

★

The sun rose between two outcrops of rock, shining its rays among the bare peaks and sparse pinewoods, bathing one slope of the valley in light.

Anna trudged out into the middle of the road, struggling to keep her eyes open. Her sleep on the roof of the coach had been short, cold and haunted by nightmares.

The Maremma was still behind her, his head down. Suddenly he started barking.

She turned round. A cloud of dust was rising on the road in the distance and moving towards her.

A car.

The dog's barks echoed off the rocks, multiplying into a din that made it impossible to hear anything.

'Quiet! Quiet! Be quiet!' she shouted at him.

He stopped barking, raised his hackles, gave her a sidelong look and raced off with his tail erect towards the cloud.

Now something denser could be seen in the middle of the golden cloud: a dark mass, like a planet surrounded by dust particles.

She stepped off the road and hid among the withered agaves that grew on the rocks.

As it drew nearer, the dark mass lengthened out, becoming two distinct thin forms advancing in parallel.

Horses.

The ground started shaking. Through the vegetation Anna saw eight weary hooves drumming on the asphalt and four wheels supporting a cart. Its wooden sides were painted yellow and bore the words 'Assuntina's Granita'. In the box seat were a boy and two girls. The boy, who was small and thin, held some ropes which served as reins. On the cart behind him was a heap of yellowish bones. The dog ran alongside the cart, barking. Having started with the wheels, he turned his attention to the horses which, restricted as they were by the yoke, whinnied and reared. Undeterred, he kept lunging between their hooves as if bent on tearing them to pieces. They tried to gallop, but the rickety frame kept swerving this way and that and swaying as it did so, leaving a trail of bones behind it.

The driver, dressed in underpants and a shirt, shouted out, trying to control the horses. Then he dropped the reins in exasperation, picked up a stick which lay by his feet and leaned forward like a knight in a medieval joust, muscles tensed, while the girls held onto his shirt. He managed to land a blow on the dog's back, but instead of being discouraged, he grew even wilder, foaming at the mouth and lunging at the haunches of one of the horses. A kick in the ribs threw him up into the air like a bale of hay, knocking him against the cart. A moment later he disappeared under the wheels.

The three children cheered.

They don't know who they're dealing with, Anna said to herself, going back onto the road.

The Maremma appeared behind the cart, shook off the dust and charged after his new enemies again, dodging the femurs and tibias that were flying all over the place. He sank his teeth into the hindquarters of the chestnut horse on the right, which reared up and rolled over onto the back of the other with a strangled whinny. The two of them fell to the ground in a tangle of hooves, tails and ropes. The cart rose up, teetering on two wheels, then came down again, heaving over in a crash of wood and iron. Bones and children flew into the air as if hurled by a capricious giant. The horses, freed of the yoke, galloped off into the hills, pursued by the dog.

★

The cart was upside down in the middle of the road. The three children lying in the dust weren't moving.

Anna put her hands to her head. *That dog's crazy.*

The same anger that had made him chase her along the autostrada had hurled him against the horses. He came trotting back, looking very pleased with himself, and sat down in front of her, sweeping the road with his tail.

Ignoring him, she went over to the driver, who was lying face down on the asphalt. His shirt was torn and he'd lost one shoe. His elbows and knees were grazed and he was groaning.

Anna crouched down beside him, but he shrank away, baring his black teeth. 'Leave me alone!'

He looked like a rat, one of those big ones in Castellammare. His face was a mass of triangles: cheekbones, protruding ears, pointed chin. He showed all the signs of Red Fever: scabs on his lips and nostrils, purple blotches under his armpits, bruises on his arms.

She took the bottle out of the rucksack and offered it to him. 'You're only grazed. Here, have a bit of water to bathe it.'

But he slapped her away with the back of his hand.

Anna rubbed her cheek, clenched her fists and walked off without saying a word.

The boy got to his feet and picked up a shinbone from

the ground. 'Stop!' He ran after her and blocked her path with his chest. 'Where do you think you're going? Look what you've done!' he shouted, pointing the bone at the cart. His eyes were black and shiny, and a strand of yellow snot hung down from one nostril.

Anna pushed him back. 'Me? What's that got to do with me?'

He coughed, spat out a gob of yellow mucus and advanced towards her. His breath smelt of rotten meat. 'Your dog destroyed the cart. That mongrel nearly killed us.' He lashed out at her angrily with the shinbone.

Anna jumped on him, wrapped her arm round his neck and squeezed hard. 'I've had enough of this. Drop that bone! Drop it now.'

But the boy was stubborn: he gasped and spluttered, but wouldn't let go.

'I'll break your neck,' she shouted, and stamped on his big toe. The boy screamed and started hopping about.

'That dog is nothing to do with me,' said Anna.

Meanwhile the two girls had got up and were staring at her. One was tall and thin, the other short and plump. The thin one was wearing a long sleeveless dress decorated with little flowers. Her two stick-like arms ended in dispropor-tionately big hands. The plump girl had short shapely legs under a large bottom, which was squeezed into a purple miniskirt. A green and blue striped T-shirt encased three rolls of fat and two large breasts. They looked like a pair of cartoon characters.

'What are you staring at?' Anna asked them.

They didn't reply, but whispered to each other.

The rat pointed to the dog, who was lying in the dust enjoying the sun. 'If he's not yours, kill him.'

'Him?' Anna burst out laughing. 'Kill him yourself! I tried and failed. He nearly tore me apart, down on the autostrada. If you don't believe me, I don't give a damn.'

The Maremma yawned loudly, bent his back and stretched his legs.

'I bet it was you that told him to attack the horses.' The tall skinny girl turned to the boy. 'My father had a dog. His name was Hannibal. He hated sheep.'

The fat girl rolled her eyes. 'For goodness' sake, Fiammetta, don't start going on about Hannibal again.'

'Several days' work wasted.' The rat was disconsolate. 'What are we going to do now? How are we going to break it to the Bear that we've lost the bones, and the horses too?'

'He'll be furious. He's got a foul temper . . .' added Fiammetta.

'We can forget about the necklaces.' The plump girl shook her head. 'We've got no chance now.' She threw her arms round her friend.

The thin girl burst into tears; it sounded like a lamb bleating. 'He said he'd let us go with him . . .'

The rat shrugged. 'He'll give me a necklace anyway . . . He won't give you one, though. Nobody likes you.'

Fiammetta didn't understand. 'Why will he give one to you?'

The plump girl shook her head. 'I'll tell you why. Because he's already got a necklace. And he hasn't told us.'

'Is that true, Katio?'

'Yes, it is.' The boy gave a treacherous smirk. 'Angelica gave it to me.'

'Damn you!' The squat one charged at him, grabbed him by the hair and started pulling it.

'Let go of me, you bitch!' shouted Katio, kicking her in the shins; but the plump girl didn't relax her grip.

'Help me, Fiammetta!'

'I'm coming, Chiara.' The thin girl took three strides with her long skinny legs and she too grabbed hold of Katio's hair like a bat. The three of them started a strange game of Ring a Ring o' Roses, shouting and pushing each other.

Anna gazed at them open-mouthed.

The fight was interrupted by a voice. 'Excuse me . . .' A boy was standing in the middle of the road. He was carrying an enormous watermelon between his shoulder blades and neck. 'Could you tell me something?'

He was wearing a long beige overcoat which trailed behind him like a cloak. Underneath it he was naked. On his feet he had a pair of lace-up shoes made of moulded leather, which must once have been very smart. 'Is this the way to the hotel?' His skull looked as if it had been put under a press which had distorted his features. His eyes were out of line: one was lower, half-closed and hidden by his cheekbone. Above his high, lumpy forehead were some tufts of fair hair which looked as if they'd been stuck on with glue.

The three kids had stopped fighting and were peering at him incredulously. The watermelon must have weighed at least twenty kilos. Chiara was the first to regain her composure: 'Where are you going with that?'

The boy paused for a few seconds, as if searching for the best answer, then put the watermelon down on the ground. 'It's a gift for the Little Lady. They say she'll cure you if you take her a special present.' He took a cloth out of his pocket and started polishing the scratched skin. 'It won't be long now.'

'What about your face?' asked Fiammetta.

'That'll stay the way it is.' He shrugged. 'Soon after I was born my father shut my head in a drawer.'

Katio went over to the boy. 'Where did you find the pumpkin?'

'It's not a pumpkin, it's a watermelon. There's not another one as big and sweet in the whole world.' He patted his chest proudly. 'I grew it myself. With plenty of fertiliser.'

Fiammetta craned her vulture-like neck, examining it. 'It's huge.'

'Are you guys going there too? We could go together.'

The rat stroked the fruit with his fingertips, as if checking it wasn't made of plastic. 'Can we have a bite?'

'No, it's for the Little Lady.'

'Go on, just a mouthful.'

'No!' The boy wrapped his arms round his treasure. 'I'm taking it to the hotel.'

Katio slapped him on the back. The slap was too hard to be friendly. 'You reckon one melon's enough to persuade her to cure you? You're crazy.' Then he suddenly turned serious. 'If you let me have some, though, I'll put in a good word for you with the Bear . . .'

Anna seemed to see the thoughts running through the head of the poor boy in the overcoat. Long, straight thoughts, running one behind the other, like the coaches of a slow, rattly train. Some ended in a question mark, some with a simple full stop. He couldn't keep them all to himself: 'Who is the Bear?'

Katio smiled, displaying a row of rotten teeth. 'Don't you know anything? He's the boss at the hotel. His real name's Rosario Barletta. He's a friend of mine. He organises the parties and he's the leader of the blue kids. If you let us eat some of the melon, I'll have a word with him. Then you'll be able to eat the ash and be cured.' He kissed his index fingers. 'That's a promise.'

The boy squatted down on the watermelon like a hen on an egg.

'Will you share it with us?' said Katio.

The poor boy looked at Anna and Fiammetta, begging for help with his eyes.

'What if it's gone bad?' the rat pressed him. 'What if Rosario cuts it open and finds it's rotten? He'll throw you off the hotel roof.'

The boy's voice was hoarse. 'It's not rotten . . .' Finally, with a pained grimace, he gave in. 'Go on then, take it.'

Katio punched the air, as if he'd scored a goal.

Anna spoke almost without realising that she was doing so. 'Leave him alone. Let him take his melon to the hotel if he wants to.'

The rat shot her a sly glance, then turned to the boy, as courteous as could be. 'I'm so sorry, she's perfectly right.' He gestured towards the road. 'Go ahead.' And with a joyful whoop he rammed his heel into the watermelon, which split open, pouring its red pulp and black seeds onto the asphalt.

The boy gave a strangled sob and threw himself down on the juicy remains of his only possession. Chiara and Fiammetta jumped on them too, like a pair of maniacs, picking up pieces of melon and stuffing them into their mouths.

'You bastard.' Anna rushed at Katio, who was watching them guzzle with great amusement, and gave him a hearty slap on the ear.

The boy quivered, his eyes bulging like a tree frog's. He opened his lips in a silent scream, clapped his hand to his ear and fell on his knees, blubbing.

The girls were too busy stuffing themselves to his give him a glance. Anna took aim at Chiara's backside and shoved her forward with the sole of her foot. The plump girl fell nose first on the asphalt. The thin girl, her face smeared with red juice, hopped backwards like a wader bird and ran away.

'Come on, let's go. Forget about it.' Anna took the unfortunate boy by the wrist. He wouldn't budge. He sobbed, hanging his misshapen head. 'Okay, please yourself.' She turned towards the dog, which was lying in the dust. She tried to whistle, but all that came out was a breathy raspberry.

The Maremma raised his head, looked at her apathetically and flopped down again.

'Okay, you can go to hell too!'

6

The silhouette of the Grand Spa Hotel Elise came into view a couple of kilometres away. It lay long on the horizon, like a cruise ship beached on a hill. Columns of smoke rose from its roof.

Anna passed under a blackstone arch which surmounted the road. Rain-bleached thighbones hanging on strings tinkled like bianzhong bells. Some large gold letters were set on a pillar: 'SP TEL ELI '. The others had fallen off. On either side of the narrow road were some ancient olive trees, now half dead. Swirls of dust danced among dark rocks and prickly pears. The wind carried a smell of sulphur and burnt plastic.

She sat down, her windpipe so tight she could hardly breathe. Her anxiety had been steadily growing. Every metre that brought her closer to the hotel had been more of an effort, and now that it was there in front of her she wasn't sure that she could go through with her plan.

What if he's been killed?

A hundred metres away from her, some children were moving among the bushes. They seemed to be picking things up from the ground.

She left the road, passing among dark boulders which surrounded the hotel like sentries; she hid between two smaller rocks, resting her chin on her knees. Her forehead was hot, but she couldn't stop shivering. She sat looking at the desolate land, tinged with red by the setting sun.

Maybe she could wait till tomorrow.

Her mother waded through the undergrowth. She wore low-waisted jeans with a black belt, leather sandals and a T-shirt made of thick white cotton. Anna saw her sit down cross-legged in front of her. A cigarette filter between her lips, a slip of paper with the tobacco between her fingers.

What's the matter?

I've got a temperature.

Her mother took the filter and placed it at the end of the paper. The tip of her tongue slid across the glue. A rapid movement of thumbs and forefingers made the cigarette. She lit it.

What about your brother? Are you just going to leave him there?

No, I'll go in tomorrow. I need to sleep now.

The paper sizzled, wreathing Maria Grazia's face in smoke. Glistening, ringed eyes, the eyes of the final days, stood out among locks of blonde hair.

I knew I couldn't trust you . . .

She was back in her room, lying among crumpled sheets in a pool of sweat.

You're weak, just like your father.

Anna clenched her fists, drying her tearful eyes with her wrist.

The dog appeared among the brambles. He looked at her with mournful eyes, his tongue hanging out.

Anna stretched out her hand towards him. 'You're back.'

The Maremma took two steps, lowered his neck, sniffed her fingertips with his chapped nose and gave her two gentle licks.

'We're friends, you and me,' she said to him, swallowing what felt like a tangle of thorns.

The dog lay down beside his new mistress, rested his large head between his paws and went to sleep.

Anna sat motionless, his dirty, foul-smelling coat brushing her thigh. Then, tentatively, she started stroking him. On contact with her fingers the dog's muscles quivered. One hind leg twitched with pleasure.

'What's your name?'

He arched his back and yawned.

'You've got such a soft, fluffy coat.' She smiled. 'That's what I'll call you: Fluffy.'

And so it was that, after Dopey and Manson, the dog took the name of Fluffy.

★

Anna switched on the torch. The beam of light was instantly filled with clouds of midges. The dog's eyes gleamed electric blue.

'Stay, there's a good boy.' She stroked his forehead. 'I'll be back soon.' The animal watched her closely and didn't move.

The hotel was enveloped in clouds of smoke tinged by the reddish glow of fires. A regular metallic drumming noise could be heard in the distance. Anna joined a small group heading in the same direction as her, dark figures laughing and chattering amongst themselves. She caught snatches of incomprehensible words, wheezy intakes of breath, fits of coughing.

Further on, the crowd was thicker. Many were resting, sitting on walls at the side of the road or lying on the ground in makeshift bivouacs.

Progress was rapid for a while, then the flow slowed to a straggling queue which moved forward in waves. Flashes from distant bonfires lit up blotched faces, toothless mouths. It was a procession of the lame, the hunchbacked and the scarred. Most had bulging plastic bags, or were pulling crammed trolley cases.

Two children were sitting away from the rest, smoking.

'I've got two tins of meat. What have you brought?' said one.

'This . . .' replied a female voice. The flame of a cigarette lighter flickered in the darkness and was reflected in the glass of a bottle with a red label.

'What is it?'

'Wine.'

'That'll never get you in.'

'Why not?'

The other laughed. 'Because I'm going to drink it first.'

They started quarrelling, but in a friendly way, with no real conviction.

You have to give them something if you want to get in.

What did she have in the rucksack? An empty bottle. A lighter. A knife. The only thing of any value was the torch, but she didn't want to give that away. It was of good quality, very powerful, and had never broken down. The batteries were still working too.

As the queue moved forward along the walls of the hotel, quarrels broke out and there were shouts and shoving.

It was the first time since the epidemic that Anna had been among so many human beings, and with all those people pressing against her, touching and pushing her, she felt suffocated and just wanted to run away. But she gritted her teeth and forced herself to stay in the queue.

Half an hour later she reached the gates.

Hundreds of candles were dripping on a row of barrels, and three boys behind the barrier checked the incomers. All three of them wore necklaces made of human fingerbones.

'What have you got for the Little Lady?' asked a thin boy whose hair was slicked down with green sludge.

Anna handed him the torch.

The boy checked that it worked and passed it to the boy next to him: 'Okay . . .'

His companion, who was small and fair-haired, dropped it into a box along with the other offerings, then peered at her breasts and let her through, while the rest of the queue jostled outside.

She went along a dark, draughty, covered passageway which led to the gardens. The walls were daubed with drawings and graffiti. On either side of the stone paving were piles of broken crockery, plastic, boxes and crushed tin cans.

She came out onto a podium which overlooked an amphitheatre. Rough concrete terraces sloped down to a pool full of rubbish and rainwater, on the other side of which, behind six Corinthian columns, the boarding of a building site was still visible. Long flames rose up from five piles of burning tyres, filling the theatre with pungent black smoke. Everything was in ruins and crumbling. Orange corrugated pipes containing electric cables ran along weed-choked channels round the semicircle and down towards the pool.

There were crowds everywhere. Those on the terraces seemed to be sleeping. Others were moving up and down the stairways. On one embankment a group of ragged children were beating a slow monotonous rhythm on some barrels.

Towering up at the top was the hotel, surmounted by a glass dome in the middle. One wing was just a skeleton of concrete columns. On the other side work had progressed further, and there were windows and roll-down blinds.

Anna ventured uncertainly down the steps, but couldn't bring herself to go on. She stopped on a tier littered with empty tins of tuna, beans and chickpeas. She picked up a couple of tins, found a free corner and scraped them out with two fingers. In her famished state, even chickpeas, which she'd always detested, tasted delicious.

Not far away, on a terrace, a girl wearing a black hood and a bone necklace held a basket full of plastic bottles. People were pushing and shoving towards them. Anyone who succeeded in grabbing one had to fend off the others.

Soon after drinking, they'd begin to sway about, head bent forward over their chest, arms hanging loose, lulled by the sound of the drums. One, walking along with his eyes closed, didn't realise he'd reached the end of the terrace, stood for a moment with one leg stretched out into the void, and then fell down – to gales of laughter.

Anna looked around. The tension evident outside the gates seemed to have vanished. Wild figures appeared among the billows of smoke, writhing about as if they were at a party or a rock concert. But there was nobody of Astor's age.

Beside her she noticed a girl's back: shoulder blades splayed like chicken wings, skinny legs.

'Excuse me.' She touched one shoulder. 'Do you know where they keep the little kids?'

There was no reply.

She pulled her arm and the girl fell back against her. Her cheeks were hollow, as if a parasite had sucked her away from the inside. Her eyes were glassy, her mouth contracted in a silent scream.

A gust of wind swept across the amphitheatre. A sea of bodies gyrated in flickering firelight.

Anna jumped up abruptly and rubbed her arms, trying to brush off the death that clung to her skin. She tripped over a boy's ankle. An acrid smell of urine filled her nostrils. The poor wretch was shivering convulsively. His face, neck and chest were covered with sores. His arms were stiff, his fists clenched, as if he were fighting.

This is a waiting room.

That's what these places were called. In Palermo there was said to be one in the stadium and another in Mondello. People who were beyond hope, close to death, would summon up their last strength just to go there and die together.

'I . . . I haven't got the Red Fever,' she stammered. She took two steps and was enveloped in a cloud of gas that filled her lungs.

She ran back up the steps, coughing. Under the skeleton of a small tree, from which pieces of cloth and plastic bags were hanging, was a cement mixer. She hid behind it and curled up on her side, her head resting on the rucksack.

If she didn't look and didn't listen, this darkness was the same as the darkness at Mulberry Farm.

Within a few seconds her eyelids grew heavy and she fell asleep.

★

The daylight dazzled her.

Anna covered her face with her hands and peeped through her fingers at a milky sky. The sun, just above the horizon, looked like a stain left by pasta sauce on a white tablecloth.

By day the amphitheatre seemed smaller. What was left of the tyres sent up straight black threads from piles of ash. The drumming area was deserted. Only a few sick children remained on the terraces.

She propped herself up on her elbows, yawning.

In front of her, a figure silhouetted against the light materialised into a familiar face. 'What are you doing here?' she said.

Pietro was sitting cross-legged. 'I came to look for you,' he replied. He picked up from the ground a bottle which still contained a couple of inches of black liquid at the bottom and held it to his nose. 'Have you been drinking this stuff?'

Anna stretched her back. 'No, what is it?'

'They hand it out in the evening. It's a mixture of all kinds of things – alcohol, tablets, sleeping pills . . . They call it "The Little Lady's Tears". I drunk half a bottle once and afterwards I put my head through a pane of glass. Look.' He showed her a dark fleshy scar behind his left ear. 'I couldn't even remember doing it. They told me about it afterwards.'

The girl smoothed down her T-shirt. 'Weren't there some dead bodies here?'

'They take them away as soon it's light and throw them in a ditch.'

Anna looked at him. He seemed tired, his face haggard and his hair ruffled. But his big liquid eyes were beautiful. 'Weren't you going to look for those trainers?'

He picked up an empty tuna tin and turned it over in his hands. 'You'll never find your brother without my help.'

Anna ran her fingers through her hair and put her head on one side.

He came here because of me.

Pietro used his forefinger to clean out the remnants, then put it in his mouth. 'He's down at the quarry. But if they catch you, they'll throw you in the tank. Only the guardians – the guys with necklaces – can go there. But I know how to get in. I'll take you there, if you like.'

Anna remained silent for a moment. 'How come you know so much?'

He turned away from her. 'I had one of those necklaces once. Then I had a problem and it's best if they don't see too much of me.' He threw the tin towards the pool, missing by a long way. It landed on the head of a boy who was lying a couple of tiers below.

The boy turned round and pointed a finger at him. 'What the hell . . .' And he started coughing.

Pietro raised his hand apologetically. 'Sorry.'

Anna applauded sarcastically. 'It's a good thing you didn't want to attract any attention.' She tied up a shoelace. 'Let's go.'

★

They walked round the pool, passing through groups of children huddled together fast asleep, like hamsters in hay. Some were wrapped in sheets of cellophane.

Going up another flight of steps, they came to an open space where a group of guardians were heating a silvery tin over a fire. They were staring at the food in silence, yawning, as if they could cook it with their eyes.

'Don't look at them,' Pietro whispered to her. 'Nobody's allowed beyond this point unless they have a necklace.'

They walked through a thicket of broom. When they emerged, a plateau stretched out in front of them, veiled by a milky mist with pale hilltops rising out of it. They went on down a narrow road. After a hundred metres the path was blocked by a barrier made of planks nailed together. There was clearly a latrine nearby: the smell of urine and excrement filled the air.

They slid on their backsides down a ridge among broad-leaved trees with spiny fruit and found themselves on a slope covered with crops. Pietro pushed his way through the wheat with his hands, turning occasionally to see if Anna was following him.

They crouched down behind some skips full of rubble at the edge of a rough clearing. A lorry and a mechanical digger stood by some prefabricated huts.

'That's where the road to the quarry begins.'

Anna peered over one of the skips.

'We'll have to run fast or they'll see us from the hotel,' he went on. 'And if they take us to Angelica, I'm done for.'

'Who's Angelica?'

Pietro bit his lip. 'She's the one who makes all the decisions, with the Bear.'

Anna remembered the Bear from her conversation with Katio, the cart-driver. 'Where is she?'

'She'll be asleep at this time of day.'

The girl tipped her head to one side and looked up at him.

Pietro waggled his hips seductively. 'She fell in love with me. She was all over me. She wanted me.'

Anna roared with laughter.

He put his hand over her mouth and hissed: 'Keep quiet! They'll hear us . . .'

Anna dried her tears of laughter with her wrist. What was that name Mama called Papa when he boasted he could dive into the sea off the priest's rock? 'You're just like my father, a bullshitter.'

'I'm telling the truth, I swear to you.' Pietro kissed his forefingers. 'That's why I ran away. She's crazy. She said she'd show me the Little Lady if I slept with her, but that was just an excuse. Look, could we talk about this later?' He tried to sound grown up. 'Listen, when I say go, we're going to run as fast as we can over to the digger, and hide behind it.'

'What's she like? Attractive?'

'No. She's too skinny. Looks like a witch.'

'How do you like them, then? All . . .' Anna drew some curves in the air.

Pietro put his hands together, as if in prayer. 'Please . . .'

She tried to put on a serious expression, but her eyes continued to laugh. 'So if we get caught, you get Angelica?'

'We won't get caught.'

'Why not?'

Pietro looked her straight in the eye. 'Because you and I are invisible.'

'I told you you're a bullshitter.'

★

Maybe they weren't invisible, but nobody saw them when they dashed across the clearing.

Anna stopped by one of the digger's caterpillar tracks. A second later Pietro rushed in beside her and gestured to her to wait. He was breathing hard. 'They've closed the road.'

The rough track that wound its way down into the valley below in a series of hairpin bends was shut off with wire netting. Where posts still supported the fence, it was still in good condition; the rest had disappeared under falling rubble.

'We'll have to go through the wood,' said the boy.

Anna hesitated. What if he was lying to her? How could she trust a bullshitter, someone who claimed a girl called Angelica lusted after him, and who spent all his time looking for a pair of shoes?

But he's the only friend I've got.

★

Trees clung to each other as if terrified of falling down into the valley. Ivy smothered the oaks and cascaded down, turning the ground, pitted with potholes and rocks, into a treacherous green tangle. The sun had come up, and with it clouds of midges which bit their ankles and arms.

Anna followed Pietro anxiously down the ridge. 'Are you sure this is the right way?'

'No, I'm not,' Pietro confessed.

'If you're wrong, we'll have to climb all the way ba—' Before she could finish the sentence, she tripped over a root and found herself sliding downhill on her backside. She clutched at the ivy, but only carried it down with her. Screaming, she came to a hump which launched her into the air. Branches and leaves lashed her face and arms.

The wood spat her out.

After several somersaults she landed on a steep scree. She tried to slow her progress with her hands and feet, but slid faster and faster, raising waves of pebbles, until the whole slope became a landslide. A small green patch, which at first seemed only a bush, grew bigger and bigger as she hurtled down. Then she was caught, like a fish in a net, by the branches of a wild fig tree poised on the edge of a cliff which fell vertically down to the bottom of the quarry. Her heart, unaware that it was safe, was pumping blood into her temples. She flexed whitened fingers and ran her tongue over dust-covered teeth.

A few seconds later, preceded by a shout, Pietro landed beside her, spraying her with sand.

Lying there under the vault of leaves, they looked at each other, amazed to be still alive. They were white from head to foot. They burst out laughing.

Anna breathed in through her nose. 'Can I ask you something? Don't be offended . . .' She cleared her throat. 'Why are you so obsessed with those shoes?'

Pietro rubbed his eyelids, took a deep breath and lay back, his head on his arm. 'There's no point in me telling you – you wouldn't believe me.'

'Try me.'

He coughed. 'I had this friend, Pierpaolo Saverioni. He was two years older than me. He got the Red Fever, badly. He was covered in blotches, could hardly breathe and never got out of bed. He didn't have long to live. One morning he gave me a page from a newspaper, the one I showed you, and told me those shoes were magic, they could save him, and asked me to go and look for them. He was quite convinced. What could I say? He was a friend of mine, he'd put me up and fed me. I went to the shopping mall and I found them. Adidas Hamburgs. There were dozens of boxes.' He batted away a fly that was buzzing around him. 'I thought it was nonsense and only took one pair, size 42. He put them on – or rather I put them on his feet, because he couldn't do it – and I went off to bed.' He fell silent for a few seconds. 'The next day he was gone. He'd left the page about the shoes on the bed. I searched for him everywhere. He couldn't have gone away on his own two feet: he was as thin as a skeleton, couldn't move. I looked to see whether he'd jumped out of the window.'

The girl scratched her cheek. 'And where was he?'

'On the other side. In the universe where everything is

as it was before, where the Red Fever has never existed and things go on the way they should. I don't know why the shoes work like that, but Pierpaolo explained to me that by putting them on you start down a road, a road that takes you into that other world.' He shrugged. 'I ran to the mall, but there were none left. They'd all gone.' He turned towards Anna.

She stared at him. 'What if you find them and they don't work?'

Pietro lowered his eyes. 'Don't you believe there's a way of surviving? Are we really just doomed to die?'

Anna's gaze fell on a brown spider quivering in the middle of its web as it shook in the wind. 'I don't believe anything. All I know is, I've got to find my brother. I promised my mother I'd never leave him.'

'But what difference does it make? Soon you'll die anyway, and he'll be left alone.'

'Yes, but before that happens I'll take him to the mainland.'

The boy rubbed the tip of his nose. 'To Calabria?'

'Maybe some Grown-ups have survived there and have the vaccine.'

'So you do believe something.'

Anna closed her eyes.

Pietro's fingers sought hers. She squeezed them.

★

They lay there hand in hand, stretched out like two salamis, and they would have lain there a lot longer if it hadn't been for a strange clinking sound.

Anna raised her head. 'Did you hear that?'

Pietro seemed reluctant to move. 'What?'

'That noise. Can you hear it?' She pushed through the branches and opened a gap in the screen of leaves. Small thick white clouds were floating in the blue sky. Below, hanging from a crane by a steel cable, was a puppet in the likeness of a human skeleton. Anna wasn't very good at calculating sizes, but it looked higher than the bank in Piazza Matteotti.

It was made of planks of wood held together by links made of rope. The chest looked like the hull of a boat and the pelvis had a hole in the middle. Apart from half of the left leg and the right arm, which was unfinished, the structure was entirely covered with bones. Humeri hung from the humeri, femurs from the femurs, clavicles from the clavicles. But the most amazing thing was the skull, which was made up of real skulls arranged in spirals. The backbone was a mosaic of vertebrae. The bones were free to move and clinked against each other, shifted by the wind.

Pietro leaned over to see. 'So they finally made it.'

Anna was full of admiration. 'It's beautiful.'

'It's for the Little Lady's party.'

Down at the bottom, around the crane, were countless piles of bones. Further away, beside a long steel shed, were a tanker, heaps of car tyres and stacks of wood.

*

Anna and Pietro crawled along the sandy edge of the precipice and went down into the quarry. The marionette looked at them with black orbits made out of tractor wheels.

The wind rushed between heaps of sand and blew on the ground, raising eddies of dust and banging the door of the shed. The tanker was in good condition and the tyre tracks it had left behind were still visible.

The smallest heaps of bones were divided up according to type. Tibias, ribs, radii, and so on. The larger ones had not yet been sorted.

Anna put her hands on her hips, dismayed. 'There's nobody here. Let's go back up.'

Pietro sat down on the ground. 'And yet . . .'

Anna interrupted him. 'What's that?' At the end of the valley a cloud of dust melted into the blue sky.

★

The driver of the tanker must have been religious. The dashboard was covered with sacred pictures of Padre Pio and Pope John Paul II. Above them was a gilded plate, which bore the inscription: THE MEASURE OF LOVE IS TO LOVE WITHOUT MEASURE.

Hunched up on the driver's seat, Pietro and Anna peered out of the side window at the cloud of dust which, as it grew in size, split up into three two-horse carts like the one Katio had driven. But instead of bones, these were carrying children. The caravan stopped under the marionette and they all jumped down, shouting.

Anna remembered when the yellow school bus used to leave her outside the gates of the primary school and she would run into the schoolyard with a bunch of rowdy schoolmates. The difference was that these children were naked, and as thin as lizards.

Her eyes skipped from one to the other, searching for Astor, but at that distance they all looked alike. She'd imagined them being chained up like the slaves in Egypt, but they were free, and seemed perfectly happy too. Six older kids followed them like schoolmistresses, struggling to keep them under control. They'd catch one and another would slip away. In the end they managed to lead them over to a row of barrels.

Pietro slapped himself on the forehead and pointed to a tall girl, who was half naked and painted white. 'That's Angelica.' Next to her a fat boy, with sloping shoulders and shapeless hips, took handfuls of blue dust out of a bin and threw it over the kids, who disappeared in a cobalt-coloured cloud. 'And that's the Bear, Rosario.'

Anna grabbed his wrist. 'I've seen those two before. They're the ones who killed Michelini.'

As soon as the colouring operation was over, a girl with a limp brought a big cardboard box and handed out bottles of Coca-Cola.

After the drinks break, Angelica blew a whistle and the blues split up into groups. Some picked up tibias and put them in bags slung over their hips, while others worked on the piles. The tasks were carried out quickly, a sign that this wasn't the first time. The ones with the bags caught hold of hooks which hung down from the cranes and were slowly hoisted up by others pulling ropes. They climbed up the skeleton like monkeys, swung about and jumped from one section to another, fixing bones to nails with wire. The older children shouted instructions from below.

Anna put her face right against the window. 'There he is. That's him.'

'Where?'

'There.' She pointed at a little boy standing on a heap of bones. 'I'm going to get him.'

'Wait . . . Wait . . .' Pietro tried to stop her, but she jumped out of the lorry and ran off.

★

The little boy had his back to her. He was holding a pelvis in both hands, in the manner of a steering wheel. Anna scrambled up among ulnae and vertebrae which gave way under her feet, stretched out her arm and managed to grab him by the ankle. He let out a yell and tumbled down on top of her.

She stood up and saw, under the blue paint, her mother's light blue eyes, her father's nose, and Astor's lopsided teeth. His eyebrows had been shaven off. She smiled at him. 'Astor.'

He stared at her blankly, seeming not to recognise her,

then swallowed hard and stammered, 'Anna . . . Anna . . .' He burst into tears.

Anna held out her hand. 'Come with me.'

He shook his head, grimacing as he sobbed.

'Astor, come with me.'

He raised his arm, to wipe away the snot running down onto his lips, but didn't move.

'Come with me,' Anna said again.

But the little boy took three steps backwards, like a lobster, sinking back into a pile of bones. 'No, I don't want to . . .'

She tried to smile. 'Come on, there's a good boy.'

She'd imagined all kinds of things on the way here, but had never dreamt her brother would refuse to go with her. In her surprise, the only thing she could manage was a forced grin. 'Let's go back to the long-haired lizards.'

Astor dropped his eyes. 'You're bad. You told me everybody was dead. There aren't any monsters. And there's no such thing as the Outside.' He burst into tears again.

Her ears were buzzing. The quarry, the bones and the puppet circled around her like a lopsided roundabout. There was a lump in her throat. Gasping for breath, she said: 'I was only thinking of you. I didn't want you to see all the nasty things. Come on now, please. Come with me.'

The blue powder mingling with tears and mucus, he gulped in air and said: 'No, I won't. There are little children here, like me.'

Suddenly Anna jumped on him. 'That's enough!' She grabbed him by the arm. 'I'm your sister, do you understand? I decide.' She dragged him through the dust. 'Do as I say.'

The wind brought a shrill whistle to her ears. Out of the corner of her eye she saw the blues charging towards her.

Astor broke free and scrambled back up onto the pile of bones.

★

The blues were pulling her hair and T-shirt, clutching at her legs. Anna fell to the ground, punching and kicking, but as soon as one dropped off, another latched on. A cluster of little children hanging off her. She took a couple of steps, trying to shake them off, but they wouldn't let go and she fell down in the dust, gasping for breath.

They pinned her to the ground by her wrists and ankles, the noonday sun in her eyes.

A slim shape, standing against the light, asked her in a hoarse voice: 'What do you want with Mandolino? Leave him alone.'

'Mandolino? Who's that?' Screwing up her eyes, Anna made out the form of Angelica. She was white all over, and so skeletal she might have stepped out of a coffin. A necklace of bones with a bird's skull pendant hung down over her small breasts. She wore an open purple gilet, and a pair of torn combat trousers draped her bare feet. Sunglasses with golden metal frames rested on her aquiline nose, across which ran a black strip, continuing onto her high cheekbones. Her stringy hair was divided into thick twists which fell onto her shoulders. She went over to Astor, who was crouching down on the bones, staring into the distance with his thumb in his mouth. She stroked his head, as you might a dog's. 'This is Mandolino.'

Anna tried to get up, but was immediately stopped by numerous little hands. 'His name's not Mandolino. It's Astor. He's my brother.'

'How old are you?'

Anna looked round and saw the Bear. A cubic head supported by a short neck. A white face as flat as the palm of your hand, with a constellation of zits showing through the paint on his forehead. A short beard stained with blue dust, linked to a helmet of curly hair by bushy sideburns. A ragged T-shirt with a slogan across the front: 'On My Way To Mexico'. A pair of green and black checked Bermuda shorts held up with string, sagging down over plump calves.

Anna spat on his feet.

Angelica crouched down beside her, a cigarette dangling from her lips, and looked at her. She took a drag, blew a cloud of smoke in her face and shoved her hand down Anna's shorts.

Anna screamed, trying to squirm out of the blue children's grasp. 'Get your hands off me, you bitch.'

The other girl grabbed her pubic hair and pulled. She held a tuft of hair between her fingers, which she examined carefully. 'Thirteen, maybe fourteen.'

Anna growled: 'You guys paint yourselves white to hide the Red Fever.'

The response was a slap in the face. Anna pursed her lips to stop herself crying.

'Let her go,' said Rosario, but the children didn't move; they looked at him uncomprehendingly. 'I said, let her go.' He pushed one away with his foot, whereupon all the others released their grip.

The Bear scratched his beard. 'He's your brother, you say?'

Anna got to her feet. 'Yes.'

'Here it doesn't matter if you're a brother, cousin or friend.' He gestured towards the children. 'They're all the Little Lady's property. So is Mandolino.'

Anna breathed in through her nose. 'Don't call him that. His name's Astor.'

'Hey you! What's your name?' the Bear asked Astor.

He mumbled something incomprehensible.

The Bear cupped his hand to his ear. 'I didn't catch that. What's your name?'

Astor looked at his sister, hesitated, then replied: 'Mandolino.'

★

Over the past four years Anna had suffered and recovered from some terrible shocks, which still weighed on her heart. After the death of her parents she'd fallen into a solitude so complete and stunning as to leave her dazed for months. But not once, even for a second, had the idea of suicide crossed her mind, for she sensed that life is stronger than everything else. Life doesn't belong to us, it passes through us. Her life was the same thing that makes a cockroach limp along on two legs when it's been stamped on, the same thing that makes a snake crawl away under the slashes of a hoe, dragging its entrails behind it. Anna, in her lack of knowledge, sensed that all the creatures on this planet, from snails to swallows, and including human beings, must live. That is our mission; it has been written in our flesh. We must go on, without looking back, for the energy that pervades us is beyond our control, and even when despairing, maimed or blind, we continue to eat, sleep and swim, struggling against the whirlpool that sucks us down. But there in the quarry that certainty wavered. That mumbled word 'Mandolino' opened up new, broad horizons of pain to her. She felt her heart shrivelling up in her chest like a flower in a furnace, while the blood in her veins dried into dust.

★

The Bear grinned smugly. Angelica winced and gave a forced smile. The children started laughing, like trained monkeys imitating their masters.

Anna walked off, hanging her head.

★

ASTOR VERSUS THE SMOKE MONSTERS

Three days earlier, Astor had still been the king of Mulberry Farm. A king running a slight temperature and with ulcers on his palate, but well enough to play games. During the night his temperature had dropped and at first light he'd woken up in a tangle of sweaty sheets.

A cool breeze came in through the window, pleasant to feel on his neck and shoulders after being so hot.

Rubbing his eyes and yawning, he wandered out onto the balcony. The sun was behind the wood, which was taking a last breath of cool air before it was overwhelmed by sultry heat. Above the treetops the sky was clear and almost white, but higher up it was darker, still holding some remnants of the night.

During the long summer Astor had discovered that this was his favourite time of day, and he liked to enjoy it in peace. It was a favourite time for the birds too, when they engaged in song contests. Many took part – sparrows, woodpeckers, robins, starlings and unmelodious crows. Those that had been awake all night, such as barn owls and tawny owls, preferred to sleep, either in their nests or, like Peppe 1 and Peppe 2 – two little owls – on beams in the loft.

Astor held onto the railing and peed, aiming at an oil drum among the weeds.

Mama had written in the exercise book that you had to go to the toilet in the wood, well away from the house, and that if you pooed you must dig a hole with the spade beforehand and cover it up afterwards. But his sister wasn't there and there were some things, like peeing from the balcony, that he could get away with; she'd never know if he didn't say anything. Pooing was different – he'd never done that from the balcony. In the first place because he couldn't get his bum through the bars, in the second because he found the idea a little disgusting.

He went downstairs and found the food Anna had left for him on top of a big box. He devoured a tin of lentils, burping contentedly when he'd finished. He picked a mobile phone up from the floor and put it to his ear. 'Hello! Is that you, Anna? Where are you? When are you coming home?'

'I've just got to kill a monster, then I'll come back,' he answered his own question in a high-pitched nasal voice supposedly resembling his sister's. 'I've found some chocolate. Do you want some?'

'Yes. I'll have the crisps too.' Then he rang the long-haired lizards. 'Hi! I'm up! See you in the wood. I won't be long.' He dropped the mobile and went back upstairs.

Going into the bathroom, he climbed up onto a stool and looked at himself in the mirror.

Every time he did this, he discovered something interesting – in his nostrils, into which he'd stick the handle of his toothbrush; in his pink gums, which turned white if you pressed them; in his ears, which clicked back into place if you bent them. He would bang on his stomach as if it was a drum, grab hold of his penis and pull down the skin at the tip. Out would come, depending on the light, the damp head of a pink tadpole, a snake's nose or a sparrow's egg.

Today his attention was focused on his eyebrows. What on earth were they for? Why did he have those two little arches of woodland, separated from the forest of his hair by the desert of his forehead?

Opening the white Formica cupboard, he took a Bic razor out from between the jars and shaved them off. 'There! That's better.' Now, instead of eyebrows, he had two pale patches of skin, which made him look like a lizard.

He kept a secret key in a box of aspirin. His sister didn't know it, but he'd found one that opened the lock of Mama's room. He turned it in the keyhole and pushed the door open. It was dark. He drew one curtain a little way, and a strip of light fell on the opposite wall.

The secret to not being found out was to put everything back where it was before, taking care not to remove the dust.

He'd never touched Mama's skeleton, though. Anna had arranged all the jewels that adorned it; he'd just made some suggestions.

He pulled *The Big Book of Dinosaurs* out of the bookcase, sat down on the floor in the sunlight and started turning the pages. He knew it off by heart, but he was always noticing new details: a funny claw, a spiny tail, the colour of a feather.

His sister told him she'd seen lots of these dinosaurs during her travels on the Outside. The smoke monsters could gas you with their smell, but these creatures could eat you whole. He could see some of them when he climbed up a tree at the edge of the wood. His favourite was the Heterodontosaurus, a small animal not much bigger than a cat, purple in colour, with a beak-like muzzle and a beautiful pointed tail. It didn't look very fierce in the picture.

He followed the printed lines with his forefinger and, with some difficulty, read out loud: 'The Heterodontosaurus had three kinds of teeth. The front ones were small and were used for tearing off leaves; the back ones were flatter and were used for chewing. Males also had two long teeth at the sides of the jaw.' In the corner of the page, there was a question in a yellow box: 'What about you? How many different kinds of teeth have you got?'

He touched his teeth and mumbled: 'I've got some good ones and some that hurt.'

His gaze fell on the wardrobe. The door was ajar. Hung up inside were Mama's dresses. One, which was longer than the others, was the same colour purple as the Heterodontosaurus. He went over to it, scratching his neck. If his sister found out he'd gone into the room and touched the dresses, he'd get a spanking. He'd have to be very careful.

He climbed up onto a chair and breathed in the smell from the wardrobe. It was like the smell of those green sweets that make your nose tingle when you chew them. It was Mama's smell.

He stretched out his arm and took the dress off the hanger, then jumped down and compared it with the picture. Exactly the same.

He put it on and looked at himself in the mirror. Perfect: the bottom part formed the tail, and the V-neck hung down as far as his belly button. On the lowest shelf of the wardrobe was a neat row of shoes.

Selecting a pair of red stilettos with ankle straps, he put them on. They were extremely uncomfortable, but the long pointed heel would be useful for killing snakes.

He walked round in a circle with his arms outstretched, as if balancing on a beam. Then he pulled the dress up over his head, so that it covered his face. 'Arrr . . . Arrr . . .' he growled, imitating a Heterodontosaurus. 'I'm going to get you . . .'

Then, barely able to see where he was going and clip-clopping on the high heels, he locked the door, hid the key and went downstairs. He stumbled across the sitting room and out onto the veranda, flexing his fingers as though they were sharp claws. 'Here I am. Watch ou—'

What was that?

Through the elasticated fabric covering his eyes he seemed to see something, a black shape moving in the distance.

'Anna, you're home! Don't worry, I'll put it back straight away.' He uncovered his face. 'I haven't damaged it.'

Some human figures were coming down the drive between the overgrown box hedges.

Astor shut his eyes and opened them again. His jaw dropped and his facial muscles tightened in an expression of terror.

Coming towards him were two older children, painted white all over, one of them pushing a wheelbarrow, and several younger children, who were all blue.

Fear thickened his flesh. The hundred thousand billion cells of which he was made up huddled together like a brood of chicks. His stomach tightened, his lungs crumpled like paper bags crushed in a fist, his heart missed several beats and his bladder relaxed.

Astor looked down. A warm trickle of liquid ran down his legs. He'd peed in Mama's dress.

Now the figures were closer.

He decided to shut his eyes and count up to six. He was good at counting up to six.

One, two, three, four, five, six.

He opened his eyes again. They were even closer. The smaller children weren't really blue; they seemed to be covered in paint, and they were making funny noises.

Ghosts.

Ghosts which for some unknown reason had succeeded in entering the magic wood. Anna had told him they were harmless, made of air, of nothing. The dust of past lives. What else could they be? The only living things in the world were him, his sister and the animals in the wood. So they must be ghosts. He decided to ignore them and go back indoors, but he found that he was paralysed. He couldn't move a muscle; all he could do was tighten his bum. A shiver ran across his scalp. His hair was standing on end and quivering like antennae.

The two big ghosts, a male and a female, were pointing at him.

They've seen me.

His legs gave way and Astor fell forward, as stiff as a tailor's dummy, leaving the red shoes behind him and hitting his forehead on the concrete. He lay there on the edge of the steps with his arms stretched out, like a worshipper prostrating himself before his gods.

Dirty feet, black toenails, broken shoes and grazed ankles filed past, stepping over him, to much laughing, pushing and shrieking. Two children, in their eagerness to enter the house, walked straight over him, as though he was a doormat. Nobody so much as looked at him or spoke to him.

What if the ghost is me?

The idea died immediately, drowned by the buzz of blood in his eardrums. He didn't move, even when he heard voices echoing in the sitting room and realised that the ghosts talked like him.

'Look at all this stuff,' said one.

'I'm going upstairs,' said another.

The secret was to let them get on with it, not disturb them, stay where he was and keep quiet. Just as they'd appeared, they'd disappear. But the more he told himself not to move, the more he longed to see them. Fear and curiosity were battling in his mind, and eventually fear surrendered.

Astor stumbled awkwardly towards the front door, holding the hem of his dress like a nineteenth-century maid of honour. He rolled his head right and left, like a doll with a spring neck.

He liked the little blue children a lot; they reminded him of the mice when they ran amok at night. They threw things to each other, climbed up bookcases, jumped on piles of rubbish. One had got into his pedal car and another was pushing him against the wall. Another was picking things up and putting them in a yellow bag tucked under his arm.

Astor watched the looting spellbound, as if this wasn't his own home. His eyes were filled with mouths, noses, eyes, hands, strange facial expressions, penises, painted buttocks, movements and utterances he didn't understand. Leaning against the door post and absent-mindedly touching his own penis, he silently watched the most extraordinary scene he'd ever witnessed.

After a while, one of the blue ferrets, rushing out of the room with Astor's big cuddly dog, pushed him so hard he fell down on the floor. And there he lay, with a smile on his face.

The big white boy, who had a bone necklace on his chest,

was sitting on a chair holding Anna's mandolin. 'Is this your home?'

He was pretty ugly. His legs were as thick as tree trunks, he had a fat belly and thick hair. There were even some long hairs on his chin.

'Do you understand what I say?'

Astor stared at him in silence.

The ghost shouted towards the stairs. 'We've found another one that can't talk.'

The female ghost replied from upstairs. 'Come and see what they've done. It's beautiful.'

She must have gone into Mama's room. Of course it was beautiful, the decorated skeleton was in there.

A hairline crack opened in his certainties, lengthened out, following a complicated but correct mental process, and suddenly everything collapsed. Astor understood that they weren't ghosts. They were as alive as him, his sister and the animals in the wood.

They weren't transparent like spectres; they were smelly, they held things in their hands; they drank, spoke, broke his car. This intuition made him happy, and a new sensation warmed his heart. There were other human beings in existence, who had escaped the smoke monsters, dinosaurs and deadly gases. He was only sorry Anna wasn't there so that he could prove it to her.

He swallowed and tried to speak: 'S-s-s . . .' He took a deep breath and finished the sentence: 'S-s-so you're alive?'

The fat boy burst into cavernous laughter. 'For the time being, yes. We won't be for very much longer, though.' He shouted to the girl upstairs: 'Angelica, I was wrong. He can talk.' Then he beckoned to him. 'Come over here.'

And Astor, as if the order had come from a god, obeyed.

The fat boy smiled at him, slapping his thighs. 'Come here.'

Astor looked at him anxiously, his blue eyes wide open.

'There's nothing to be frightened of.' The god stretched out his hand.

The little boy examined it; it was short and broad, the nails thick and yellow. He touched it hesitantly with his middle finger, as if it might give him an electric shock.

'See? I'm flesh and blood.'

Astor looked at the T-shirt with the slogan: 'On My Way To Mexico'.

'Mexico . . .' he stammered.

The boy shook his head incredulously. 'No! You can read too? What a clever boy!' He picked Astor up by the hips and lifted him onto his lap.

Astor felt faint. His head seemed as heavy as lead, but the thoughts inside it were as light as gas and merged into one another. He looked around. The blues were quarrelling over a scarf. He studied the boy who was holding him on his knees – the hairs on his chin, the white paste on his cheeks. 'Are you good guys?' he asked him.

The other squeezed him hard, as if trying to guess his weight. 'Who taught you to read?'

'Anna.'

'Good for Anna. This is the first time I've found a little kid who could read. My name's Rosario. What's yours?'

'Astor.'

'What kind of a name's that?' He pointed to the mandolin. 'Can you play this?'

The little boy took it and plucked the sole remaining string.

Rosario said: 'Do you know what it's called?'

'A guitar.'

'No, it's not a guitar, it's a mandolin.' He tilted his head to one side, sizing him up. 'That's it . . . I'll call you Mandolino. I like that better.' He put him down on the ground and shouted in a tenor voice. 'Angelica, we've got to go, it's late.' He put his hand in his pocket and took out a Mars bar,

· 141 ·

unwrapped it and took a bite, looking around as if searching for something to take with him.

Angelica came downstairs, draped in jewels like the Madonna of Trapani. She had Maria Grazia Zanchetta's skull in her hands.

And everyone, large and small, left the house laden with loot.

Astor found himself waddling after them like a duckling. He didn't stop to ask himself any questions, but walked barefoot among the others, trailing the dress behind him. He'd forgotten everything: Anna, the house, who he was.

The blues ran on ahead, but he stayed beside Rosario, who was pushing the wheelbarrow full of food, smoking a cigarette. Angelica stopped, examined the skull, shrugged and tossed it among the weeds.

Astor ran to fetch it and brought it back to her. 'It's my mama.'

'Throw it away,' she said.

The blues had gone through the gate. Angelica let Rosario pass and looked at Astor standing in the middle of the drive with the skull in his hands, like a basketball player preparing to take a free shot.

'Get moving,' she ordered him.

Astor stood there, staring at her.

Beyond the boundary was the Outside. He couldn't cross it, he'd be suffocated.

'Get moving,' the girl repeated.

He shook his head.

Angelica called to Rosario. 'He won't come.'

Rosario stopped, put down the wheelbarrow and after one last drag threw away the cigarette. 'Mandolino? What's up? Aren't you coming?'

Astor didn't move.

The girl turned back, rolling her eyes, and grabbed him by the wrist.

He took two steps, then dug his heels in with a cry of protest.

Angelica pulled hard. The skull rolled into the grass. 'You idiot. Come on!' she snarled, showing gappy pointed teeth and dark gums. She grabbed him round the neck, but Astor sank his incisors into her arm.

She screamed and slapped him across the head with her other hand, knocking him over. 'I'll teach you . . .'

Astor couldn't understand it. There was no way he could go through that gate. Did they want him to die? He felt a lump form in his throat. He raised his hands to defend himself and Angelica kicked him in the backside.

He tried to get up, tripped over, crawled along for a few metres on hands and knees, then got to his feet again. Whirling his arms and legs, he jumped over a dog rose bush and ran off.

The wood welcomed him.

Behind him he could hear whistles, shouts and Rosario's voice. 'Catch him! Catch him!'

Astor slipped between holly bushes which snatched at his dress, stepped through a maze of fallen branches, jumped over moss-covered rocks, sank ankle-deep in mud.

They couldn't catch him. He was in his own territory, he'd been born there, he'd explored those four hectares of land centimetre by centimetre, finding holes, burrows, trees to climb. Those guys might be special creatures, but none of them knew the wood better than him. If only he wasn't wearing that damned dress that kept getting caught on things. He tore it off, slipping out of it like a snake from its skin, and started galloping faster through the thickest part of the wood, stark naked.

The sun penetrated the green vault, dappling the under-wood with patches of golden light; balls of midges buzzed among the tree trunks. Astor ran through them with his mouth open, and found some on his palate.

He turned round.

Well done. You've given them the slip, the long-haired lizards whispered from up on a branch.

Deafened by his own breathing and by his heart beating beneath his breastbone, he sat down on a rock and removed a thorn from his heel.

In his headlong flight he'd gone a long way from the house, into a more open area, close to the Outside. The fire had consumed the younger trees; there were only charred trunks, jagged spikes and the twisted wire netting of the fence. A big, gnarled dark-brown oak, which had withstood the flames, leaned out beyond the boundary, where the fire had burnt its fingers.

When the whirl of thoughts had died down, Astor checked his wounds. Red welts across his thighs and calves and the tender skin of his belly. They didn't hurt yet, but he'd feel them soon enough.

He was sure he'd shaken them off. But he was wrong.

He spotted them because the blues stood out in that mixture of browns and greens.

There wasn't a single hole to hide in.

Up the tree.

He scrambled up the trunk and with an agile leap caught hold of the first branch, and from that another and then yet another. He didn't stop till he thought he was out of reach.

The blues were pointing up at him from the ground.

Two of them started climbing up the oak tree exactly as he had.

He tried to go higher, but the next bifurcation was too far up. In desperation, he started walking along a branch, with his arms stretched out on either side, but soon it became too thin to support him. He crouched down, clinging to the dry foliage and grinding his teeth.

Down below, Angelica and Rosario had joined the others.

'What's the matter, Mandolino? Don't you want to come

with us?' said the fat boy. 'We'll take you to see the Little Lady.'

His two pursuers, as agile as Barbary apes, started crawling along the branch towards him.

Astor backed away, the wood swaying between his buttocks, then, without any thought of the height, the harm he might do to himself and the fact that he would fall right into his enemies' laps, he jumped. Turning an untidy somersault in the air, he landed on his side on a carpet of grass soft enough to stop him breaking his back.

His head was pulsing as if someone had put his heart where his brain should be. Flashes of yellow light kept hitting his pupils. The acid taste of lentils coated his tongue. He struggled to his feet.

The world around him was swaying. The sun between the yellowed leaves of the oak tree. The wood. Rosario. Angelica. The blue children. The scorched fields. The remains of the fence.

He was in the Outside.

He opened his mouth in a silent scream, put his hands to his neck and fell to his knees. The toxic air, the invisible gas, seeped into his pores, the holes of his ears, his nose, his bottom. He couldn't breathe. He was dying. He gasped for breath, inhaling the poison. In the distance, with heavy, earth-shaking steps, the smoke monsters were advancing, as big as mountains and as thick as the fear that was suffocating him. *Tramp. Tramp. Tramp.* They were coming. Soon, very soon, he would die. He would join all the ants, grasshoppers and green lizards that he'd killed. He would go to his mother, wherever she was.

Rosario was standing in front of him. Talking to him, hands on hips, shaking his head. Why was he laughing? There was nothing to laugh about.

Astor was dazed by the buzzing of a million bees, yet a flurry of words reached his ears.

'You're not dying, are you, Mandolino?'

He opened his eyes and nodded.

'Are you sure about that?'

The little boy raised his arm towards the sun. 'They're coming . . .'

'Who's coming?'

'The monsters . . .' He let himself fall back on the ground, stretching out his arms and legs, grinding his teeth and making guttural noises.

'What on earth is he doing?' asked Angelica.

'I've no idea.' Rosario turned towards the blue children, who had gathered round Astor. 'Pick him up, it's late.'

7

'Stop. Wait a minute.'

Anna was walking, with her fists clenched, up the slope from the quarry to the hotel, followed by Pietro.

'Where are you going? Stop.'

She speeded up.

Pietro tried to keep up with her. 'Wait . . .' He grabbed her by the shoulder. 'Anna!'

She twisted out of his grasp and started climbing up a bank of loose earth from a landslide which covered a hairpin bend. Her feet sank into the earth. After two more steps she kneeled down, out of breath.

'Anna, will you let me speak?'

'What do you want?'

He swallowed. 'Angelica was there . . . I couldn't let her see me. We'll get him during the night. I know where they sleep.'

A bitter smile curled her lips. 'Him? Who are you talking about?'

'Your brother. We'll wait until nightfall, then we'll get him. Me and you. I promise you.'

Anna cocked her head on one side, as if Pietro was speaking a foreign language. 'You're a bullshitter. In fact, you're a coward. And what's all this talk about me and you? Who do you think you are? And what do you want from me?' Her voice grew louder, and was breaking. 'Do I know you? Are we friends? Brother and sister?' She pushed him, and he fell down on his backside. 'You'd better keep away from me. I'm tougher than Angelica. Go away and look for your shoes.' Scrambling up on all fours, she got over the rubble and started walking again.

Pietro didn't follow. He shouted: 'I took you to your brother. You just dashed out . . . I tried to stop you, but you . . .'

Anna put her hands over her ears.

He hadn't helped her, the coward. If there was one thing she couldn't stand, it was a coward.

★

She walked past the hotel and started along a path which ran down a hillside shrouded in mist.

She must banish Astor and Pietro from her mind and go away. She imagined her heart covered with mud, like a giant wasps' nest.

You can do what you want now. You're free.

A gust of wind cleared the scene. On a slope covered with burnt rubbish there were three large concrete pools, arranged stepwise one above the other, surrounded by palm trees wrapped in blue plastic and by big yellowish-brown rocks. The lowest pool, covered with a pall of steam, was full of water that smelled of bad eggs. A smoking yellow stream gushed out of a concrete pipe into the pool, encrusting the sides with limescale. Heads bobbed up and down among the clouds of steam, like buoys in a foggy harbour.

Anna went down the steps, passing a group of children asleep around the ashes of a bonfire. She picked up a bottle half-full of black liquid, like the stuff she'd seen being handed out in the amphitheatre.

She stripped naked, bundled up her clothes and hid them behind a row of barrels. Then she sat down on the edge of the pool and, with a push of her arms, dropped in. The warmth pressed on her chest and spread through her aching muscles, making her sigh with pleasure. Half a metre down, a seat jutted out from the side. She sat on it, her head still above the surface. With her legs floating free, the back of her head against the side of the pool, and the sound of water sloshing in her ears, she put the bottle to her lips. The thick concoction flowed down into her stomach. It was sugary and bitter.

She heard the low voices of other bathers, sparrows in the trees, the wind in the palm trees.

Astor had grown up and left home. He didn't want her any more.

So much the better.

'What do they call him? Mandolino,' she whispered, amused.

The black liquid was taking effect. She was floating not just in the water, but inside herself.

Some heads came towards her, as if carried on the current, and clustered around her.

Her eyelids were heavy and in that opalescent vapour she couldn't distinguish the faces. They looked like seals.

An alarm bell rang in her sluggish brain, but she didn't listen to it, tired of keeping up her guard.

They snatched the bottle out of her hand. She wanted to protest, but the words didn't come out of her mouth. She thought of moving away, but it was too much effort. She shut her eyes. Dazed and distant from everything, she dreamed of taking her sad thoughts, rolling them up into balls and throwing them down a dark tunnel.

The sun printed a glow on the clouds of sulphur. The warmth that rose from the bottom of the pool brought up seaweed, lazy bubbles and earth. It seemed to her as though the other side had moved away and the pool was a big saucepan of steaming broth into which a cook had put all this stuff to stew.

At Christmas, Mama used make tortellini with boiled meat and potatoes. Here she is, placing the soup bowl on the living-room table. 'This is a recipe from Bassano.' She fills Anna's dish with little green frogs swimming in broth streaked with olive oil.

She rocked up and down inside her body, fell down through it, undulating slowly, like a feather in a well with flesh walls, and found herself in a warm cosy cavern. If she looked up, above her there was a round dark hole, ending in her mouth. Through the arches formed by her teeth she could see clouds drift by.

The people pressed in on her, rubbed against her; someone spread mud on her face and spoke to her in a distorted voice that seemed to be coming out of a pipe. She felt fingers touching her nose, her cheeks, her lips. They made grooves in her skin, like a ploughshare cutting through wet earth.

'I want a drink,' she moaned, spitting out the foul water that filled her half-open mouth.

Now the concoction tasted salty. The mist changed colour, from grey to green and from green to pink.

'You're beautiful. Have you had the blood yet?' asked a voice.

She couldn't speak. Words reached her palate without the requisite strength to become sounds. They collected in her mouth like sour-tasting silver jewels. Her tongue touched the sharp edges of rings and earrings. She raised her hand. It was transparent. Golden streams flowed under her skin between sheaves of new-mown hay.

'You're very beautiful,' the voice whispered.

Anna burst out laughing.

Hands slid over her legs and her stomach, squeezed her breasts and nipples. Fingers explored her mouth, searching for her tongue, pulling her lips; others slipped between her thighs. She arched her back. Twisting her body and stretching out her arms, she grabbed one boy's neck and buried his face in her wet hair, scratching his back. They breathed in her ears, pressed their lips against hers. They fought over her, opened her legs, holding her feet and supporting her by the armpits. She screamed when someone bit one of her nipples hard, but a hand was clapped over her mouth. In a surge of anger, consciousness re-emerged and she started to kick out and thrash about with her arms; she writhed, gasping and swallowing the liquid, which ran warm and fetid down her throat. Coughing, she grabbed the side of the bath and reached out over the poolside, but a vice-like grip closed on one of her calves, trying to pull her back.

Anna stretched out her arms and dug her fingers into the earth. She rammed her heel into a nose and succeeded in breaking free, to cries of protest.

Panting and shivering, she stood up, with her hands on her stomach, still coughing and spluttering. Her pink skin was steaming, as if it had been boiled. She took a few uncertain steps in the cold, rubbing her chest, her teeth chattering. She went to the barrels where she'd hidden her clothes, but they weren't there any more.

Leaning over a wall, she opened her mouth and released a warm, acid gush of vomit which wetted her feet. That made her feel better immediately, but her head was still spinning and she couldn't stop shaking. She ran round the pool, threading her way between bodies. Finding a tattered red cardigan which reached down to her knees, she rolled up the sleeves, put on a pair of shoes and staggered over towards the steps.

The hill skewed to one side and she tried to straighten it up by leaning the other way. There were black figures everywhere. The hotel walls bent over and rolled towards her like concrete waves. Terrified, she raised her arms to defend herself and backed away, bumping into someone who pushed her away, saying, 'Easter ducks.'

Bent double, as if she'd been stabbed in the stomach, she made her way to a shed.

The door was bolted. She walked around the prefabricated building, hammering on the metal walls with her fists. With her forehead against the drainpipe, she burst into tears, exhausted, and slid down to the ground.

The building rested on two concrete blocks, and she slipped underneath. No one would find her there.

The effects of the concoction evaporated from her body in slow green fumes.

*

The Fire Festival was held on 2 November 2020, All Souls' Day. The fact that it fell on that day was certainly a coincidence.

According to Sicilian tradition, during the night between the 2nd and the 3rd the dead returned from the afterlife to visit their relatives, bringing gifts and sweets for children. The little ones would wake up and, with the help of their parents, find 'Dead Man's Bones', chocolates, crunchy *pupatelli* filled with toasted almonds, and other treats, hidden beneath bedclothes, in wardrobes or under sofa cushions.

Some of the orphans of the Grand Spa Hotel Elise perhaps still remembered the hunt for sweets, but all sense of time had been lost. Public holidays, name days and birthdays no longer had any meaning. Now it was the Red Fever that marked out the intervals of time with blotches, lumps and pustules. If anyone wore a watch, it was out of vanity. On the exchange market a watch was worth as much as a mobile phone, a computer or a Boeing 747. Less than a packet of Smarties.

*

When the sun appeared in the dip between two hills oppo-site the hotel it was ten past seven in the morning, but few were able to enjoy the sight.

Many had ceased to suffer during the night. Many were asleep, knocked out by alcohol, medicine and The Little Lady's Tears. Others, nearing the end, stared into space with frozen pupils and open mouths, like mystics experiencing visions; or tossed and turned, coughing, feverish and choked with catarrh. Others wandered about on thin, stork-like legs, hunched under blankets, searching for leftovers, something to eat.

The solar dot melted like butter in a black frying pan, grew into an orange dome, left the hills, tingeing the sky with purple foam, and extended its rays as far as the hotel. At ten past eight it crept under the shed.

Anna, suspended between wakefulness and sleep, felt it on her neck and through closed eyelids. Her head was being crushed in a vice and her stomach ached, but the effect of the drug had worn off. Clenching her fingers, she ran her tongue over her teeth. She couldn't remember how she'd got there, nor what had happened in the pool, but the feeling of the boys' marauding hands on her body was still there. A shudder of embarrassment. She opened her eyes and brought into focus, a few centimetres away from her nose, the cobweb-covered underside of the shed.

She had to get out of this place.

Coming out from under the shed, she was dazzled by the sun and screwed up her eyes. The crowd had grown bigger and there wasn't a single free seat. Everyone was huddled around dead fires, wrapped up in nylon sheets, blankets and cardboard boxes in an attempt to keep warm. The narrow path to the exit was filled with interweaving streams of people going in opposite directions.

Her way towards the gates took her across the top of the amphitheatre. The sun glinted on shards of broken bottles, tin cans and coloured foil snack wrappers. The terraces were a mass of sick children emitting a chorus of wheezes, coughs and groans. The guardians dragged away the ones who hadn't survived the night and piled them up under the columns. A girl with long red hair was singing beside a lifeless body.

Anna entered the covered passage that led to the gates, but as she was going against the main flow it was hard to make any headway. She found herself squashed against the wall. Nobody was checking the entrances any more.

Where was she was going?

Mulberry Farm had been desecrated, and there was no sense in going to Calabria without Astor. There was no sense in anything without Astor. She'd grown up with her brother as a tree grows around barbed wire; they'd fused together and were now a single entity.

She stared at the gaunt faces and blank expressions of children pushing to get in.

She was one of them, one of the many, mixed up in that desperate crowd, one sardine in a shoal of sardines which the Red Fever would devour indiscriminately, like a hungry tuna fish.

She let the flow of the crowd carry her back again.

*

Between two rusty mechanical diggers, a group of children – all boys – had created a sheltered niche for themselves and were feeding a fire with pieces of cardboard and wood. They were handing round tins and packets of biscuits.

Anna watched them from a few metres away, her mouth watering. Plucking up courage, she moved closer and asked: 'Will you give me something?'

The boys exchanged glances.

Anna put her hands together in silent prayer.

Who knows? Maybe they could see the beauty hidden under the clumps of greasy hair and the dirt that covered her face, or maybe they just felt sorry for her; the fact is, they motioned to her to sit down and passed her a small jar.

She pulled out a soft slimy pickled gherkin, which she found delicious. She finished it in an instant and searched the bottom of the jar with her fingers for remnants.

Seeing her so hungry, a shaven-headed boy with feminine features rummaged in a big bag between his legs and handed her a bigger jar.

Without even stopping to read the label to see what it was, she unscrewed the top and stuffed the mush in her mouth. It was tasteless. Without asking if anyone minded, she picked up a bottle of Sprite from the ground and took a swig from it. She looked at the boys. Each of them wore a close-fitting red vest with a number on the back, and among their possessions was a big orange ball.

She learned that they were the survivors of a youth basketball team from Agrigento. After the epidemic they'd assembled in their gym and they'd lived there together for the last four years, sending out small groups to find food. The oldest boys were dead now. It had taken them a long time to get to the hotel, and they'd had all kinds of trouble. They'd been attacked by dogs, then by a group of kids who'd robbed them one night and beaten them up for no reason. Their point guard had been stabbed, their power forward bitten by a viper while they were crossing a field.

'Do you know when the party starts?' a fair-haired boy asked her, brushing aside the fringe in front of his eyes.

'No, I haven't got the faintest idea.' Anna had spotted a jar of pesto near the embers. She loved that green sauce.

'They say the Little Lady's incredibly tall. More than two metres,' said another boy. Long and thin, like a stick insect, he appeared to be the team captain.

The shaven-headed boy didn't agree. 'No, I've heard she's

beautiful. They keep her locked up in Room 237 of the hotel.'

Each boy had his own theory.

Anna took another swig of Sprite. 'Do you know why they never show her?'

The others gazed at her in silence.

'Because there's no such person as the Little Lady. It's a lie. The Grown-ups are all dead.'

The thin one protested. 'But this one's special. She managed to survive. She's . . . What's the word?'

'Immune,' said another boy, who had a woollen hat pulled down over his forehead. 'She has the substance that destroys the virus in her blood.'

Anna grinned sarcastically and repeated: 'The Grown-ups are all dead, have you guys forgotten that?' She pointed at the hotel. 'All this mumbo-jumbo is just a way for those guys with necklaces to get people to give them stuff when they come in. I bet there won't be any party. They're making fools of you.'

The boys fell silent, their eyes fixed on the flames.

One boy, whose lips were covered in pustules and scabs and who'd kept in the background till now, spoke in a faint voice. 'It's you that's wrong. There is such a person as the Little Lady. She does exist.' He coughed violently, as though he was going to spit out his lungs. 'They'll burn her, we'll eat the ashes and we'll be cured of Red Fever.'

'If you want to believe that, please yourselves.' She picked up the jar of pesto, dipped in her finger and licked it.

The atmosphere had changed. The eyes staring at her were less friendly now.

Anna ran her tongue along her lips. 'I always used to have pesto with pasta.'

The sick boy sighed in a barely audible voice. 'Why are you here?' He must have been fat before the disease; now the skin hung off his skeleton like a dress on a coat hanger.

'I came to look for someone . . . But he wasn't here. I'll be leaving soon.'

'Leave straight away,' said the captain. 'We're sure we'll survive, because we're the greatest . . .' He looked at the others and put his hand to his ear. 'Who are we?'

'The San Giuseppe Club!' they all shouted together, raising their arms.

Anna got up and went to find a free wall to sit on.

A few metres away, a group of children were rooting about in the rubbish, squabbling over a blanket.

*

She spent the rest of the day searching for food and dozing. She'd tried to get into the hotel, but she didn't have a bone necklace and they'd turned her away.

A rumour was going around that the Fire Party would take place that night. Someone had seen groups of guards erecting barriers down at the quarry and there was even talk of a lorry moving.

Even Anna was becoming convinced that something was going to happen. The place was packed and expectations had grown too high – there was a risk of a riot.

She wandered aimlessly among the crowd. Cigarette lighters, candles and electric torches shone in the darkness, and sheets billowed like bright sails over recumbent bodies. Bonfires scattered sparks as they devoured wheels, wood, plastic, anything combustible. Drums beat a rapid unchanging rhythm. Twice she passed Pietro going in the opposite direction. He was hovering near her, not daring to approach.

Tiredness had slowed down her thoughts, which just drifted aimlessly.

Someone touched her shoulder. 'Excuse me . . .'

She turned and found herself facing a kind of big ape. He had an oval head which looked as if it was made of plasticine, a pug nose and two small black eyes. His shoulders sloped down steeply like the sides of a roof. He'd painted his face red and white and his mouth green, as if he was on his way to an Italy match. He was naked except for a pair of long johns that encased his buttocks, held up by a strip of black elastic which bore the words: 'Sexy Boy'. He pointed at her. 'That cardigan's mine. You took it, down by the pool.'

Anna pulled out the tattered garment with both hands. 'Do you mean this?'

'Yes. Could you return it, please.' He had problems with his *r*s and *p*s.

She shrugged her shoulders.

'It was my grandpa Paolo's,' Bigpants explained. The flames of the bonfire shone on an improbably perfect white smile which moved independently of his lips.

A sensible little voice implored Anna to keep quiet, but she ignored it. 'Were your dentures your grandpa Paolo's too?'

The other changed his tone and started spluttering. 'Give it back. Or I'll . . .'

'Or you'll what?' Anna realised that the lethargy she'd felt all day had disappeared. The adrenaline roused her, she felt alive and quarrelsome. 'All right. Here it is.' With a shout, she charged at him head-down, butting him in the stomach. It was like hitting the door of a fridge. She bounced back and found herself lying on the ground among a small crowd of spectators who turned their torches on them, anticipating a show.

Bigpants looked at her hesitantly, hands on hips. 'What was that supposed to be?'

Anna got up, shook her head and charged again, but a hand as wide as a pizza shovel was waiting to slap her across the face.

She spun round on one foot like an ungainly ballerina and fell down, hitting her collarbone on the edge of the wall at the side of the path. A sharp pain shot through her shoulder.

The people around them shouted, encouraging Bigpants, who spread his arms and clenched his fists. 'Are you going to return it to me or not?'

Anna looked at the sky. The stars were tiny quivering holes through which the light of a huge sun shone, from where it lay hidden behind the curtain of night. There was a metallic taste of blood on her teeth.

This guy's going to kill you. Give him the cardigan and stop this, the sensible little voice advised her.

But the audience were urging her to fight on and she couldn't let them down. He was only a fat ape, like the other one who'd taken her brother.

She spat blood. 'Now I know who you are. You're the Little Lady's twin brother.'

Bigpants was not amused. He clamped his hands round her arm and calf and lifted her up in the air like a rag doll. Anna clenched her fingers and landed a well-aimed punch on his flat nose. The giant's eyes goggled, he spat out his false teeth and put his hands to his face, dropping her on the ground.

Treacherously, the audience began to shift their allegiance to her. Two spectators fought over the false teeth, as if they were a tennis ball that had landed on the terraces at Roland Garros.

Anna got up, hopped forward and aimed a kick at his crotch. She caught him on the inside of the groin.

He bent double, yelping with pain. Anna raised her arm, whipping up the crowd and forgetting the only rule that matters when you're in a fight: never take your eyes off your opponent.

Bigpants rushed at her with his arms outspread and hit her on the side, slamming her down on her back among rubble and litter. The impact knocked the wind out of her lungs. The ogre climbed over the wall and brought a gigantic fist down on her shoulder.

Anna's back arched and her head rose. She gave a hoarse yell and fell down again, gasping. Faces, arms and flames blurred and sharpened in flashes of yellowish light. She saw her opponent towering over her, holding a stick in both hands, and the crowd undulating in slow motion like balls on the waves of the sea.

Of all the possible deaths, this was the stupidest: being killed by a boy who wanted his grandpa Paolo's cardigan back.

Anna covered her head with her arms and shut her eyes tight.

An explosion shook the hill.

She opened her eyes.

On the starry vault of the sky a bright red hydrangea fired out curving yellow tendrils which faded beyond the walls of the hotel. This was followed by a green sphere which shot out white quills, and by less colourful but noisier bangs, which echoed around the valley.

Bigpants, his small eyes gleaming with coloured lights, dropped the stick and started clapping with his pudgy hands. Everyone looked upwards, open-mouthed.

Somebody shouted: 'The Fire Party has started.'

★

Like a multicellular organism, the crowd camped around the hotel sent its human offshoots out along the ridges of the hill – they clogged up paths and tracks, crossed seas of rubbish, walked through woods, scaled heaps of rubble and headed towards the quarry, shouting as they went.

The fence that blocked off the way had been removed. A river of children poured onto the road, guided by fires lit on the valley floor. Some, in the darkness, fell down onto rocks and slid down screes, others were trampled underfoot.

Groups of fevered, limping, scab-covered individuals also

converged on the scene from the amphitheatre. Some hobbled along, supporting themselves on crutches, others leaned on a companion, some gave up and let themselves be overrun by the flow.

Anna, aching all over, found herself struggling against hundreds of arms, shoulders, terrified faces, bodies squashed against each other. A wave from behind pressed against her, pushing her forward.

She turned and saw a camel, its large head swaying smoothly from side to side. Clinging onto its back were three children with flaming torches. Bellowing desperately, the animal knocked down anyone who blocked its path. Its tongue hung out of its mouth like a huge blue slug. Anna dodged to one side and threw herself on the ground, letting it pass. When she got up again and started running, she saw the camel's mangy hindquarters already far away, framed between crowds on either side. A couple of wretches had caught hold of its tail and were letting themselves be pulled along, while trying to stay on their feet.

*

Anna came to the end of the road and found herself looking at a dark undulating sea of heads which covered the floor of the quarry, spreading even onto the mounds of sand and the scree. The valley was divided in two by a long strip of burning rubbish, from which tongues of fire rose up. Squeezed onto one side was the audience; on the other, veiled by a curtain of thick smoke, were the crane holding up the skeleton, the piles of bones and the tanker where she'd hidden with Pietro the day before. She tried to push her way through the crowd, but after gaining a few metres, she gave up. The warehouse loomed over the crowd like a metal island. In the reddish gleams, small antlike figures climbed up the pylons that supported the structure.

She skirted the crowd and pushed her way up among the children attempting the climb. A human column had formed on the pylons, and some, finding nothing to hold onto, fell back on top of those below them.

Anna grabbed rusty crossbars, shoulders, arms, stepped on heads and reached the corrugated iron roof. The metal was sagging under the weight of hundreds of kids. She found a small space on the ridge of a roof tile and sat down.

The barrier of fire crackled as it devoured tyres and plastic, blotting out the stars and the moon. Now a strange silence reigned, broken only by the roar of an internal combustion engine clanking somewhere in the darkness.

'What happens now?' asked a girl sitting next to her. One of her arms was swathed in dirty bandages and one of her hands had only three fingers.

'I don't know,' Anna replied.

A short time passed and the crowd grew restless again.

Suddenly loud music blared out and a woman's voice, amplified and distorted, started singing. 'If you want to leave, I understand you . . . Yes . . . Again . . . Take me back again . . . Sensual on my heart . . . Because I love you still . . .'

The crowd roared.

Someone on the roof shouted that it was the Little Lady's voice.

One after another, three electric spotlights came on, transforming the smoke into an iridescent pall, reflected on thousands of astonished faces.

The audience gasped and responded with a spellbound 'Wow!'

'Who's that over there?' The girl with three fingers pointed at something above the curtain of smoke. 'Look!'

A huge dark silhouette materialised in the haze. A gust of wind blew through the valley, revealing the big skeleton floating in the air, suspended by its head.

Its movements were slow and gangling. It raised one arm

and lowered the other, bent one leg and straightened the other, like an astronaut in space. Teams of little blue devils, hanging from ropes attached to the marionette's wrists, elbows, knees and ankles, were pulled up into the air and swung down again, counterbalancing the weight of the limbs.

The giant seemed about to step over the curtain of fire. The bones that adorned it shimmered like a fur coat in the floodlights.

The excited crowd jostled each other, pushing forward against the flames, but the heat drove them back.

Now a male voice started singing: 'The Americans will hear my song, our friends who left just yesterday, whose flowery shirts lent colour to our streets and to our springtime . . . And your lovely eyes . . .'

At this spectacle of music and electric light, everyone on the roof stood up and hugged each other, with tears in their eyes.

Only the Grown-ups could do something like this, thought Anna, while her neighbour squeezed her hand, saying over and over again: 'It's not true . . . It's not true.'

A floodlight dipped down, sliding over the thousands of heads, bathing them in light and making them jump excitedly. Then the beam moved up, dazzling the children on the roof, who stamped their feet, turning the warehouse into a drum.

Inside the building an engine came on and a siren started up.

Anna clung to the roof, dazzled by the light. Below, hundreds of children hammered on the walls with their fists.

The engine revved up and the doors opened, driving them back. The green nose of a lorry emerged.

Anna saw it cut slowly through the crowd like an ice-breaker, heading for the skeleton. The sides of the long trailer were lowered. On top were dozens of blue children waving sticks and flaming torches, as on a carnival float.

In the middle, chained up on a platform, among billows

of black smoke, between Rosario and Angelica, who were whipping up the crowd, was a strange tall, gaunt figure. Its skin was so white it could never have been in the sun. Its arms dangled long and straight. A row of pointed humps ran up its back. Its long, bald skull was too big for its small fleshy ears. A sparse beard, streaked with grey, hung down like a bib over female breasts, which fell limply over skinny ribs.

'The Little Lady!' shouted the children on the roof, leaning forward to get a better view.

Five or six of them, pushed by those behind, fell down on the crowd, which swallowed them up.

Anna was finding it hard to keep her balance, but couldn't stop looking at the strange creature.

Its forehead was low, rounded and devoid of eyebrows. A stupid smile hung on its toothless mouth, from which a stream of drool ran down onto its grizzly beard. Its eyes, as dark as onyx, were frightened. It shook its great head, as if trying to drive away a swarm of wasps.

Anna recognised its expression as of one afflicted by idiocy.

She remembered Ignazio, the son of the woman who used to come to the farm once a week to do the cleaning. The poor boy had been starved of oxygen at birth, and had been left retarded. He would roll about on the ground drooling, his head sunken into one shoulder, and he would eat anything he found, including shit.

Anna wondered why the Red Fever had spared the Little Lady. Maybe because she was half man and half woman. She certainly wasn't a real Grown-up.

She's not going to save anyone. Not even herself.

A bitter smile formed on her lips as the crowd surged wildly towards the trailer, trying to touch the deformed creature – only to be beaten back with sticks by the blues.

Her brother was at the back of the trailer and, like the others, was fighting off countless hands trying to pull him down.

Anna called out to him with all the breath she had, but her voice was lost among the shouts, the siren and the roar of the fire.

She looked down. For a moment she was tempted to jump, then she set off on all fours towards the pylon she'd climbed up. The central part of the roof had caved in, and a mass of bodies was writhing inside the shed.

She fought her way down through the others, tugging at hair and T-shirts. Halfway there she gave up the struggle, dropped onto the crowd and was absorbed into it. Then she rushed after the lorry, along with hundreds of other children.

She was pushed forwards, and then backwards, by colliding, screaming waves of human beings.

A long way ahead, the lorry honked its horn as it made for the skeleton, with clumps of hysterical children clinging to the sides and the cab. It entered the fire with all its retinue.

Anna didn't see what happened next – it was too far away. But the marionette caught fire, and within a few seconds was burning right up to its head, a human torch lighting up the whole quarry. One blazing arm broke away from the bust, and a huge fire spread, engulfing the tanker.

There was pandemonium. People were running in all directions, while Anna stood motionless, staring at the inferno into which her brother had gone.

The world exploded.

There was a loud bang, and the tanker turned into a red ball. It rose and swelled in the darkness, sending out meteors which left luminous trails behind them, whistling into the crowd or into heaps of sand, and setting fire to pine trees at the top of the quarry. The blast was like a red-hot slap in the face. It threw Anna backwards, scorching her face, neck and eyelashes, entering her mouth and going right down to her lungs.

The sphere imploded, releasing a thick black pall which settled over the valley. Swirls of fire emerged in the pearly mist. Black figures appeared and disappeared again, sucked back in by the smoke.

Anna got to her feet and started walking forward. She screwed up her eyelids, trying to wipe the tears from her eyes. She coughed, choked by the acrid petrol fumes. A little girl running with her head down collided with her, and she was dumped on the ground again. She stood up again and walked on towards the fire. Her brother was there. The heat was burning her legs and she wondered if her hair was on fire.

Someone grabbed her shoulder from behind. 'Anna!'

She shook her head and didn't turn round.

'Anna!' This time he grabbed her wrist.

Pietro, black with soot, his T-shirt torn, was carrying a little boy in his arms.

She moved closer, putting her hands to her face.

The little boy lifted his head slightly, looked at her and stretched out his arm. 'Anna.'

Part Three

The Strait

8

The sand was warm on top, but if you dug down a little with your feet, it was cold and wet. Anna was lying on a beach towel, enjoying the sun on her forehead and limbs. The undertow slowly dragged the shingle. Seagulls screeched out at sea.

She felt drowsy and apathetic.

Turning her head, she opened her eyes a little and saw the tail and bony haunches of Fluffy, lying beside her. The scaly black pads under his paws twitched as if he was running in his sleep. Down by the water's edge, Astor was running about naked, jumping and kicking at waves. His arms projected from two green water wings like little sticks. He drew lines in the sand with his toes which the waves washed away.

'What are you doing?' she shouted.

He looked at her for a moment, picked up a long gnarled branch and ran up to her, spraying her with sand.

'Be careful . . .' Anna complained, brushing her face.

'Look at this! Isn't it great?' Astor waved the branch in the air.

'It's a stick.'

'No, it's not.' He pointed to a darker crack in the pale wood. 'It's a snake. See the head? It's got a mouth, too.'

'Are you hungry?'

'A bit.'

'Shall we go home?'

'You said we'd go for a swim.'

'When? I don't remember saying that.'

'Yesterday.' Her brother grabbed her forefinger and tried to pull her to her feet.

'Are you sure?' Anna sat up and stretched her back. Out at sea some clouds like tufts of white steam had appeared. At the end of the bay, where Cefalù stuck its rocky old nose into the sea, a flock of seagulls were swooping down on a shoal of fish.

'Come on . . .' the little boy whimpered.

'All right.'

Astor triumphantly displayed his array of lopsided teeth and rolled in the sand, like a meatball covering itself in breadcrumbs. He jumped to his feet, ran over to Fluffy and grabbed hold of his tail. 'We're going for a swim!'

Anna puffed out her cheeks. 'Leave him alone.'

But he wouldn't let go; he grunted, trying to drag him along.

That dog was a saint. They'd found him waiting outside the hotel, and he and Astor had instantly made friends. He would ride on his back, pull his ears, explore his jaws like a lion-tamer. And yet the Maremma was so gentle when he played with Astor you'd have thought he was afraid of breaking him. He pretended to bite him, but didn't apply any pressure. During the long trek to Cefalù, he'd never let him out of his sight. If Astor lagged behind, Fluffy would be constantly going backwards and forwards between him and Anna.

'Why won't he go into the water?'

Anna shrugged. 'He doesn't like it.'

'Why not?'

'I don't know. Do you like tinned peaches?'

Astor made a face. 'Those mushy things in that clear liquid? No, I can't stand them.'

'And he can't stand the sea. So don't keep pulling him

about, or one day he'll lose his temper and bite you, and it'll serve you right.'

They made their way down towards the wash, hand in hand. Near some overturned boats there was a small polystyrene surfboard, spattered with tar. The front part was missing, as if a shark had taken a bite out of it.

Anna took off her denim shorts and was left in her swimming costume, a green two-piece with white polka dots, and a padded top that made her look grown-up. She took a mask and snorkel out of her rucksack, picked up the surfboard and entered the water, while Astor ran past her and did a belly flop, uttering squeals of joy.

Although it was a mild winter, the water was freezing cold. Anna walked gingerly, as if crossing a carpet of broken crockery. Her brother, unconcerned by the temperature, tried to dive down, holding his nose with his fingers, but the water wings kept him afloat.

Anna pushed the surfboard till the water came up to her thighs, then lay down on it. 'Start up, engine,' she ordered, pulling down the mask.

Astor gripped the rear end of the board and started making raspberry-like noises.

'Forward. Slow down. Straight on.' She put her head under the water, biting on the snorkel. Below her there appeared an expanse of grey pebbles and strips of sand combed by the current. A silent landscape which had little to offer, but which Anna never tired of observing. When she breathed into the tube, with the water sloshing in her ears, she felt at peace.

'Hey, what's going on?' she shouted into the snorkel, bending her back as though she'd been whipped. Through the steamed-up glass she saw Astor kicking his feet like a madman. 'Stop it! You're soaking me. Are you the engine?'

'Yes,' her brother replied, very serious.

Anna spoke slowly and clearly. 'Well then, engine, listen

to me carefully: go slowly and don't splash, or I'll puncture your water wings and you'll drown.'

'All right.'

She resumed her exploration. Shoals of grey mullets chased each other, while red mullets brushed the sea bed with their whiskers. Thoughts, with your head underwater, formed slowly, grew bigger and burst in abstract bubbles. How wonderful it would be to lose your bones, turn your flesh into transparent jelly and be carried along by the current like a jellyfish. How wonderful to sink slowly down to the bottom of the sea and find, among the luminous creatures that live there, Cola the Fish, the boy who carried Sicily on his shoulders.

Further out, the sea bed, mottled with clumps of Neptune grass, turned a deeper blue, and suddenly she saw a big concrete cube covered with green and brown and with clusters of mussels, and surrounded by myriad little fish with coloured heads. A tiny planet teeming with life in the middle of a sandy desert.

'Stop, engine.'

She'd seen these big things before, but didn't know what they were used for. Maybe for mooring boats. Close beside it she noticed two small yellow pebbles with a black stripe in between. She looked at them from all angles and gradually made out a camouflaged form. It was the same colour as the sand, yet slightly different. Around those two little pebbles, evidently eyes, was a ring of fleshy tentacles.

'An octopus! There's an octopus!' she said excitedly, and felt her brother's fingers grip her ankle.

'No! What's it like? Is it big?' Astor was as excited as if she'd said there was a basket full of salami down there. He'd never seen a real octopus, though he'd once had a toy one.

'It's hiding in the sand.' She passed him the mask. He started spluttering and gulping seawater, and Anna was scared there was something wrong with him.

'Please, please, will you get him for me?' Astor fluttered his lashes, with his eyes wide open, playing the good little boy. He reminded her of herself standing at the window of the toyshop in Via Garibaldi and asking Mama if she could have the Chinese Barbie with the panda and the red dress.

'I can't reach it. It's too far down.'

'But you can swim.'

'Swimming and deep-sea diving aren't the same thing. Anyway, how would I pick it up?'

'With your hands. It's friendly. It won't bite.'

Once her father had caught an octopus in Zingaro Nature Reserve. He'd come back to the shore immensely proud of the little creature which stretched out and curled round the barbs of the spear, and he'd slapped it on the rocks as if he was washing clothes. To soften it, he'd explained, but when they cooked it, it had become a pathetic fleshy flower.

'I want to play with it,' said Astor.

'I could try.' Anna slid into the water. Millions of icy pins pricked her skin. She looked down. She was no longer sure that it was an octopus, and she didn't know how many metres it was to the bottom. At least three – four Annas, one on top of the other. And as well as going down, she'd have to come up again.

She started breathing in and out, filling her lungs. It'd be a miracle if she could just get to the bottom and grab a handful of sand. Counting up to three, she closed her mouth and went down. After a few strokes the pressure squeezed the mask against her face. Then she felt a pain in her ears; she tried to ignore it, but it was like two bradawls boring into her ears. She swam back up to the surface and grabbed the board, gasping.

'Did you catch it? Let me see it!'

Sometimes Anna suspected her brother was soft in the head. 'Can you see it? Am I holding an octopus in my hands?'

Astor thought about it. 'Well, you might have stuffed it

inside your swimming costume, so you could spring a surprise
on me later.'

'Listen, engine, instead of thinking, switch yourself on and
take me back to the beach.'

'Won't you try again? Please?'

'I'm freezing cold.'

Disappointed, Astor switched himself on, blowing a raspberry.

★

'Hey, Anna, how many tentacles does an octopus have?'

'I don't know.'

'Ten?'

'Maybe.'

'Why does it have ten and not nine? And how many
suckers does it have?'

'Lots.'

'Why does it have lots?'

'Because that's the way octopuses are.'

Since his time with the blues, Astor had changed; his
tongue had loosened and he never stopped talking. Coming
into contact with the world had made him less introverted
and more tiresome.

'And if a sucker sticks to you, will it tear your skin off?'

'I don't know.'

Her brother ran alongside her and grabbed her by the
wrist. 'Hey, do octopuses have willies? And why don't they
come out and live in the air instead of in the sea?'

Anna stopped. 'What's the matter with you? That's enough!
I don't know anything about octopuses.'

A question mark crossed the little boy's mischievous
eyes.

Anna put her finger to her lips. 'I don't want to hear any
more questions. Don't say another word till we get home. If

you do have any questions, keep them to yourself for the moment, choose four and ask me them tomorrow.'

Astor looked at her, puzzled. 'Why four?'

'Shhh . . .'

★

So here they were, the three of them, on Cefalù promenade. The dog out in front, Anna in the middle and Astor bringing up the rear with hundreds of questions in his mouth.

The road, the pavements and the iron benches were buried in sand; only a few concrete walls and rusting lamp posts stuck out of it. On the landward side, rows of restaurants formed a solid mass. Many signs were still there, The Seagull, Nino's, The Pirate's Den, but in four years of dereliction façades had faded and paint on windows had peeled. Many places had lost their glass fronts and the sea had pushed plastic, wood and deckchairs into the rooms. In one there was even a capsized rowing boat.

'Will we go and see the octopus again tomorrow?'

'Be quiet.'

In front of them was the bay, which ended in a small harbour hemmed in by the village. Stone houses, squeezed together, overlooked the sea in a jumble of arches, windows and little balconies. Towering up behind the dark pantiled roofs were the two square bell towers of the Duomo and the sheer sides of the Rocca, a round mountain resembling a panettone.

They walked across a car park crammed with cars white with salt and guano. From there they went down a narrow street flanked by buildings sprouting balconies, street lamps, electric cables and lines that had once been used for drying clothes. The shops' shutters were lowered and most Persian blinds barred. Street signs still pointed the way to the cathedral, bars and hotels.

Looting, destruction and fires had raged all over Sicily, but not in Cefalù. She'd found few skeletons in the houses, as if the inhabitants had left the village before the epidemic could kill them. Now it was a refuge for rats, ducks and colonies of seagulls. Most of the cats had been chased away by Fluffy.

Anna stopped outside the bookshop, The Compass. She tried to lift the shutter, but it was locked. To one side, the fanlight above a green door was open.

She made a stirrup with her hands and Astor shot through to the other side like a squirrel. A few moments later the door opened onto a yard paved in stone. A green forest grew out of pots standing against the walls. The bar, The Comet, was still in one corner, its iron tables next to a small wooden dais. A poster announced that the Mariano Filippi Jazz Trio would be playing there next Thursday.

Anna went over to a small window. She picked up a chair and smashed the glass. Climbing over the windowsill, followed by her brother, she switched on the torch.

The bookshop was full of display cases containing postcards, painted dinner plates, human–head–shaped vases and ceramic suns with smiling faces. The tables were laden with stacks of coloured tiles and boxes of souvenirs. If Cefalù had a fault, it was that of being our enormous container of ceramic trash.

Continuing her inspection, Anna found some shelves in a corner with some books on them – manuals on Sicilian cookery, tourist guides and a small volume with a plasticised cover.

'Here we are.' She showed the book to Astor.

'What is it?'

'Read.' She shone the torch on the title.

Astor scratched his nose. 'Ap . . . ne . . . a . . . fi . . . shing. Apnea fishing.'

During these months they'd spent on the road she hadn't been able to make him practise his reading. They must start doing it again.

'What does that mean?' asked Astor. 'Is it like apple-picking?'

'It means diving underwater to catch fish.'

Astor's eyes lit up. 'Including octopuses?'

'Well, we'll have to see about that.'

They went back out into the yard and Anna sat down at a table.

Her brother strutted over to her. 'May I take your order, madam?'

After listening to all the stories about bars and restaurants, Astor had decided that if he grew up he was going to be a waiter, because waiters were involved with food all day long.

Anna couldn't make up her mind. 'What's on the menu?'

'Meat with tomatoes, and almond milk.'

'I'll have some almond milk.'

The little boy ran over into a corner and fiddled about with some imaginary glasses. 'Here you are.'

Anna downed the non-existent drink. 'Mmm! Delicious!'

The book devoted three pages to the octopus, king of the invertebrates. They learned that it had eight tentacles and was very intelligent, even being able to solve problems of geometry. And in particular that it was a solitary creature: it would choose a den and stay there. Anna showed the photograph to her brother, who shook his head in disbelief. He'd never seen such a strange animal.

'It's even stranger than the long-haired lizards.'

★

'There you are at last! What took you so long?' Pietro rushed out of a garage at the side of a narrow street. He was covered in white dust, like a baker who's been busy kneading. 'You'll never guess what I've found . . .'

Astor didn't let him finish. Speaking too fast, and mumbling his words, he told him about his adventure in the sea. Then he pulled him by the hand and made him sit down on a step to look at the photographs in the book.

Anna leaned against a wall, crossing her arms. Pietro raised his eyes and gazed at her.

She lowered her head at once, embarrassed. She waited a few seconds, but when she lifted it again he was still looking at her, with that smile like . . . Even she didn't know like what. Then she bent her neck forward and silently mouthed: 'Are you an idiot?'

9

Since leaving the Grand Spa Hotel, the three of them had never been apart.

After retrieving the exercise book and the thighbone from the restaurant, A Taste of Aphrodite, they'd decided to spend the night in a small terraced house in Torre Normanna. During the night the wind had picked up, rattling the houses' shutters and making their gutters creak. The sight of Pietro wrapped in a blanket and the sound of Fluffy's hoarse breathing hadn't been enough to reassure Anna. Lying beside her brother on a battered sofa, she floated in a sleep disturbed by dreams and thoughts. Staring at the dark ceiling, she heard the wood and the mulberry cottage calling to her.

Stay with us, Anna. You're the queen of the bones.

Then her mother's footsteps upstairs, clicking rhythmically across the floor.

Are you leaving, Anna?

Yes, Mama.

Be careful, then.

I will, I promise.

How many of the promises she'd made to Mama on her deathbed had she kept? Maybe not even one. But she still had her brother with her. She'd succeeded in getting him back. And now she must keep the promise she'd made to herself, to take him to the mainland.

Pietro and Astor had woken up to find her standing there looking at them. 'We've got to make an agreement,' she'd said.

The two boys had yawned, their eyes swollen with sleep.

'What agreement's that?' Astor had asked.

'That we'll go to the mainland, all three of us.'

'And on the way there we'll look for the shoes,' Pietro had added, rubbing his eye.

Astor had picked his nose. 'Can we go home first? I want to get my cuddly toys.'

'We'll find some new ones,' Anna had replied.

So one cloudy morning, rucksacks on their backs, they'd set off eastwards along the autostrada, escorted by Fluffy.

★

They walked quickly, and if they came to a tunnel they went through it hand in hand, singing. They often made detours looking for shoe shops and shopping malls. They broke down doors, smashed shop windows, opened hundreds of boxes, but Pietro's Adidas trainers were nowhere to be found. As the days passed, Anna became convinced that either those shoes didn't exist or they'd never reached Sicily. But Pietro never lost heart.

'Don't you understand? It's proof that they're magic. We'll find them in Palermo, you'll see.'

She bit her tongue. She wanted to reach Calabria as soon as possible, and wasting time like this drove her crazy. But she'd made an agreement, and she was going to stick to it.

As they walked along the A29, the landscape changed.

With a wide sweeping bend, the autostrada approached the coast. To the right was a wall of tall rocks, with occasional patches of greenery. At sunset the top glowed bright orange and the veins of the rock were tinged with blue. The mountain chain followed the shoreline, which was indented with gulfs of varying sizes. Between the mountains and the sea was a strip of land scattered with roofs and terraces of small blocks of flats which stood out among the undergrowth like

Lego bricks strewn on a green carpet. The villages merged into each other, and only the autostrada road signs broke them up into Terrasini, Cinisi, Capaci, Sferracavallo.

The few solitary travellers that they came across gave them a wide berth when they saw the great hound that was escorting them. If they met a gang, however, it was they who kept their distance, holding a growling Fluffy back by the scruff of his neck. The dog walked alongside them, but sometimes he'd vanish and not come back until dusk. During the night he'd curl up beside the three of them, with his ear cocked, ready to bark at the slightest noise.

It took them two weeks to reach Palermo.

The autostrada ran straight into a city choked with columns of trucks, tanks and jeeps with dirty windows. They came to what must once have been a road block. Concrete barriers and barbed-wire fences blocked the carriageway and ran on between the countryside and the houses. Everywhere notices riddled with bullet holes warned travellers to stop for health checks: 'Infected area. The penalties for attempting to cross the barrier range from thirty years' imprisonment to the death sentence.'

A long line of sheds which had housed the medical teams were full of computers, yellow protective suits and breathing equipment scattered all over the place and covered in mouse droppings.

They entered the silent city. Nothing had been spared by the fury of destruction. Not a shop, not a building, not a flat. All the locks on the doors had been forced. All the kitchens had been emptied. All the cupboard doors opened. Pictures thrown on the floor, windowpanes broken, crockery smashed to smithereens. Some areas appeared to have been bombed. Sections of wall were still standing, like sea stacks among heaps of rubble which filled the streets and buried cars. They passed the burnt-out wrecks of two helicopters that had been shot down.

As they approached the sea they had to scale barricades of furniture and rubbish bins over which the tattered remnants of black flags were still flying. Nobody seemed to have survived. Or if they had, they'd left. There weren't even any dogs or cats. The only living creatures were some green insects which formed wriggling balls of legs and got into your face and hair.

Pietro walked hand in hand with Astor, who had been struck dumb and was staring wide-eyed at the tangles of burnt bodies, with his thumb between his teeth. Anna felt as if the city didn't want them. It was still steeped in its inhabitants' suffering; all it wanted was to be forgotten. But nature was having trouble burying it. Only limp grass grew in cracks in the asphalt, pellitory was slow to creep between bricks, saplings were feeble and stunted, as if rooted in poisonous earth. Even the ivy, which usually proliferated everywhere, laying a green veil over the ruins of the Grown-ups' world, here sent out feeble runners with yellowish, shrivelled leaves.

The sea front had been used as a refugee camp, which now, four years later, was an unbroken layer of plastic, canvas and stiff cardboard. It no longer held any interest even for seagulls and rats. There were heaps of bodies in the piazzas and lime-covered corpses lay in mass graves. The harbour had been consumed by a fire so fierce it had twisted the iron railings and reduced the quays to blackened expanses. The only things still standing were cranes and stacks of rusty containers. Two ships lay on their sides like beached whales.

When they stopped outside the Sports Shop, a huge store as dark as the entrance to hell, Anna couldn't stop herself saying, 'We won't find your shoes here.'

Pietro stood for a moment in silence, then said, 'Let's go.'

They spent the night in the Politeama Theatre. The foyer was full of barrels, boxes of medical supplies, drip stands and camp beds. Someone had drawn a skull with purple eyes over the box office.

They pulled back the thick velvet curtains. The torch's

beam passed over red seats, shone on gilded columns of boxes, on dusty chandeliers and on frescos of rearing horses that emerged from the gloom. A flock of pigeons fluttered up in the darkness, banged into the big blue dome and fell down dead in the stalls.

Astor clung to his sister's arm and asked: 'What did they do here?'

Anna wasn't entirely sure, but replied: 'Elegant people used to come here. Mama came here too, with her smart skirt and her high-heeled shoes.' She shone the light on the stage, where there were still some pieces of scenery. 'And up there people used to dance and tell stories.'

They went to sleep hungry in one of the boxes.

Anna was the first to wake up. Pietro and Astor were stretched out stiffly on their seats like two young vampires. She left a note telling them to wait for her outside.

The sun was somewhere beyond the row of buildings. In the large Piazza Ruggero Settimo spirals of coloured plastic bags and paper whirled about among jeeps and tanks lined up around the marble monument. All that was left of the statue was its feet.

She started down a long straight road flanked by churches, looted shops and nineteenth-century palazzi with cloths and tattered flags hanging out of the windows. At the end, the black silhouette of a mountain stood out against the blue morning sky.

She recognised the remains of the gelateria, 'Dreamland', where her grandpa had often taken her, and of the shoe shop where her father had bought her some fur-lined boots. Then she turned down a side street and, proceeding partly at random and partly from memory, came to Via Ottavio D'Aragona.

The grey and pink palazzo where Papa used to live was there, its balconies looking out onto an underground garage and a burnt-out modern building. She pushed open the big dark wooden front door and entered the lobby. A toppled Christmas tree lay against the door of the lift among broken pieces of red glass. She switched on the torch and climbed the stairs.

On the second floor, the glass door of an insurance company was broken, revealing overturned desks and a carpet covered with sheets of paper, keyboards and monitors. The drinks machine had been smashed open and emptied. On the wall a poster featuring a blonde woman said: 'Assure yourself of a trouble-free future with us.'

Anna stood staring up the flight that led to the third floor. The door of the flat was ajar, and the vase with the cactus was still beside the mat. She rubbed her eyes and walked up the steps. As if floating in a dream, she went down the long hall with its marble-chip floor and stuccoed walls. Light filtered in from the windows of the rooms, painting bright strips on the walls. The white cupboard was open and all the windcheaters were on the floor, together with shoes, hats and gloves. She recognised the belted black jacket her father used to wear when he drove his work Mercedes. She stopped in the doorway of her own room. The drawings still hung on the wall. One showed a ship with three figures standing on it, and their names written above: me, Mama, Papa. Grandpa and Grandma's heads were sticking out of the sea. She smiled to herself. Why on earth had she put them in the water? Her pencil case containing her felt-tip pens was still on the red Ikea bedside table, along with the water colours and a drinking glass encrusted with limescale.

Every object in the room conjured up a recollection in her mind. Fragments of memory rose out of forgetfulness like broken pieces of glass, reassembling themselves into a prism of images. She was Annina, the little girl who came here twice a month.

Seeing the little room again now, she realised she'd never missed it. Never felt it was really hers. It was full of lovely things, but they only seemed to have been put there as decoration, like the plastic palm trees in the turtles' tanks. And she hadn't played with these toys and dolls often enough. They were her Palermo things; she wasn't allowed to take them to Castellammare. They weren't the products of tantrums, nor rewards for being good. Papa had simply stocked up in a shopping mall after splitting with Mama.

She looked out onto the street. There'd never been this silence in the old days. Back then, the traffic had flowed all day, and in the summer, with the windows open, you could hear what people said when they passed by. She went into the kitchen. The empty fridge was open, some dusty crockery piled up in the sink. Coffee powder was scattered over the worktop, and the wall above the sink was covered with patches of green mould. In a wall unit she found the box of alphabet-shaped cereal that she used to eat with milk. She opened it and moths flew out. She scooped out a handful of pieces and laid them on the Formica table. She put them in a row and managed to make ATOR; there was no S. She ate them one by one, crunching in silence.

Somebody must have slept in Papa's room. It was strewn with dirty sheets and empty bottles of alcoholic drinks. The curtains and carpet had caught fire and the wall around the window was framed with soot. She opened the drawer of the bedside table. The nasal spray for sinusitis. A watch. Photographs. Anna as a little girl in the car with Papa. Mama holding the newborn Astor in her arms. Mama and Papa with an ancient Roman in front of the Colosseum.

There was also a crumpled, open envelope.

Darling,

How are things with you? It's lovely here, and very cold. It snowed for three days, and this morning the car was like a white ball, but the sun was beautiful. I went skiing with Adriana, who keeps asking me about you. I think she's scared of being left on the shelf. And she remembers how everyone thought I was the one in the family who was going to remain single. Skiing is always great, especially today with the fresh snow, and I was sorry you weren't here too. I know you're Sicilian and you feel uneasy about putting on tights, but promise me you'll come one day so I can teach you how to do the snowplough. Adriana says I've got a Sicilian accent now, and you know what, I'm glad. I can't stand the Veneto dialect any more. I think of you and I wish I could have you in bed to warm my cold feet.

Over the past few days I've often wondered why I love you, and I realise you make a enormous effort to accept me for what I am. To adapt to me. I'm sorry we quarrel. You're a special person, and I want to try and see things through your eyes. Will you let me? We mustn't lose each other. I can learn to make you happy. How about that? I've written you a letter with pen and paper! I'm sure it'll give you more pleasure than an email when you find it in the box.

Annina is very well. My mother loves being a grandma and spoils her rotten. I've told her if she doesn't come to Palermo this summer to meet you she'll never see Annina again. What a nice girl I am, don't you think?

Kiss you all over,

Maria Grazia

★

She took the letter and the photos, put them in the rucksack and went out.

Later that morning they left Palermo.

On reaching Cefalù, they decided to take a few days' rest.

Anna snatched the book out of her brother's hands. 'Stop thinking about the octopus. Let's go and see what Pietro's found.'

Pietro took them into a garage with lime-plastered walls. Most of the space was occupied by a grey BMW covered by a tarpaulin. Among jars of food, big cardboard boxes and tools there was a light blue Vespa with a sidecar. The saddle was white, the handlebars fringed. The sidecar seat was made of woven plastic straw.

Pietro mounted the saddle and gripped the handlebars. 'This will start, I'm sure of it. Even the tyres are pumped up. And there's room for all of us.'

Anna, who had been expecting a new stock of Nutella at the very least, couldn't hide her disappointment, but tried to compensate by saying, 'It's lovely.'

'Don't you see?' Pietro pointed to the engine. 'We could travel more quickly.'

She said nothing.

He lowered his head and looked at her, coughing. 'What's the matter?'

'Nothing. Where would we go?'

'Where do you think? To Messina.'

'Yes. But . . .' *Aren't we happy here?* She kept the rest to herself.

'But what?'

'Nothing.' She realised that her voice had hardened. 'And what about Fluffy?'

Pietro slapped his forehead. 'I hadn't thought of that . . . We'll put him in the sidecar with Astor!'

'It's nowhere near big enough.' Anna picked up a screwdriver and made a face. 'I'm going home.'

'I'm going to stay a bit longer. I've got to clean the engine.'

Astor clung to his sister's arm. 'I'm hungry.'

★

Anna was furious.

What a bastard . . .

He didn't want to stay in Cefalù any longer. He wanted to go away because he was tired of her.

Astor ran along beside her, panting. 'Slow down. Why are you angry?'

'I'm not angry. Hurry up.'

The mere thought of Pietro wanting to leave her was terrifying. She couldn't imagine being alone again. What was happening to her? She had never needed anyone, and now she depended on that bullshitter. Her mood fell in with his. If he was happy, she was happy; if he was too quiet, she'd become gloomy. And he only had to call her Annina for her to melt away like an idiot. If she found a mirror, she'd stand in front of it; she no longer liked her nose, and she loathed the little mole on her cheek. She laughed without opening her lips to hide her chipped canine, and she spent hours trying on clothes. She was so exhausted by her own feelings that sometimes, in order to let off steam, she'd snap at Pietro and then regret it immediately. Or she'd try to run away, but an invisible elastic cord would pull her back.

It was a hellish situation, which nothing in the world would ever change. Her life had been broken down into minutes and every minute she spent by Pietro's side was a gift. Boredom had disappeared. That idiot made her laugh; he showed her the world through eyes less serious and anxious than her own. What's more – she had to admit it – he was very good-looking. During those months his nose, eyes, mouth and chin had found their correct proportions. Now they were perfect.

But one thing, more than any other, drove her to distraction: she still didn't know if she was his girlfriend. She'd have liked to slam him back against a wall and ask him: 'Listen, are we a couple or aren't we?'

Only she was afraid of the answer.

*

Wandering around the village, the four of them had found a flat at the top of an old building which overlooked the small harbour. A dimly lit staircase ended in a little door which opened onto a sitting room with a terracotta floor. Three white sofas formed a 'U' around a glass table and a long window gave onto a terrace full of plants. Many had withered, but others, such as the lemon trees and the sago palms, had continued to grow and were bursting out of their pots. In the middle was a wrought-iron table with a majolica top and on either side of it a row of camp beds with wooden slats. To the left there was a view of the new village that had spread around the bay. Below the building, framed by a small concrete quay, was a small beach of firm sand on which a couple of boats had survived. The sea was so clear it hardly seemed to be there. From the sitting room you passed through an arch into a kitchen with red lacquered units. The cutlery was tidily arranged in the drawers, and the glasses and dishes on the shelves. In the hall cupboard the sheets were neatly folded.

Nothing, however, compared with the bedroom, with its four-poster bed veiled by curtains as thin as gauze. On the polished ceramic floor there was a carpet embroidered with an image of a tiger emerging from some long grass. Fluffy had made that his bed. When you lay on the mattress you could see the vaulted ceiling, which was painted blue, with hundreds of little gold stars. The airtight windows and doors had kept the flat in immaculate condition, free of dust, insects or patches of damp. The owners certainly hadn't lived there during the epidemic. Everything in there, apart from the electricity, water and gas, was in perfect working order, and Anna tried to keep it like that. But with those three pigs it was impossible.

That filthy beast Fluffy hadn't learned to pee outside and, when he needed to go, would simply raise a leg and do it on the sofas. Once he'd even crapped on the coffee table. Astor, by contrast, loved doing it in the toilet 'like the Grown-ups'; unfortunately there was no water in the flush, so the toilet had been declared out of bounds. Pietro wasn't much better; but at least he did it in the flat below, and took off his shoes before going to bed.

★

Pietro came home and found Anna and Astor sitting on the sofas.

'What are you doing?' he asked them.

The little boy jumped to his feet. 'We were waiting for you.' He ran over to the drinks cabinet and took out a bottle of bilberry liqueur. 'We've got to drink it all – we've seen the octopus.'

'Quite right!' Pietro never said no to a drink. Sometimes he got so plastered he couldn't even stand up, so Anna would put a blanket over him and leave him to sleep on the sofa.

They started passing the bottle round and within ten minutes they were all drunk. Conversation was halting and interrupted by yawns, while the wind outside pressed against the windowpanes.

Anna looked at Pietro, sunk deep in the cushions, with his legs stretched out on the coffee table. He was wearing his windproof jacket, a shirt, long trousers and socks.

He never took off his clothes, never came to the beach. Always had something else to do. Anna suspected he was trying to hide the blotches, but preferred not to think about it. Since they'd left the hotel, the subject of the virus had been put to one side. Both of them, in an unspoken agreement, had pretended it didn't exist. As the days passed, the Red Fever had become background noise, like the sound of the sea which seeped through closed windows, and which you only heard if you concentrated. But the slightest thing was enough for the raven to start beating his wings again, obliterating all happiness.

Suddenly Pietro jumped to his feet and clapped his hands. 'Aren't we going to have supper? It'll be dark soon.' He shook Astor, who had gone to sleep.

In a daze, Anna rubbed her eyes and went into the kitchen, took out the cutlery and put it on the table, then picked up the candlestick covered with melted wax and placed it in the middle.

Pietro stepped forward with three tins. 'No chickpeas this evening.'

Anna turned them over in her hands, incredulous. 'Chicken soup . . . Where did you find this?'

He raised his hand, nodded his head with a knowing smile and pulled out a dark bottle with gold foil on its cork. 'Champagne. The very best. The brand my father used to drink when he won races.'

Astor grabbed at one of the tins, but was stopped by Pietro. 'Wait. First you've both got to answer a question.'

Astor's put his forehead on the table. 'I'm hungry . . .'

'What day is it today?'

Anna shrugged her shoulders. 'I've no idea.'

'The 8th of July.' For Astor it was always the 8th of July.

Pietro shook his head. 'Today, while you two were lounging about on the beach, I went for a walk and I came across Cammarata the jeweller's. There was a big watch in the window with a notice beside it, explaining that it was a Solar Quantus, the solar-powered watch used by explorers. The numbers moved, and it showed the date too.' He gazed at the brother and sister as if trying to hypnotise them.

'And?' Astor was all agog.

Pietro took a watch with a black rubber strap out of his pocket. 'What day of the year were you born, Anna?'

She was beginning to suspect where all this was leading. 'On the 12th of March,' she stammered.

Pietro clapped his hands. 'Happy Birthday, Anna.' And he started levering at the champagne cork.

Astor jumped up onto his chair. 'It's your birthday! It's your birthday! It's my sister's birthday!'

Fluffy, excited by the noise, started howling. The cork shot out with a bang, and champagne frothed out onto the table.

Anna's hands were over her mouth. She wanted to say thank you, but felt a lump in her throat. She mumbled something incomprehensible, then bowed her head and swallowed.

Pietro passed her the bottle. 'Have a drink. It's your party.'

She sniffed and gazed at him. 'How did you know?'

'You told me. In Palermo.'

'And you remembered?'

'Of course I did. How old does that make you?'

She looked at him uncertainly. 'Thirteen, I think. Or maybe fourteen. I don't know . . .'

'Never mind, it doesn't matter.' Pietro put his hand in his pocket. 'The important thing is that today's your day.' He pulled a gold necklace out of his pocket. The pendant was a little starfish decorated with blue enamel. 'Happy birthday.' He strung the necklace round her neck.

Anna clapped her hands over her eyes, staggered out into the hall and locked herself in the bathroom. Resting her forehead against the door, she let the tears come.

Pietro called out from the other side of the door. 'Anna! Anna! What's going on? Open the door.'

'Open the door! Are you cross?' Astor joined in, peering through the keyhole. 'You'll suffocate in there. It's full of my shit.'

'I'll come in a minute. You start eating,' Anna managed to stammer.

'No, we'll wait for you,' said Pietro.

'Not for long, though,' Astor added.

*

When she returned to the table, Anna had regained her composure, but her eyes were swollen. The starfish hung on her chest.

She sniffed as she ate, while the two boys wolfed down their food, pouring out champagne and burping at each other.

Pietro raised his glass. 'Today Anna is queen and can do whatever she likes. We're her slaves.'

'We're always her slaves,' said Astor.

'Don't argue,' the older boy silenced him. 'Those are my Aunt Celeste's rules for birthdays.'

'What have we got to do, then?' asked Astor.

Anna was at a loss for ideas. She looked around and her gaze fell on Fluffy, who was sitting beside the table, licking out a tin of chickpeas. 'We'll play the animal game.'

Astor jumped around the room like a monkey. Pietro mimed a mayfly which sounded very much like a motorbike.

When it was her turn, Anna lay down on the floor waving her arms and legs about, then hid under the table.

Her brother was baffled. 'What is it?'

'A spider?' Pietro suggested.

She shook her head.

'A snake with arms?' said Astor.

'A drunken sheep?' said Pietro.

Anna kept writhing about, opening and shutting her mouth.

Astor burst out laughing. 'Is it a toad that's eaten a drunken sheep?'

'No. It's a snake with arms that's eaten a toad that's eaten a drunken sheep,' Pietro went on.

Astor couldn't help himself: he collapsed on the sofa, roaring with laughter.

'And that's trying to imitate Anna,' Pietro concluded, sitting down beside him with tears in his eyes.

Anna put her hands on her hips, offended. 'It's an octopus.'

Astor burst out laughing, pointing his finger at her. 'An octopus. Yes, a drunken octopus.'

The two boys pushed each other, helpless with laughter.

'So much for me being the queen,' said Anna sharply.

Astor rolled on the floor, clutching his stomach.

Anna told them to go to hell and went into the kitchen to tidy up, clattering with the dishes. She heard them talking in low voices in the other room.

'Is she cross?' said Astor.

Pietro couldn't keep a straight face. 'Yes, I'm afraid she is.'

'Why?'

'Oh, women are like that. She'll get over it.'

'Women are like what?'

'Temperamental.'

'What does that mean?'

'It means they get cross if you tease them. My father was a bit of a Casanova and he used to say there's nothing worse than an angry woman.'

'What's a Casanova?'

'A man who has lots of women. And he used to say that

if you want to have lots of women, you have to give them presents.'

'Is that why you gave my sister the necklace?'

'Of course.'

Anna smashed a jar on the floor and came back into the living room, as wild as a lioness. 'Oh, so you gave me the necklace because you want to have lots of women, did you?'

Pietro gulped, at a loss for an answer. Astor sat beside him, gnawing his fist.

Anna pointed her chin at Pietro. 'Well? Say something!'

'No. Not me. That was the way my father behaved. I don't want lots of women. You're enough for me. I gave you the necklace because it's your birthday.'

She glowered at him, trying to make out if he was telling the truth. 'Admit it: you want to be a Casanova.'

Pietro put his hand on his heart. 'No, I swear I don't.'

'Nor do I,' Astor assured her.

Anna pointed towards the kitchen. 'All right then, since I'm the queen, get down on your knees, slaves, and beg for forgiveness. Then go and clean up in there.'

★

With one puff the candle went out and darkness as black as liquorice filled the room. Not a star, not a sliver of moon, not a small light in the distance, only the sound of the waves breaking against the quay.

Anna rearranged her pillow and pushed away Astor, who was sleeping up against her, with her bottom. Pietro was lying on his back to her right, and Fluffy was snoring under the bed.

Although she was tired, she couldn't get to sleep. Her hand was around the starfish. She turned on one side, her hipbone sinking into the latex mattress. She heard Pietro breathe in, hold the air and breathe out again.

'Are you awake?' she whispered.

'Yes.'

'Can't you sleep?'

'No. What about you?'

'I can't either.'

She shifted so she was lying next to his shoulder. 'What are you thinking about?'

'Dogs. And the fact that they never live beyond the age of fourteen.' He remained silent for a few seconds. 'Like us.'

Anna pushed at Pietro's calf with her foot. 'Yes, that's true . . .'

'In fourteen years they do everything. They're born, they grow up and die.' She heard him sniff. 'In the end, what's important is not how long your life is, but how you live it. If you live it well – to the full – a short life is just as good as a long one. Don't you think so?'

Anna's hand slid under the blanket and sought Pietro's. She squeezed it, stroking his fingers with her thumb.

*

Anna opened her eyelids in a flood of light. Pietro and Astor were asleep, one with his head under the pillow, the other wrapped in blankets at the edge of the mattress.

She got out of bed, stretched her back and shuffled into the living room. Picking up the book on apnea fishing, she yawned and went out onto the terrace.

Another windless day, the sun pulsing in a blue sky, with a few white patches here and there. The sea was calm, and even more transparent than the day before, if that were possible. Fluffy came out, head drooping, tail wagging listlessly, and rubbed against her.

Anna turned the pages, lying on the camp bed. One chapter explained the technique of compensation, whereby you compensate for the pressure of the water on the ear, so it's not painful when you dive down underwater. The trick was simple:

just hold your nose and breathe out through your mouth.

'Shall we go?' she said to the dog. He wagged his tail happily.

She went down the road to the beach, escorted by the Maremma, who found himself face to face with a black cat behind a car. Contrary to every law of physics, the cat shot up the front wall of a house and took refuge on a balcony. The dog whined in frustration, paws against the wall.

Anna walked along the promenade, singing a song she'd often heard in the car when her mother drove her to school: 'You come round to my place when you like, usually at night. First you sleep here, then you leave, do what the hell you like. You know you can always have me, if you want, for a night.' She started jumping up and down. 'Na na naaaaa.'

She felt carefree, ready to catch a whale. Bubbling with happiness: everything seemed beautiful – the crushed boats, the crumbling ruins of the restaurants, the cars half-buried in sand, the rows of seagulls motionless on the shore. She shut her eyes and tried to imagine what Cefalù must have been like a few years earlier. Tourists stepping out of coaches with cameras, tables laid with checked tablecloths, waiters with napkins over their arms carrying steak with salad, bands playing on the promenade near black men laying out hand-bags on the paving. Pedalos down at the shoreline. Teenagers playing volleyball on the sand.

She spread out her arms as though to embrace it all. *Now things are so much better. Cefalù is all mine.* Which of those tourists, those waiters, those teenagers could have said the same? Or even imagined it? She turned towards the old village. The sun shone on the terrace outside their flat, glinting in the window of the room where Astor and Pietro slept.

'Well? Are you coming for a swim with me?' she asked Fluffy. But as soon as he understood what she meant, he retreated to the other end of the beach and sat down to watch her.

Taking off her T-shirt and shorts, she put the mask over her forehead and lay down on the surfboard in her two-piece. Then she started paddling with her arms towards the concrete cube. It took her a while to find it. Finally it came into view behind a shoal of small fish. The octopus had gone, but after coming all this way she was determined to try out the technique explained in the book. With a grimace she jumped into the icy water. She filled her lungs and went under. As soon as she felt a pain in her ears, she held her nostrils between her fingers and breathed out through her mouth. It felt as if air was coming out of her eyes, then a small explosion in her eardrums removed the pain. She swam on down into the blue water, while the cold stripped all the warmth out of her body. Around her the sun formed bands of light linking the sea bed to the surface. Freed of the force of gravity, she flew. With slow movements, almost without realising it, she reached the bottom. Here it was even colder. She looked up and felt a kind of vertigo. The sea's surface was a silvery mirror in which the surfboard was floating. Pity Astor wasn't there, he'd have been proud of her. The pressure had stuck the mask to her face, and her ears began to hurt again. She was running out of breath. She repeated the compensation exercise and quickly grabbed a small seaweed-covered stone as a souvenir. Then she crouched down, and was about to push herself upwards with her legs when she saw the octopus's two yellow eyes peering at her from under a rock which lay against the concrete block. For a moment she hesitated, thinking of her brother. She put her hand under the rock. The octopus, quicker than her, backed into his den. Anna put half her arm into the hole, feeling the octopus's cold slimy flesh with her fingers. She tried to grasp hold of it, but it seemed stuck to the rock.

You tried. Go back up.

As she withdrew her arm, a dark tentacle as thick as a hawser curled round her wrist. She would never have imagined a soft, boneless creature would dare to challenge a human being. It was true the book said they were intelligent animals, but they were still related to mussels and snails. And it said nothing about them being dangerous. These thoughts ran through her brain like sparks and came out in a scream. A whirl of bubbles slid across the glass of the mask. She was running out of breath. In her panic, she grabbed the tentacle with her free hand, trying to remove it, but the octopus instantly wrapped another round. She used up what little air she had left in a desperate gurgle. The pressure had risen from her chest to her throat. She was suffocating. She started struggling, turning full circle, and found herself without the mask in a blurred universe where everything appeared and disappeared in scarlet flashes, swirling bubbles and the rumble of her screams. Water flooded down her throat and into her lungs, and her body, deprived of oxygen, started to shake. But something tough prevented her from giving up, an indomitable will to live took hold of her limbs, making her put her feet against the rock and her back against the concrete block. She found herself pulling and pushing harder than she'd ever done in her life. A lazy cloud of sand rose from the bottom, surrounding her, and a muffled sound with a scraping of stones told her something was moving, giving way. The big rock under which the octopus had been hiding rolled over. The animal found itself exposed, and faced with a choice between rock and arms chose the arms.

Anna started rising back up, kicking her legs, wriggling like an eel with that creature clinging to her and reaching out, encircling her neck and shoulders. The surface seemed to be moving further away rather than closer. The lack of air was devouring her. She kicked until she resurfaced with a hoarse intake of breath, swallowing the life that would oxygenise her blood. She spat out water, coughing. Holding the octopus, which was now trying to escape, she looked around.

The surfboard had been carried away by the current. The

beach was a long way off, and holding the mollusc's slippery head in her fingers was draining her strength.

Let go of it.

But instead she rolled over and started swimming back-stroke, breathing through her mouth, spitting, churning the water with her feet, keeping her eyes tightly shut and repeating: 'One, two, three. One, two, three.'

She knew she'd arrived when her shoulder blades brushed against the bottom. Gasping and staggering like a shipwrecked sailor, she walked a few steps and collapsed face down on the beach, exhausted. The octopus, now in the air, tried to break free with its last remaining strength, but she held on, smothering it in the sand. She lay against the octopus with her heart beating, filling her lungs, amazed to be alive.

'I did it,' she kept saying, her teeth chattering from the cold. 'I'm a real fisherwoman.'

She couldn't wait to run back and show those two boys her catch.

Fluffy walked towards her in his indolent way, inspected her and started licking her face with a tongue as wide as a shoe's insole.

When she realised that the octopus had stopped moving, she lifted it up by its head between her finger and thumb. Death had reduced it to a pathetic, dirty thing, like the tip of a paintbrush immersed in gelatinous liquid. She took a plastic bag out of her rucksack and dropped the octopus inside.

She'd lost the top of her two-piece, but thank goodness still had her starfish, which was dangling on her chest. Her stomach and breasts were streaked with slime and ink. She slipped off the swimsuit bottoms and took three steps towards the shore, then she stopped. On the inside of her right thigh was a long trickle of dark blood right down to her calf.

I must have cut myself.

Presumably she'd grazed her leg on the rocks when she'd been struggling to free herself underwater. But it didn't hurt.

Maybe it's the octopus's blood.

She looked up. A flock of seagulls was circling above the village rooftops. She didn't see them; her blurred gaze took in only the cliffs.

Does an octopus have blood?

She opened her legs, sinking up to her ankles in the warm sand. She closed her right hand, except for the index and middle fingers, making a pistol shape. She put her fingers into her vagina and slipped them right in, her eyes on the clear sky.

She took her fingers out.

They were covered in reddish-brown blood.

★

Anna walked down Vicolo San Bartolomeo feeling scared, trying to swallow. Rucksack over her shoulder, plastic bag with the octopus in her hand. The trickle of blood still running down from her denim shorts.

She must find some of those tubes, the ones Mama used to keep in the bathroom cupboard with bags of little doll-sized nappies.

She'd come across thousands of them in her searches over the years – in bathrooms next to medicines or packets of toilet paper; in chemists' shops and in supermarkets, where they'd have a whole shelf to themselves. She'd used them as torches, after soaking them in alcohol, as swabs for cleaning wounds, as pretend cigars, or as straws, after emptying them of their cotton wool. For every imaginable purpose except the right one.

Pietro and Astor must have woken up by now and would probably be wondering where she'd got to. They mustn't see her like that.

She turned round the first corner, with Fluffy close behind. She went to the Muzzolini pharmacy, next to the Duomo. A Range Rover Sport had crashed straight through its window. She climbed over the bonnet and entered. The walls were covered in mahogany panelling, and there were old blue and white earthenware vases on the shelves. She found some packets of tampons on the floor, among some over-turned display cases. She took some Tampax, the ones Mama used to use. The instructions said that the first time you put a tampon in it was important to relax and not be tense.

She sat down on the bonnet of the car to insert one, and was surprised to find that it was quite easy and not particu-larly painful. After cleaning herself with a T-shirt in a boutique, she put on some dark shorts and a striped shirt that came down to her knees. Then she headed for home, feeling rather relieved. Having a box of tampons in her rucksack gave a sense of security.

She was amazed that her period had arrived so suddenly, and painlessly. When Mama had had 'her trouble', she'd always been ill and had to take medicine. Anna wondered if going underwater had had something to do with it, whether it had tipped some balance in her body or burst some sac inside her, like the one containing the octopus's ink. And how strange that it had happened the day after her birthday!

At the hotel she'd seen children of her own age, and often younger, already showing signs of the Red Fever. When people had looked at her, they'd always been amazed that she had breasts and pubic hair, yet not a single blotch. At first she'd tried not to think about it, but she'd been increas-ingly tempted by the fantasy that she might be different, special. Sensing that it was about as realistic as someone who's hurtling down towards the ground hoping they'll sprout a pair of wings, she dismissed the thought every time it came into her mind. But as everyone knows, illusions bloom like poisoned flowers in people with short futures.

Thinking about it now, with that tube inside her, she felt like a fool. She was the same as all the others. She remembered what Mama had written at the end of the chapter on water:

When you're thirsty, don't hope that it will rain. Think about the problem and try to find a solution. Ask yourself: where can I find some drinking water? It's no use hoping to find a bottle in a desert. Leave hopes to the hopeless. There are questions and there are answers. Human beings are capable of turning problems into solutions.

Lost in thought, she found herself in a little piazza overlooking the sea. She sat down on a bench and started absently stroking Fluffy.

She needed to think about it. Having the blood didn't mean anything. Before the virus, menstruation had simply meant that the body was ready to have children; only after the epidemic had it become a sign that you were about to die. She mustn't mistake the blood for Red Fever.

So there's still a chance that you're immune. Oh, for goodness' sake don't start that again.

What was certain was that a period of time always passed between the blood and the appearance of the blotches. Sometimes short, sometimes long. At any rate, long enough for them to reach the mainland.

Messina wasn't far away. A week's walk, at the outside. And judging from the maps, the land on the other side of the sea wasn't far away. Nobody knew what was happening across the Strait. Sicily was an island inhabited by a few survivors, and in five years, or six at most, there'd be nothing left there but animals and plants. Maybe the rest of the planet had defeated the virus.

Cefalù was a lovely place, but they'd die if they stayed there.

★

She had another look to check that her shorts weren't stained, took a deep breath and entered the garage.

In the half-light, the two boys were busy pouring petrol into cans.

'Bring me the funnel, or it'll spill all over the place,' Pietro was saying.

Straightening up, Astor saw his sister silhouetted against the light. 'Where have you been?' Before she could reply, he rushed over to take a big blue funnel off the tool bench.

Anna held up the plastic bag. 'I've got a surprise for you!' Neither of them turned round. 'Hey! Did you hear me? I've got a surprise.'

Astor glanced into the bag. 'The octopus. You caught it. Well done.' He fished it out and dropped it back in again. 'I'll have a look at it later. We're starting her up.'

Anna leaned back against the car.

Pietro was completely focused on the job, his lips pushed forward as if sucking from a straw. His long hair straggled down over his forehead. A shaft of light fell on his neck. Near his head he was tanned, but lower down, where it was usually covered by the T-shirt, the skin was a milky colour.

'How are you getting on?' Anna asked, trying to sound interested.

'I've got to clean the carburettor and change the spark plugs.' Pietro picked up a can and poured some petrol into the tank through the funnel.

Anna let a few seconds pass. 'We could eat the octopus with peas. Or tinned tomatoes. But we're out of them. And we'll have to make a fire on the terrace.'

'Okay. You do that,' said Pietro, laying the funnel aside.

Anna looked out of the garage. She'd woken up at dawn, gone out quietly so as not to wake them, nearly drowned fighting that bloody octopus and started her first period.

Pietro turned towards her. 'I've got to check the brakes.' His speckled hazel eyes tempered the seriousness of his expression and added a touch of doubt. It was as if he didn't have much faith in what he was saying.

'You're doing a great job,' she said, with a faint sarcastic smile.

Pietro either didn't see or ignored it. 'I think the spark plugs are dirty. That's why it won't start, and . . .' He stopped and stared at her, his head on one side.

Anna stiffened, looking down at her shorts. 'What's the matter?'

'You're wearing a shirt.'

'So? What's wrong with that? Don't you like it?'

'I've never seen you in a shirt.' He rummaged about on the work bench and picked up a hammer. Meanwhile Astor had started polishing the sidecar with a cloth. The first time she'd seen her brother clean anything.

'I'm going home.' She turned round and walked away, but stopped when she reached the shutter. 'We're leaving tomorrow.'

Pietro opened his eyes wide. 'Tomorrow? I don't know if I can get the engine to start that soon.'

'That's your problem. If you can, fine. If you can't, we'll go on foot. As we've always done up to now.'

'Oh, I see. You're in a bad mood.'

She raised her arms. 'In a bad mood? No, I'm not. It's just that we're leaving tomorrow.'

He banged the hammer down on the bench. 'Why should it be your decision?'

'Because that's the way it is.' Anna clenched her fists. 'And if you don't like it . . .' She didn't finish the sentence.

Astor stamped his foot. 'But Anna . . .' He caught hold of her arm. 'Why?'

'Because that's what I've decided.' And she pulled her arm free.

Astor swung his foot at a scooter, which crashed down on the ground.

Anna exploded. With a scream, she flung the plastic bag with the octopus at her brother, hitting him between the shoulder blades. He dropped onto his knees in tears.

Anna whistled to Fluffy and marched out of the garage.

★

She entered the flat, slamming the door behind her, went out onto the terrace and lay down on one of the camp beds with her arms crossed, muttering to herself. Then, puffing out her cheeks, she tore off that awful shirt, pulled down her shorts, extracted the blood-soaked tampon and threw it over the railing. How often did you have to change the stupid things? She put in another, weeping tears of frustration.

She could have killed Pietro. She always noticed every little change in his mood, but he never noticed anything. He'd hardly even looked at her. Hadn't taken the slightest interest in the octopus.

'That's it. I've finished with him,' she said to Fluffy, who slept serenely on.

Going indoors, she made her way to the bedroom and flopped down on the bed, with her arms round the pillow. Listening to the sea and the wind in the leaves of the lemon trees, waiting for sleep that wouldn't come.

★

She woke up abruptly. Called out to Pietro and Astor, but there was no reply. Fluffy was lying on the bed, with his head on the pillow. She pushed him away, with a grimace. 'Get away from me, you smelly mutt.'

The windows shook under the gusts of a north-westerly wind. A bank of low, bluish clouds had approached the coast, shrouding the sun.

'Why don't they come home?' she asked the dog, who scratched his neck.

She'd gone too far in the garage, and felt guilty. Her hand went to the starfish. She squeezed it against her palm. With eyes closed, she thought about last night, when they'd slept huddled up together.

A stream of languid warmth rose up through her chest, stifling her.

★

The sun had already set when the boys came home, laden with tins of tomatoes, which they dumped on the sofa, looking very pleased with themselves.

'Will that be enough for the octopus?' Pietro held up the bag with the slimy ball inside.

'Oh yes, that'll be plenty!' Anna clapped her hands idiotically; she wanted to make amends. 'We'll have to cook it first, though. Let's make a fire on the terrace.'

Pietro's irises refracted the light; they looked like those of a wild animal, but he wasn't angry. Maybe with him she could just carry on as normal, but there was someone else she was going to have to apologise to.

Astor was playing with Fluffy on the terrace. She came up behind him and whispered: 'Are you cross?'

He turned round. A childlike quality had gone from his blue eyes, and been replaced by an adult seriousness.

She took both his hands in hers, with an embarrassed smile. 'I'm sorry.'

He threw himself into her arms. Whatever faults she might have passed onto him, they didn't include resentfulness.

Like a mother dog with her puppy, she hugged the skinny little boy, smothering him with kisses on the neck and forehead, till he started trying to wriggle free.

'What's the matter? Don't you like kisses? Would you

rather have bites?' She jumped on him and bit him on the arm. Astor gave her one of his lopsided smiles. She tickled him, pressing her thumbs into his sides, and he thumped her on the back, roaring with laughter. The sudden wrestling match excited Fluffy, who clung to Anna's bottom with his paws, wagging his haunches. She gave him a slap, and he ran off behind the lemon tree pots, tail between his legs.

Brother and sister lay on the majolica tiled floor looking at the stars. They seemed so near that if you reached out your hand you could take them and put them in your pocket.

'Well? Are we going to make this fire or not?' Pietro's head blotted out the sky. He was holding a half-full can of petrol. They piled up some chairs and camp beds, sprinkled them with fuel and set them alight. Red and blue tongues rose up higher and higher, crackling and sending out sparks. Carried away with enthusiasm, they dragged the living-room furniture outside and threw it onto the flames. The smoke blackened the attic windows and went into the flat. Before long the fire had burnt down to ashes.

'Let's put the mattress on too!' suggested Astor.

'No! Not the mattress!' Anna and Pietro answered in unison.

Anna opened the plastic bag with the octopus inside and a pungent aroma filled her nostrils. She'd thought she could handle bad smells; she was so used to the stench of rotting flesh that she no longer even noticed it. But this she found quite unbearable.

'Is it really bad?' asked Pietro.

Anna shrugged her shoulders and flung the bag over the railing. The tentacled monster that had nearly killed her flew through the darkness and landed on the beach not far away from her Tampax.

They heated the tomatoes and peas in a big saucepan, taking turns at stirring them and competing to see who could stay longest near the fire. When the soup was ready, they poured it out into their dishes and devoured the warm, tasteless but filling mixture.

Neither Pietro nor Astor had said anything about the motorbike, and Anna was dying to know. 'How are you getting on with the Vespa?' she said casually.

Pietro ran his finger along the edge of the saucepan to polish off any remaining sauce. 'Not too badly. It started for a moment, but then it cut out and we couldn't get it going again.'

'Well, you can try again tomorrow.'

He stopped, his finger smothered in sauce. 'What? I thought you wanted to leave? You kicked up such a fuss . . .'

'One day more won't make much difference. And it's true that we'd get to Messina more quickly.'

Astor tapped his forefinger against his temple, looking at Pietro. He stroked Fluffy, who opened his jaws in a yawn. 'What about him?'

All three of them became pensive.

'Sleeping pills!' Anna said suddenly. 'Mama wrote that some sleeping pills can knock you out for a whole day. We'll give him some, wait till he goes to sleep and put him in the sidecar. By the time he wakes up, we'll be in Messina.'

Pietro wasn't convinced.

'It'll work, you'll see,' she reassured him. 'I'll go and look for some at the chemist's tomorrow. And if I can't find any, we'll go on foot.'

'On foot!' Astor repeated, aghast.

Too tired to talk any more, and full of doubts, they sat and watched the glowing embers.

11

The clouds lay on the horizon, passive observers of a sunny day warmer and clearer than the one before. Doves were cooing in the little pine wood behind the restaurants.

Anna was sitting on the beach, wearing a new blue balcony bra with a pretty white ribbon in the middle. It was too big for her, and her breasts fitted into it like scoops of ice cream in two bowls. Lower down, she'd kept the shorts. The tampons were doing their job, but the blood showed no sign of stopping.

A big black insect flying out of season hit her on the forehead, fell down, stunned, and lay quivering in the sand. Anna took the exercise book out of the rucksack, put it on her lap and started turning the pages, looking for the name of the sleeping pills she had to give to Fluffy.

It was the first time she'd opened the book since retrieving it in Torre Normanna. There'd been no need for it on the journey. She knew it by heart and there were many things in this new world that Mama could never have dreamed of.

She found the page about sleeping pills. There was a list of names: Minias . . .

The other names had been washed away by a splash of water.

It didn't seem likely that she'd find them in any pharmacy: sleeping pills had been among the first medicines to run out. But there was no harm in trying. She skimmed through the book and came to the final pages, which had been left blank. She gazed at the horizon, the wind ruffling her hair.

Could I write something in it myself?

It was like a revelation. She'd never dared to contemplate such a thing before. This was the book of Important Things which Mama had given her before she died.

And which I'll pass onto Astor.

She counted the blank pages. There were thirty-two. Would Mama mind if she wrote on them? She gazed at the clouds, took out a pencil and began.

MAIZE

Never eat maize, Astor – those little yellow balls that give you tummy ache and make you shit all day. Don't even think about it. Just forget about maize, for goodness' sake. All other kinds of food . . .

★

'Anna!'

She looked up and saw Fluffy racing along the promenade, followed by her brother. 'Anna! Anna!'

She put the book in her rucksack and started walking, then running, towards him.

Astor stopped in front of her, bent double and panting hard.

'What's the matter?' Anna asked him.

'Pietro . . .' The little boy put his hand on his chest. 'Pietro managed to turn on the engine. It started!'

Somewhere in the old village an engine was roaring. It seemed only yesterday that the sound of motorbikes racing along the road beyond the wood had been a common experience.

'Come on,' said Astor, running off.

Anna ran after him, with the dog at her heels.

Pietro came out from between the houses on the Vespa. With the sidecar attached, it was nearly as big and cumbersome as a car.

He advanced slowly, trying to avoid the sand which covered much of the road.

He reached them in front of the restaurant, The Fishing Lamp, pulling up next to what was left of a fishing boat. The sidecar bucked and the engine cut out with a loud bang.

'I'm not very good with the gears.' Pietro was dripping with sweat, his face was red, and there were big dark patches on his shirt under the armpits.

'That's incredible . . .' Anna murmured, walking round the sidecar. It was a beautiful blue colour, with chrome mirrors glinting in the sun. There was an advert on the side: 'For hire'.

Pietro was bubbling. 'The lights work, so we can travel at night too.' He dismounted and pushed down hard on the kickstarter. The engine obediently started roaring again. 'How about that?'

'Fantastic,' Anna applauded.

Astor jumped up and down in delight.

Pietro grinned knowingly. 'Be honest, you didn't think I could do it, did you?'

'Yes, I did. It's just that . . .'

'What?'

'It's funny. That's all.' Anna ran her hand over the bodywork.

'It's a Vespa 125, with four gears. You change gear by twisting the handle.'

Astor jumped onto the saddle and gripped the handlebar eagerly. 'Can we go for a ride? Can we go for a ride?'

'All right, but we'll have to get it out of the sand first. Give me a hand.'

Astor and Anna pushed from behind while Pietro steered,

perched on the tip of the saddle. The scooter kept getting stuck and the engine cutting out.

Exhausted with the effort, they reached the beginning of a straight, upward-sloping road towards the hills. As soon as the back wheel touched the asphalt, the scooter moved off, skidding from side to side and spraying gravel, with the dog behind it, barking and trying to bite the tyres.

'Fluffy!' shouted Anna. 'Come back!'

Pietro smiled and accelerated away, pursued by the Maremma.

Anna watched them, still out of breath. 'That stupid dog will never let us put him in that sidecar.'

The combo swerved erratically, just missing the cars parked on either side of the road, then, somehow, Pietro managed to get it under control, steered out into the middle, slowed down as he approached a hairpin bend and disappeared round the corner.

Anna and Astor listened to the sound of the engine grow ever fainter, until silence returned.

'Has he gone for good?' Astor asked.

Anna shrugged her shoulders. 'I've no idea.'

'What about Fluffy?'

'No, he'll come back all right.'

A few minutes later they heard the engine revving up again, then the combo came back round the corner and accelerated down the straight.

Anna and Astor waved their arms, like fans cheering on the winner of a race.

Pietro came racing down the middle of the road, sounding the buzzer, but suddenly something happened. As if blown by some invisible giant, the Vespa swerved to the left, and without slowing down, without braking – without any reason – ran into the kerb. The sidecar broke off and smashed into the stone wall at the side of the road. The scooter and its rider were flung into the air, turning over and over, and disappeared down the embankment with a crash of crumpling metal.

The whole thing took no more than a few seconds.

★

Anna and Astor leaned over the wall, breathing hard.

A three-metre drop ended with a spur of rock covered with prickly pears, caper bushes and litter.

The wreck of the Vespa was near the edge overhanging the beach.

'Where's Pietro?' the little boy asked.

'He must have fallen down below.' Anna felt the blood running down through her legs and was afraid she was going to faint. She dropped down on her knees and brought up the chickpeas she'd had for breakfast.

Astor leaned further out. 'I think I can see him.'

Anna wiped her mouth with her hand. Her head was spinning, but she managed to say: 'Where?'

'Under the scooter.'

She tried to get up, but her legs wouldn't support her. 'Go and see, but be careful.'

Astor climbed down, clinging onto rocks and bushes. On reaching the spur, he crawled through the prickly pears and approached the Vespa. 'He's down here.'

She straightened up and climbed to her feet.

The sky was blue. The clouds white. The sea grey. The beach yellow. The calm indifferent background which hadn't changed since their arrival. Underneath it all, she was certain now, was something evil.

'Is he alive?'

'I don't know.'

As she climbed over the wall, fighting off the nausea, she saw Fluffy to her right. He was whining and rocking forward, trying to summon up the courage to jump down.

'Please,' she begged him. 'Be a good boy. Stay there.'

He flattened down obediently on the ground, moaning.

She threaded her way between the pads of cacti. Astor was sitting beside the Vespa, biting his thumb and looking at Pietro's arm reaching from the wreckage, the hand on a blackened bottle of bleach. The rest of his body was hidden by the metal. The wind had dropped and the silence was broken only by Fluffy's whimpering.

'We've got to pull him out,' she said to her brother, though there was a risk of him being crushed when they moved the scooter. 'Do you hear me?' She turned towards Astor, who was gazing blankly into space. 'Pull yourself together! Help me! Take his hand and hold onto him while I lift the scooter.'

Automatically the little boy gripped Pietro's wrist with both hands.

'Now don't let go, whatever you do.'

Anna took hold of the rear end of the Vespa and pushed with her legs. She managed to lift it about ten centimetres, but had to lower it again. It was just too heavy. She tried again, but without success; it seemed to be stuck somewhere. She sat down, put her forehead on her knees and whispered, 'I can't do it.'

Why on earth had she let him repair the scooter? She was the one who'd said, 'You can try again tomorrow.' All she'd have needed to say was: 'I'm sorry, but we're going on foot.' Just a few different words and they'd be walking towards Messina now.

She gazed at the two yellow towers of the cathedral. 'We'll both have to lift it. Me at the back and you at the front.'

At the first attempt they only managed to move it a little way. One of Pietro's shoulders and one of his hips came into view, with his striped shirt. There was no blood. The second time Astor changed his grip slightly, and Anna pulled with a desperate scream. The scooter rose up, but didn't roll over.

Anna pushed forward, supporting the frame with outstretched arms. 'Astor, here. Come here. Quickly.'

He let go of the handlebars and came to stand beside her.

'On the count of three, we push. We shut our eyes and push. Even if we hurt him, it doesn't matter.' She gazed into his blue eyes. 'Like you're the strongest man in the world, okay?'

Astor nodded.

'One . . . two . . . three!'

The scooter swung over, carrying a cloud of earth and prickly pears with it, and crashed down onto the beach.

Anna instinctively threw her arms round Astor and hugged him against her chest.

Pietro lay with his arms spread out. His head was turned to one side, buried under pieces of cloth and plastic bags. Below the knees his trousers were soaked in blood. One ankle had been crushed into a mixture of socks, bones and flesh. A jagged piece of pink bone protruded from one elbow.

Anna knelt down and put her ear to his mouth.

'He's alive.'

Three days later he was dead.

★

During those days Anna tried to carry Pietro up to the road. She found a ladder and some ropes, but as soon as she tried to move him he'd start screaming in agony and quiver as though an electric current were passing through him. Then Anna would take fright and withdraw.

They cut down the prickly pears, lit a fire and carefully laid him on an inflatable mattress. Anna slit his trousers and T-shirt open with a knife. There was a dark bruise starting below his navel, covering his stomach and running down one side. On his bottom and under his armpits there were, as she'd suspected, the scarlet blotches of the virus.

He lay unconscious, with a high fever. When they tried to get him to drink, he spat the water out as if it were poison.

During the night he started screaming.

In pitch darkness, escorted by Fluffy, Anna walked down Cefalù's narrow streets in search of medicines. There wasn't much left in the drawers of the chemists' shops. Skin creams, deodorants and boxes gnawed by rats. She found a bottle of melatonin, some paracetamol and some antibiotics, but nothing that could alleviate the pain.

The next day Pietro fell into a state of panting drowsiness from which he would re-emerge shrieking, as if waves of pain were breaking over him. He kept saying he was cold; not even the fire and blankets could warm him.

The following morning a pale cold sun rose out of a sea as grey as the rocks. Astor and Anna were sleeping curled up beside Pietro, who had lost consciousness. The blood had coagulated into a dark, pitch-like substance, sticking him to the surface of the mattress. The purple patch on his distended belly was warm.

Towards midday he became delirious. He kept talking about someone called Patrizio. He said he must stop typing – the tapping of his keyboard was driving him mad.

'I'll tell him straight away,' Anna reassured him, raising his head. 'There! Do you hear that? He's stopped.'

Pietro's mouth stiffened in a grimace of horror, and he stared at the grey sky with frozen eyes, as if something terrifying were hovering above him.

Anna ran back to the chemist's, opened all the boxes in the storeroom and found pills and some ampoules to inject, but no syringes. She poured the liquid between his cracked lips and tried to push a handful of pills into his mouth, but he clenched his teeth, as though to spite her. She tried over and over again, but without success. Finally she threw the pills in the air and started kicking empty jars and prickly pears and uprooting bushes, screaming all the time. Astor clung to her legs, begging her to stop.

They crawled around picking up the pills and put them into his mouth one by one, until he calmed down. His face relaxed and he fell into a deep sleep.

On the third day Anna was woken up by Pietro's voice calling to her: 'Anna . . . Anna . . .'

She threw off the blankets, knelt down beside him and held his hand. 'Here I am. I'm here.'

He screwed up his eyelids, as if dazzled by a headlight, raised his head a fraction and directed his unseeing gaze at her. 'The wheel. It jammed. I tried . . .' A fit of coughing shook his chest and he spat out a gob of dark blood. He touched her fingers, seeking her in the darkness. 'You must find the shoes.'

Anna dried her tears and stroked his sweaty forehead. 'Yes, I will.'

'You must find them, do you understand? They'll save you.'

'I understand. Now you rest.'

Anna's words seemed to reassure him. A hint of a smile curled his lips, and for a few minutes he lay there in silence. Then he spoke with his eyes closed. 'Anna . . . Get two plastic bags.'

'What for?'

'Two plastic bags. Without any holes in them.'

★

TWO PLASTIC BAGS

Vita is an inland village in the province of Trapani. In one of the village streets, Via Aleramo, there was a small block of flats surrounded by a garden of fruit trees, owned by the Lo Capo family. The ground floor was occupied by Signora

Costanza, the widow of Domenico Lo Capo, a prosperous builder who had died of a heart attack when he was sixty. The first floor was the home of their eldest daughter Laura, Pietro's mother, who was divorced from Mauro Serra, a mechanic in the Ducati motorcycle racing team. The second floor was divided into two flats for the other two daughters, Annarita and Celeste.

Annarita, the youngest, was studying architecture. Celeste was in her early thirties and single, and ran a china shop in the centre of the village. People said Celeste was neither fish nor fowl: one of those creatures who are simply not interested in sex, with either gender. Annarita, by contrast, was rumoured to be a lesbian, and her university studies were said to be just an excuse for going to Palermo and seeing her girlfriend, who worked for the city council. Such was the village gossip.

At any rate, after Domenico's death the house in Via Aleramo was inhabited exclusively by women who doted on Pietro, a little king pampered by his aunts and spoiled by his grandma.

Only one other male was allowed to stay in this gynaeceum: Mauro, the little boy's father. The mechanic, constantly travelling around the world, would find a weekend every month, and two weeks in the summer, to return to his son and his ex-wife, who with the help of her sisters would fatten him up on helpings of *caponata* without too much vinegar, *frittedda* and *cannoli* and sheep's milk ricotta. During those days Pietro's star was dimmed and his papa's shone.

Mauro Serra was tall and red-haired, with blue eyes and a thick beard framing his face. He wore flannel shirts and pointed Texan boots. The sisters said he was the spitting image of Robert Redford. He was a consummate ladies' man.

When the three of them watched the Grand Prix on Sundays, they'd try to guess which of the umbrella girls on the podium next to the riders Mauro had seduced.

'One every race,' snorted Laura, serving the parmigiana.

Laura Lo Capo was an attractive woman, dark-skinned with two coal-black eyes, but since the divorce she'd put on weight and allowed regrowth to whiten the roots of her long hair. She referred to her ex-husband as 'the Playboy', but far from being jealous, she was proud of the fact. 'Is it possible to stop a lion hunting? You'd have to lock him up in a cage. I can't do that. It'd be a crime against the female sex.' The fact that she was the only lioness Mauro had had offspring with flattered her self-esteem, and was enough for her. As long as he didn't forget Pietro, and brought her magnets to stick on the fridge whenever he returned from his travels, she was happy. The younger sisters were susceptible to their brother-in-law's charms too, and whenever he came home would put on their best clothes, doll themselves up and play at who could be the most seductive. The dream of living in a harem and sharing the mechanic's favours stimulated their libido.

'Right! Since he liked the cannelloni I made with my own fair hands, tonight the Playboy's coming to bed with me,' said the younger one, casting aside all modesty.

'What would he want with a skinny little thing like you?' said Celeste. 'I'm the – what's the word, Mauro? – the cougar.' And she made a gesture as if to support her ample bosom.

'There's no need to quarrel! If you squeeze up together, there's room in bed for all three of you. Oh yes, Mauro, I know you're not averse to that kind of thing!' cried Laura, warming to the game as she rinsed the dishes.

As excited as schoolgirls, they burst into fits of giggles, feeling unconventional and modern.

The mechanic could already see himself in retirement, in a state of grace, with the three women serving him and kowtowing to him, like some Babylonian king.

Little Pietro, too, grew up revering this handsome, special

father who brought him Ducati T-shirts and gadgets. He'd spend hours in the garage watching him repair an old Laverda Jota.

On sunny days the two of them would ride out to the seaside, with the little boy astride the petrol tank.

In short, things were going very well, but as in every self-respecting plot, an event occurred which shattered the harmony of the Lo Capo family. The arrival in Via Aleramo of Patrizio Petroni, Annarita's new boyfriend. He was from Rome. Weight: over one hundred kilograms. Short and wide, a guy it would have been quicker to jump over than walk around. A mass of black curls stuck to his forehead, a few centimetres above one long continuous eyebrow. Thick-rimmed glasses on a pug nose. A fat stomach, bulging out over surf shorts which hung down from low buttocks, and calves as plump as turkey legs slotting into a pair of black high-top trainers without the mediation of ankles.

Annarita was reluctant to talk about how they'd met, but it was clear from some details that Facebook had played its part. Patrizio explained to the sisters in his inner-city drawl that he and Annarita had loved each other since the beginning of time, since the Big Bang. They had finally managed to meet up in this life, after spending thousands of other lives searching for each other.

'Those two are about as well suited as crusty bread and a blunt knife,' old Costanza observed, sadly.

'Patrizio is going to stay with me for a while; he's got to finish his novel,' Annarita explained to her sisters, who listened open-mouthed.

The writer settled into his girlfriend's flat and converted the living room into his study. Before the week was out he'd contrived to turn the whole family against him.

Pietro didn't like him because he ate his Kinder Buenos. Grandma complained that he was domineering. Laura hated him because, she said, he was dirty and as ugly as sin. And

Celeste because he'd duped her sister, who was a little naive, poor thing.

Patrizio was about as sensitive to the Lo Capos' scowls as a buffalo to a bite from a sandfly. He'd sit down at the table and scoff food, then sprawl on the sofa with his arms round his girlfriend, watching barbecue competitions on TV. The rest of the time he spent writing. The sound of his keyboard echoed down the stairs day and night. He only left the flat for sporadic trips to the takeaway to buy French fries and kebabs.

Celeste and Laura held a conspiratorial meeting on a patch of waste land to work out a plan for getting rid of the 'Universal Shitbag' (that was the nickname they'd given him) without hurting their sister too much. They decided it was Mauro's job to convince him. By fair means or foul.

The mechanic invited Patrizio out for a pizza and a man-to-man chat, and when he came home he found the two sisters still up in their nightdresses. 'How did it go?'

'He scoffed two patapizzas, a calzone with ricotta and frankfurters, and four jugs of beer.'

Laura flopped disconsolately on the sofa. 'What's a patapizza?'

'A pizza with chips on top.'

Celeste walked round and round the room, pulling on a cigarette. 'Did you ask him when he's leaving?'

'He said he's got to finish his novel.'

Laura cut a slice of jam tart and handed it to her ex-husband. 'Did you manage to find out what this novel's about?'

'He's rewriting the whole history of the world, with giant hamsters instead of humans.'

The two women gazed at him expectantly.

The mechanic took a bite from the tart. 'He's just finished the prehistoric era.'

Nothing changed over the next three months, until the TV news reported that an unknown disease was raging in

Liège, and that children, for some obscure reason linked to their lack of puberty hormones, seemed to be immune to it.

Mauro had been in the Netherlands for a month, carrying out tests on a new motorbike, and on the plane back to Palermo he started to feel really bad. It was as if two knives were stabbing at the base of his nose and an iron clamp gripping his temples. When he went to the toilet to throw up, he noticed a red blotch on his hip.

Laura went to pick him up at the airport. She saw him emerge from Arrivals looking worn out, and with his eyes glistening. On the way home in the car he started coughing. They put him to bed, but despite lemon juice and aspirin his temperature shot up. He was examined by Dr Panunzio, the family doctor, who reassured the sisters. 'It's nothing serious. A touch of flu. He just needs to rest.'

The news from northern Europe was not encouraging: the virus had crossed the borders of Belgium and was spreading inexorably throughout the continent. A team of German scientists was trying to develop a stable vaccine.

Fortunately the few cases recorded in Italy had been isolated ones.

Two days later Mauro suffered an acute respiratory failure, and Laura went with him in the ambulance to Palermo. She returned with a fever and a runny nose. She said the hospital was in chaos and Mauro had been parked in a corridor along with hundreds of other patients who had the same symptoms.

A week later the Lo Capo family, with the exception of Celeste, who was confined to her room with a heavy cough, were sitting together in front of the TV waiting for a message from the Prime Minister which was due to be broadcast simultaneously on all channels. In the event it was the Minister of Health who appeared before journalists. Coughing, he apologised for the Prime Minister's absence and advised the population to stay at home, going out only if it was strictly necessary. 'Anyone who suffers from acute respiratory syndrome, associated with blotches on the skin, a high temperature and symptoms of pneumonia or other respiratory conditions, must be isolated at once, because they may have contracted the virus and constitute a threat to those around them.'

Laura, worried and feverish, and having received no news of her husband for several days, asked Annarita to go to Palermo. Her sister found the autostrada blocked by an interminable queue of cars piled high with luggage, all trying to leave the island. She was told the regional capital had been placed under army guard and it was impossible to get out or in. The airport had been closed too, and the ferries to Calabria weren't running.

The first person to die in the block in Via Aleramo was Grandma. It took the virus less than a week to finish her off. Annarita was the only one of her daughters who was able to go to her funeral. There was hardly anyone else in the church, except Patrizio and Pietro. Even the hearse failed to show up, and one of the girls' cousins loaded the coffin into his station wagon. The village was deserted and most of the shops were closed. Everyone in Vita who was not in bed was either in front of the TV or on the phone to distant relatives.

Patrizio would spend all day on the computer, searching for news. The whole planet had been contaminated, from India to the United States; not even Australia had been spared. By now it was clear that the original infection had occurred much earlier than the cases documented in Belgium. There was a terrible – human, according to some people – deviousness in the way the virus was propagating itself and in its long quiescence, which had transformed it into a biological bomb. The speed at which it mutated made creating a vaccine impossible. Not even the researchers working on it, despite rigorous anti-contamination procedures, could avoid succumbing.

Vita, which before the epidemic had had a population of 2,500, lost half of it in less than a month. Some people died waiting hopefully for a vaccine; others, more sceptical, barricaded themselves in their homes, sealing them up with duct tape, but still didn't escape the disease. Children, the only healthy inhabitants, went round the village in search of food and water for their parents and grandparents.

The television had suspended news broadcasts and only showed old films. The telephone networks failed, one by one. When the electricity supply failed too, the bird of the Apocalypse spread its dark cold wings over Vita.

In the apartment block, after the death of Signora Costanza, it was Celeste's turn. The body was thrown into a common grave without any funeral rites. Laura and Annarita lay in their beds, racked by fever, and unconscious. Pietro sat for hours beside his mother in a sweltering silence, playing with toy soldiers. One morning, making an excuse, Patrizio took hold of his hand, led him into his room, locked the door and said: 'They're dying. We can't do anything for them; they're doomed. We must stay here and wait.' Inside the room he'd stacked boxes of food and cans of beer.

But Pietro would cry: he wanted his mother. Then the fat man would lose his temper and start kicking the wardrobe, ripping arms off teddy bears, pouring Lego bricks over his head. 'Why don't you understand? Why can't you accept things for what they are? Forget about the old world. You've got your whole life in front of you. We've entered a new era.'

As soon as the first light crept between the curtains, he'd sit down at his desk and start filling reams of paper with his old Olivetti typewriter. He was enthusiastic: 'This is a masterpiece.' He'd go over to little Pietro and stroke his head. 'It's a no-holds-barred chronicle of the Apocalypse. I haven't censored anything.'

Pietro didn't know what the Apocalypse was.

'It's when everybody dies because God has said that's it. I gave you a game and you ruined it. I gave you a beautiful planet and you messed it up.'

The epidemic, in Patrizio's opinion, was the most amazing thing that could possibly have happened to humankind. He walked round and round the small room like an orang-utan, talking, talking, asking questions and answering them himself, until he fell back drunk on a small chair, with his legs apart.

Pietro knew Patrizio kept the key to the door in his trouser pocket. One night he got out of bed and tried to take it. But his fingers struggled to get into the pocket, buried beneath layers of flab.

The ogre woke up with a grunt. 'Looking for the key?' He pulled it out. 'Pretty, isn't it?' He opened his mouth and swallowed it like a Saila Mint. 'Magic. All gone.' He folded his arms and went on snoring.

On another occasion it was Patrizio who woke the little boy up. 'Pietro . . . Pietro . . .' He was whispering, as if there were hidden microphones in the room. 'Do you hear that?'

The little boy, clutching his panda, hadn't heard anything for days. Not even the muffled groans of Aunt Annarita and Mama. Even the cars had disappeared.

'Well? Do you hear it?'

'The wind?'

'It sounds like the wind, but it's not. It's the rustle of millions of souls leaving the planet, a constant stream of spirits who rise out of our atmosphere, fly across the solar system and join up together again.'

Pietro was worried. 'Are you sure you're all right? You're not dying, are you? You're not going to leave me in here on my own?'

'No, don't worry. I'm different. Look.' He did a pirouette.

'I haven't got a single blotch on my body, and I've never felt better in my life. I'm imbued with grace. There's a small number of chosen people whom God spares and whose job is to found the human race anew. I'm a bard. My mission is to tell the story of the end and the new beginning. And you're going to be my assistant.'

The food was beginning to run low, and Patrizio decided to ration it. As soon as darkness fell, the two of them would lie down among the soft toys on Pietro's blue camp bed. His breath reeking of alcohol, Patrizio would tell him tales of hamster armies fighting against ancient Egyptian gods. Or whistle Queen's 'We Are The Champions' to him.

One morning Pietro woke up to find Patrizio sitting there staring at him. He'd changed his T-shirt and shaved. The bedroom door was open.

'Good morning, assistant. Did you sleep well? Today we're going back into the world. A bard can't tell his story if he's locked up in a room.'

The little boy trotted out to see his mother. She wasn't in her bedroom, or in the living room. He went out into the stairwell and found her lying on her back on the landing. Swollen and covered with flies. He shrank back against the wall, covering his eyes with his hands.

Patrizio picked him up. 'You see what happens to a body when the soul leaves it? It becomes smelly. Food for worms and flies. You mustn't cry. That thing there isn't your mother. Your mother has been set free. Right now she's flying over Alpha Centauri.'

'What about Papa? Where's my papa?' sobbed the little boy.

'Same thing. He's gone too. His atoms have merged with your mother's in a world of perfection.'

They found Annarita still alive, lying on a double bed. The virus had shrivelled her into a panting little skeleton. Pietro went up to her and stroked her hair. She opened and closed her mouth like a fish, her eyes veiled by a grey patina.

Patrizio put his ear to her lips. 'She's asking us to help her.' He took the little boy into the living room and sat him down on the sofa. 'That sick body is keeping Annarita's soul prisoner. We must set her free. In the end she'd manage it on her own, but she could suffer for a long time yet, and we don't want her to suffer, do we?'

The little boy sat in silence, with his head bowed, then looked at Patrizio. 'Are you going to kill her?'

Patrizio sat down beside him. 'Have you ever seen those videos of wild animals when they're released? Sometimes the gamekeepers open their cages, but the animals don't go out, and they have to drive them out with sticks. Do you know why they don't go out? Because they're scared of freedom. It's the same with the soul.' Patrizio rippled his stubby fingers as if writing on a keyboard. 'The soul, that mysterious essence – that particle of God that has made your aunt's flesh live – is frightened by the idea of leaving the body. But as soon as it does, it'll feel an infinite joy. We're going to be the gamekeepers. Do you understand? We're going to set her free.'

The little boy nodded.

Patrizio looked around. The sun was cutting the living room in two and the dust was shimmering in the musty air, making everything golden. 'Where do you keep the plastic bags?'

'In the kitchen. Under the sink.'

'Go and get two. Without any holes in them.'

Patrizio stood at the head of the bed over Annarita's shrunken skull, clutching two plastic bags, one inside the other. He looked at his little assistant who was standing beside the mattress, holding his aunt's hand. 'Now I'm going to put it over her head. She'll struggle. I want you to jump on her and hold her down; use all the strength you have. You mustn't let go.'

The little boy nodded, seriously.

'When your aunt's soul leaves her body, it'll pass through you; it'll live for a few more seconds inside your body. You'll feel it slip through you, like a caress. That'll be her way of saying goodbye. Are you ready?'

Pietro climbed up onto the bed, lay on top of the dying woman and put his arms round her. 'Ready.'

It didn't take his aunt long to die.

Patrizio, dripping with sweat, took a deep breath. 'Did you feel her go?'

'Yes.'

'What was it like?'

'It was nice.'

Annarita Lo Capo was the first. Over the next few days the two liberators of souls dealt with all the dying people in Via Aleramo, then in the rest of Vita. They went out early in the morning and came home at dusk. They proceeded in order, according to the house numbers. Often they had to break down doors, climb up walls of buildings. The sick people had locked themselves in for fear of being burgled. There were still quite a number who were teetering between life and death. The few adults who could still walk would take them to their dying relatives. The notary Botta's Ferrari 458, which Patrizio drove, shattering the silence of the village, was often chased by gangs of orphans.

The double-bag method worked; the only trouble was that sometimes the liberatees, as they called them, would go into convulsions, and Pietro would be thrown onto the floor. So the two perfected their immobilisation techniques, strapping patients down onto their beds with bungee cords before the little boy lay on top of them.

One day Patrizio decided to extend their range of action to a hamlet near Vita. They parked the Ferrari outside a bar and got out armed with plastic bags and bungee cords. The road was straight, with a row of two-storey buildings on either side. The continuity of the buildings was broken by small fenced gardens planted with palm and lemon trees. A pack of stray dogs slipped away between the houses as soon as they saw them.

'We've got to kill those brutes. They go into the houses and eat the dead.' Patrizio went back to the Ferrari, took out a shotgun and loaded it. 'One of these days I'm going to teach you how to use this.'

The virus had cleaned out the flats; they found nothing but corpses. Patrizio flopped dejectedly down on a sofa. 'Our job will soon be done.'

'What will we do then?' asked Pietro, toying with the still hands of an old grandfather clock.

'We'll go to Palermo, then onto Paris.' Patrizio turned and reached out over the back of the sofa to take a box of chocolates from a table. His T-shirt rode up, and his trousers slid down over his buttocks, revealing a red blotch. Pietro had to catch hold of the clock to stop himself falling over. He wondered if Patrizio knew he had the blotches. He'd always said he was immune, that he would never fall ill.

'Would you like one?' The young man held out the box, after wolfing down three *gianduiotti*.

Pietro shook his head.

'What's the matter? I've never heard you say no to sweets before.' And with his teeth stained with chocolate, he unwrapped a nougat.

The little boy bit his lip, swallowed and, with the little breath he had in his body, whispered: 'You've got some blotches.'

Patrizio jumped to his feet, grabbed him by the T-shirt and lifted him up in the air as if he was made of cloth. 'What did you say?' His mouth, too small for his big round face, was trembling, and his wild eyes had sunk back between his under-eye shadows and his bristly eyebrows. '*What* did you say?' He raised his fist. It was the first time he'd ever laid hands on the little boy. 'Where?'

Pietro closed his eyes. 'On your back.'

Patrizio let go of him and went over to a large mirror with a mahogany frame. He took off his T-shirt, then had a long look at himself, breathing in through his nose. He pulled down his trousers. His hairy white buttocks, too, were covered with red blotches.

The little boy had retreated into a corner of the living room. Patrizio looked at him for a few moments, then pointed to the door. 'Go.'

'Where?'

'Away. Go away.'

Pietro burst into tears and didn't move.

'You've got to go away. At once,' barked the fat man. He picked up a glass lamp from the side table and smashed it on the floor.

Pietro slid his back down the wall and clasped his legs between his arms.

'Do what you like, then.' Patrizio sat on the sofa, picked up the shotgun, stuck the barrel in his mouth, put his thumb on the trigger and looked at him.

Pietro covered his eyes with his knees and his ears with his hands. He tried to think about something pleasant. Him and his father on the Laverda. That time they'd stopped by a lagoon as flat as a table with mounds of white salt rising up out of it. In the distance there were some pink birds with S-shaped necks, banana-like beaks and legs so thin they could have been billiard cues.

'Come on, get up.' A powerful hand clamped round his arm.

'Where are we going?'

'I'm taking you home.'

The assistant followed his master, who marched out with his legs wide apart, the shotgun over his shoulder.

They didn't speak in the car. Patrizio drove fast, and Pietro shut his eyes every time they approached a bend. They pulled up sharply outside the house in Via Aleramo, leaving thick skid marks on the road.

The young man opened the door. 'Get out.'

'Where are you going?'

'Get out.'

'Can I come with you?'

'I said, get out.'

The Ferrari roared off, scaring flocks of rooks out of the trees.

He didn't come back.

Pietro joined the other children of the village. They all lived in the school. There were about thirty of them, boys and girls, aged between five and thirteen. They played football in the playground, slept on the big mattresses in the gym and ransacked houses in search of food.

One day Pietro and two other boys decided to venture out to a discount store on the main road outside the village, where rumour had it there was still some Coca-Cola. The store was a concrete box in the middle of an expanse of asphalt.

One of his companions pointed at something. 'Look at that.'

A Ferrari, its bonnet rammed into a row of rubbish bins, one of its doors wide open.

'You go on, I'll join you later,' said Pietro.

Patrizio was sitting in the driver's seat, surrounded by empty beer cans and a sickening smell of excrement. His arms were covered with blotches and bruises, his stomach sagged like a punctured football. His double chin, formerly pudgy, now drooped down, greasy and yellowish, over a swollen neck. Eyes as opaque as marrons glacés stared at a windscreen spattered with dry vomit. A cavernous wheezing sound came from his open mouth.

Pietro was amazed he was still alive. He touched his shoulder. 'Patrizio. Patrizio, can you hear me? It's Pietro.'

Patrizio closed his eyelids, but his face remained expressionless. 'How are you doing, assistant?'

Pietro swallowed. 'I'm fine . . . What about you?'

Something, perhaps a smile, ran across the thin lips covered with sores and scabs. 'You haven't got two plastic bags, have you?'

12

They'd been on the road for four days.

Before leaving, they'd pulled Pietro's body up to the road with ropes, loaded him onto a supermarket trolley and pushed it down to the beach. There they'd dug a hole in the sand, buried him and overturned a boat on top.

Every now and then Anna would turn round to look for him, but see only Astor shuffling along in her wake and Fluffy sniffing at the sides of the road. Then she'd clutch the pendant and squeeze it so hard the points of the starfish dug into her flesh.

Pietro had exploded in her heart, and thousands of splinters were tearing through her veins.

There was so much talk about love in her mother's books. Now she understood what it was.

To know what it was, you had to lose it.

Love was losing someone.

Without Pietro the world had become threatening again. Silence, once her comforting companion, was now deafening and painful. It had been so stupid, the way he'd died, his long agonies, and she couldn't find any meaning in it.

It was as if someone watching her from above was writing her story, inventing ever crueller ways of making her suffer. Pushing her further and further, to see when she'd finally collapse. They'd taken her father and mother and left her alone with a little boy to bring up. They'd arranged for her to meet Pietro, made him indispensable to her, then taken him away from her. The truth was she was running along a fixed path, like a hamster in a wheel. The idea that she could choose whether to turn right or left was just an illusion.

She remembered something Pietro had said to her many times. 'This world doesn't exist. It's a nightmare we can't wake up from.'

★

It was about a hundred kilometres to Messina now. Another three or four days at most, she reckoned. Under her feet the never-changing autostrada, on either side the slow, monotonous landscape, broken only by an interminable series of tunnels.

She turned towards Astor. Head drooping, he was trailing a stick on the ground. Talking to him had become difficult; words were too heavy for utterance.

'Are you all right?'

He gazed blankly at the green slope which ran down towards the sea in the morning haze.

'Answer me when I speak to you.'

Astor puffed out his cheeks, folded his arms and ran on ahead, stamping his feet.

He always seemed to be sulky. If she scolded him, he'd run away and hide.

As if it was my fault.

She caught up with him and put her hand on his shoulder. 'Are you hungry?'

He shook his head.

'Well, I am.' She sat down at the side of the road and took out of the rucksack two tins of tuna, one tin of dog food and a bottle of water.

Fluffy sat down obediently, wagging his tail. Drool trickled down from the sides of his mouth. Anna poured the meat out onto the asphalt, and he devoured it, his body trembling.

She opened a can of tuna, poured off the surplus oil and started spooning it out with a knife.

Astor kept whacking the guardrail with the stick.

'Will you stop that?'

He pulled the hair at the back of his head.

She was worried. He'd started tearing his hair out and talking to himself. He'd have long conversations with himself in a made-up language, punctuated by exclamations and bursts of laughter. With Pietro, Astor had become talkative and sociable, and the long-haired lizards had disappeared. But now, since the accident, he'd retreated into his own world of little things – stones, insects, dead animals and sticks.

'Pietro had the Red Fever. He would have died anyway.' She tossed the tin into the gutter. 'We've got to keep going. We're still here, the two of us.'

He shook his head. 'The three of us.' He pointed at the dog.

Anna offered him the other tin. 'Are you sure you don't want any?'

'I'll have a bit,' said Astor.

How would he cope when she was no longer around? It was pointless writing in the exercise book for him; he'd never open it. He wouldn't even read the road signs.

She wasn't even sure he'd be capable of finding food for himself.

★

In the afternoon the rain started. Cold and relentless, out of a blanket of grey clouds. From the autostrada, which followed the sinuous line of the coast, they could see the rough sea, grey like the sky, foaming against black rocks far below. Soaking wet, they took a slip road down into a small village on a hillside under one of the autostrada's viaducts. A land-slide had come down onto the houses, filling streets and uprooting trees. Rivulets of rainwater had cut beds through the debris and ran down towards the beach, joining together in a torrent which melted into the sea, turning it ochre brown.

There was no sign of life here either.

They entered one of the few surviving buildings, a white cottage surrounded by agaves. The walls were black with soot and in the bedrooms the wallpaper hung down in thick mouldy strips. Not a single windowpane was intact, and there was a cold draught. In the kitchen they set fire to the units, hung up their clothes to dry and huddled round the flames to get warm. They had no food, but were so tired they fell asleep at once, the embers reddening their silhouettes in the darkness.

★

At dawn they set off again. It had stopped raining, but the clouds still hung there menacingly. After only ten kilometres they came to a collapsed viaduct. There was nothing left of it but two stumps. Below, a rain-swollen torrent ran between the piers. The paired wheels of an overturned articulated lorry protruded from the muddy waters.

They went down through a thick thorny wood which grew at the foot of the hill. The stream was too fast-flowing to be fordable; they had to go upstream to a bend where a fallen poplar formed a bridge. Anna led the way, balancing precariously on the trunk. Astor and Fluffy followed her on all fours.

The rain waited for them to get back onto the autostrada before starting again. They sheltered inside a Volvo parked in a lay-by. Its warning triangle was still standing nearby. Fluffy lay down on the back seat and Astor sat in the driver's seat. The car's interior filled with the sound of the rain, which drummed on the roof and poured down the windscreen.

Anna searched the luggage for something to eat, but the only thing even remotely connected with food was a book of recipes for pressure cookers. She chucked it out of the window. By the time the downpour finished it was too dark to start walking again, and they slept there, curled up on the seats.

During the night Anna woke up. She needed a pee. She got out and saw a light shining in the distance. Maybe a fire. When she got back into the car, she found Astor awake.

'I'm hungry,' he said.

'Don't think about it. We'll look for something tomorrow. Go to sleep.'

'Why don't we go home?'

Anna hugged him. 'We've got to go to the mainland.'

'I liked it at home.'

'So did I. But you'll see: it'll be even better on the other side.'

'How do you know?'

'I just do. Now go to sleep.'

★

The sun had opened a gap through purple clouds, but the wind felt cold on their wet clothes.

Anna was beginning to have serious doubts about crossing the Strait. She had no idea how wide it was. As wide as a river? A sea? And how were they going to cross it? By boat?

They reached the slip road to Patti. Rising up to the right were some low, barren hills. To the left, beyond a strip of green land crowded with roofs, lay the sea. They passed the remains of a burnt-out tollbooth and a column of abandoned cars, and started along the main road into the city.

When they'd gone a hundred metres, Anna stopped and turned round.

A low noise, like a rumble, was growing in intensity.

'Do you hear that?' she asked Astor.

He nodded and looked at his feet.

The asphalt was shaking as if an earthquake was starting. Some rooks rose up from a cedar.

Fluffy growled, baring his teeth and pricking up his one good ear.

A herd of cattle swept round the bend and came thundering down the road towards them.

Anna pulled her brother back behind the guardrail.

The mass of hide and horns passed by, hemmed in by the metal barriers. It lasted nearly a minute, then, in a cloud of dust, dozens of children appeared, running after the animals, brandishing sticks, shouting and whistling.

Astor gaped at his sister, then jumped back onto the road and mingled with the shrieking mass, with Fluffy following behind.

'Where's he going?' said Anna, and she too started running.

The herd ran down to the end of the road and into a car park, where a hundred or so other children were waiting, to steer them with their shouts towards the King Arthur shopping mall, a big pink building in the form of a castle, complete with battlements and four round towers at its corners.

Terrified, the cattle ran between two lines of children, who beat them with sticks. Without slowing down, they went through a row of open doors and into a dark tunnel, which led into the heart of the big mall. Kiosks advertising Fastweb, Sky and Super-Mop: the Magic Broom were knocked down by the animals to the thunder of hooves and the sound of mooing. Those at the sides ended up in the clothes shops, banging into empty display cases, smashing the windows of the Zecchino snack bar, skidding into the Bosphorus kebab house and upending counters, grills and tables. Others slipped over and were trampled. Behind them, thin arms waved torches which threw gleams on the signs for Big Burger, the shops and the Wurstelleria Liebe. Lamed, wounded and terrified, the cattle found themselves at the end of the tunnel on a huge circular balcony. In front of them the balustrade was missing; on either side two flaming barricades made escape impossible.

One after another, without even slowing down, the cattle leapt into the void, like the mammoths driven over cliffs by primitive human beings. The only difference was that, after a flight of some fifteen metres, they landed not in the frozen undergrowth of the Pleistocene, but on the tables of the restaurant, The Trawler, crashing like living bombs onto a big glass tank which had once housed a pair of small blue sharks, and onto a boat that served as a display stand for fresh fish.

Anna reached the end of the tunnel, befuddled with smoke and dust. Gasping, she looked down from the balcony.

Below her was a heap of cows in their death throes, gashed by horns, their backs broken and their heads crushed. Many had died on impact, others writhed on top of their companions. A stench of excrement, blood and petrol rose out of the mass. An army of children covered in filthy rags cheered from the balconies and escalators. Some had painted their faces with black stripes, and all them – male and female – had long hair that reached halfway down their backs.Some were crippled, others blind, others disfigured with scars.They shouted, beat their hands on their chests and stamped their feet louder and louder, drowning the piercing screams of the animals. When the room was filled with deafening noise, those who were below started climbing the mountain of flesh and bludgeoning the animals that were still alive, urged on by the spectators on the terraces.

They're all so small . . .

Anna's heart leaped in her chest.

Astor!

From the smoke that flooded the tunnel, unrecognisable

figures emerged and blended together. Anna looked for her brother, pushing her way through the bodies, tripping over marble benches. But in the darkness everyone looked alike.

She circled round the columns of the lifts and elbowed her way towards the stairs.

Astor was leaning over, looking down and stroking his chin.

She shook his arm. 'You must stay with me, do you hear? You must stop running away!' And she hugged him tight.

He was trembling with excitement. 'Did you see that? Did you see what they did? They drove them over.'

'You weren't even listen—'

Fluffy's barks exploded in the tunnel. Squashed against the window of a mobile-phone shop, hackles raised, he was showing his teeth. A small group of children were pointing sharpened sticks at him.

Anna ran over to him. 'He's friendly. Leave him alone.' She gestured to them to calm down, but one boy, bolder than the others, tried to hit Fluffy, who leaped forward, knocked him over and sank his teeth into his arm.

Anna grabbed the dog by the neck and pulled him back.

Those around them, excited and scared, shouted, grunted and ground their teeth like a crowd of macaques, threatening them with their spears, while the unfortunate boy got to his feet, clutching his elbow.

'Astor! Astor, where are you?' shouted Anna, holding the dog.

Astor slipped through the group and joined her.

'Make him sit, at once.'

He pushed Fluffy's haunches down on the ground and threw his arms round him.

'Stroke him. These guys will kill us.' Anna raised her hands. 'Look, he's not aggressive.'

The group parted to allow the passage of a skinny little blonde girl, who gazed at the three of them, holding her arms out in front of her like a preacher. The others fell silent and stepped back. A pair of green-framed sunglasses covered most of her face. Her thin legs emerged from some tattered booties; above them, a tartan skirt and a dirty fur coat.

With a forced smile, Anna stroked Fluffy's head. 'He's a good dog.'

'Good?' said the little girl, unconvinced, and pointed to the boy who'd been bitten on the arm. 'Bad.'

'No, no. Good. Good dog.'

The little blonde girl went over to Fluffy. Around her the hunters were ready to plunge their spears into the animal. Without hesitating, she reached out her hand towards the Maremma's head.

Anna shut her eyes, sure he was going to bite it off, but instead he peered at her with his big clear eyes, stretched out his neck and sniffed her.

The little girl retreated a step, put her fingers to her nose and looked around, amused. 'Good,' she said to the others, who were looking at her, holding their breath. 'Good.'

They all burst out laughing. Only the poor wretch who'd been bitten laughed with a little less conviction.

Anna realised that those children were too small to know that dogs had once been pets. Or perhaps they'd forgotten.

She felt old.

*

The hunters of Patti organised a barbecue in the car park. Some dragged the carcasses out, some cut the meat, while others fed the fires with clothes, furniture and pallets.

A light breeze swept plastic bags, paper and leaves across the asphalt, as the sun, an orange oval, sank behind the barren hills.

The columns of smoke attracted other children who arrived in the mall alone or in small groups. As darkness fell, the area was swarming with black figures lined up by the bonfires, waiting for a portion of meat.

Astor and Anna queued up with the others. They hadn't eaten for two days, and the smell of roast meat made them faint. Fluffy, too, was impatient. They'd tied a rope round his neck and were keeping a tight hold on him. At first he'd tried to wriggle free, digging in his paws and shaking his head, then he'd accepted it.

Thanks to him, Anna and Astor had become the evening's central attraction. Everyone, keeping a safe distance, admired them, commenting with guttural noises and grimaces on the size of the beast who stood so docilely beside his owners. Astor looked around, standing up straight and feigning insouciance. Anna felt like laughing. It was the first time she'd seen her brother try to look cool.

When their turn finally came, they received three enormous pieces of meat, charred and dripping with fat, but still bloody inside.

They sat down on a concrete kerb and devoured them in silence.

'What's it like?' Anna asked her brother.

Astor, his mouth full, mumbled something incomprehensible, rolling his eyes.

The girl searched for the starfish under her T-shirt. She pulled it out and turned it over between her fingers. For unpleasant things she could do without Pietro – she could handle them herself – but now that it was a question of celebrating, laughing, enjoying a steak, his absence became more painful. She remembered the time they'd thrown the smelly octopus off the balcony, and felt like laughing.

Astor nudged her with his elbow. 'I want some more.'

'Let's go and see . . .' She was about to stand up when the little blonde girl with green glasses appeared in front of her. She had a torch in one hand, and in the other a big charred shin of meat, which she held out towards them.

'Thank you,' said Anna, but the little girl threw it to Fluffy, who caught it in his teeth and tore off the meat, holding it with his forepaws.

The thin girl pointed at him. 'Good.'

'Good.' Anna wasn't sure whether she meant Fluffy or the meat.

The little blonde girl pointed at the dog. 'Mine?'

Anna knitted an eyebrow. 'What?'

'Mine.'

Anna tapped herself on the chest, with a forced smile. 'No, mine.'

The little girl stared at Fluffy. 'Dog good.'

'Good.'

'Dog mine.'

Anna pointed at herself. 'No. Dog mine.'

Astor whispered anxiously in his sister's ear. 'She wants Fluffy.'

'Smile.'

The little boy flashed an over-friendly smile, displaying his lopsided teeth. 'Dog ours.'

The little blonde girl took off her glasses. Her right eye was glassy and looked to one side.

'Dog ours?' She walked away, scratching her head and repeating: 'Dog ours? Dog mine?'

Anna pulled Fluffy with the lead. 'Let's get going,' she said to Astor.

'Where to?'

'Out of here, before she makes up her mind.'

Astor looked around. 'What about the meat?'

'Forget about it. Get moving. Quickly. No, slowly. Calmly. As if everything was perfectly normal.'

They walked a short distance, then, as soon as the darkness swallowed them up, they started running.

★

It took them two days to get from Patti to Messina, walking from dawn to dusk. The first night they spent in a small block of flats beside the autostrada. The ground floor was occupied by a job centre, but on searching through the kitchen drawers in a first-floor flat, they found some mouldy stock cubes, which they crushed and dissolved in water. Then they pulled the curtains off the windows and used them as blankets.

On the last day of the journey a cold wind was blowing, the sky was blue and the air so clear that everything seemed nearer.

The autostrada ran over viaducts linking one wooded hill to another and through dark tunnels.

Closer to the city, an unbroken queue of traffic blocked all the lanes. The cars were still full of luggage. Searching through suitcases in an SUV, they found some heavy pullovers, clean T-shirts and windproof jackets.

Finally, at the top of a long slope, the sight they'd been waiting for all these months spread out in front of them. The Strait.

They both started jumping up and down and twirling round and round, hand in hand. 'We've done it!' They climbed up onto the roof of a lorry to get a better view.

The island ended in a strip of tall buildings overlooking a big harbour and a stretch of blue sea, beyond which there arose a chain of dark mountains. The mainland. The two shores were so close to each other, the channel between them seemed no wider than a river.

Anna had imagined it as immense, impossible to cross, but now, looking at it, she thought she could swim it.

They ran the rest of the way, stopping only to get their breath back. They left the autostrada along a slip road and went on down suburban streets which progressively filled with blocks of flats, shops, filling stations and traffic lights.

Messina was a solid mass of cars, even in the narrow streets of the city centre, and yet, closer to the sea, you didn't feel the same sensation of death and anguish that had been so strong in Palermo. Here, nature was taking over the city again. Saplings and hawthorn bushes grew in cracks in the asphalt, avenues and pavements were covered with earth and leaves, grass and wheat were putting down roots. Climbing plants spread their blooms over the façades of apartment blocks. There were animals everywhere: flocks of sheep grazing beside monuments, bearded goats climbing over rubbish bins, flocks of birds spilling out of windows, herds of horses and foals threading in and out between cars. Only the harbour, sealed off by coils of barbed wire and surrounded by army vehicles, recalled the violence of the days of quarantine, but the wind brought the briny smell of the sea, and the waves beyond the harbour walls were crested with foam.

It was late, and they decided to wait until the next day before attempting the crossing. They searched shops and supermarkets for something to eat, but without success. Exhausted, they entered an old aristocratic palazzo with a marble doorway, a porter's lodge and a lift in an iron cage. At the very top they found an open door. The brass nameplate said: 'The Gentili Family'.

The attic was full of pictures, frames, furniture made of dark wood and armchairs with flowery patterns. The windows looked out onto the promenade. There were two skeletons in the bedroom. Black membranous clusters of bats hung from the pelmets and crystal chandeliers in the living room. The wall cabinets of the kitchen were empty, but in the dresser they found some bottles of Schweppes, peanuts, pistachios and a shrivelled *pandoro* cake, which they shared with the dog.

They lay down on the sofas in the living room in front of the television screen.

Astor fell asleep at once. Anna kept dropping off and waking up again, out of a tangle of dim, disturbing dreams.

She lay on the velvet cushions, breathing through her mouth, listening to the waves breaking against the quay.

She knew nothing about Calabria. What would she find there? Were some Grown-ups really still alive there? Maybe they wouldn't let them come ashore.

Go away! We don't want you here! You're infected.

And she thought fondly back to her home, the wood, Torre Normanna. Those four years of solitude, the make-believe Christmases, the roads she'd travelled along and the thousands of decisions she'd had to make with no help from anyone else.

One way or the other, everything was going to change, starting from tomorrow.

The air in the room was musty. Opening a window, she went out onto the balcony and let the wind blow her hair. Then she leaned on the railing in the dark starless night, shivering. Calabria was switched off.

Don't hope for too much.

Then she saw a small red light in the distance, going on and off at regular intervals. As though someone had been listening to her thoughts.

A signal.

She stared at it, rubbing her arms. Who was capable of doing such a thing?

Only Grown-ups.

She went back indoors and sat down on the edge of the sofa by her brother. He was sleeping with his face pressed against the back of the seat, the lines of the material imprinted on his cheek. She called out to him softly.

'Astor . . . Astor . . .'

He rubbed his eye: 'What's the matter?'

Anna shrugged her shoulders. 'I love you.'

He yawned and ran his tongue over his lips.

'Were you dreaming?' she asked him.

'Yes.'

'What about?'

Astor thought for a moment. 'Hotdogs with wurstel.'

Anna took a deep breath. 'But do you love me?'

He nodded, scratching his nose.

'Move over, then.'

Lying beside her brother, she finally managed to get to sleep.

13

It was the right kind of day.

The wind had dropped, the sky was clear, the sea calm, and the mainland was there.

They explored the docks, but there were no boats on the quays. Further out, at the harbour mouth, near the breakwaters, rusty hulls, propellers and funnels of sunken ferries protruded from the water. Colonies of seagulls had made their homes there, covering them with guano.

They walked along the promenade, which was divided in two by a flyover. To the left, a long row of tall modern buildings looked out onto stumps of palm trees, lamp posts and a strip of pebble beach eaten away by the sea. But there were no boats there either. What had happened to them? Had they all been used to escape from the island?

The mainland, which had seemed so near the day before, was becoming unattainable, and the city that lay like an opalescent strip below the mountains on the other side of the sea, just a mirage.

Anna sat down on a bench, disheartened.

It was impossible to swim across. And even if they found a dinghy, she didn't know how to row. They wandered on, Astor talking to himself, Fluffy peeing on lamp posts to mark out his territory.

A series of filling stations gave way to a row of low buildings: The Sailor's Tavern, The Squill Restaurant, Scylla Bar.

Behind the salt-encrusted windows were dusty tables, piles of chairs and empty fish tanks.

Astor went down a sandy passageway between two restaurants and Anna followed him. Behind the buildings, on a tiny promontory, a funfair was rusting among the eucalyptuses. A roundabout with hanging seats. Dodgems. A hall full of wrecked video games.

They'd seen others like it on their journey, and every time Astor had got into the little cars and tried desperately to start them up, then asked Anna to tell him what they were like with their coloured lights, music and other children. But this one he walked straight through without a word.

The little wood ended in a desolate car park bordered by a row of burnt-out rubbish bins. The long space looked out onto a stony beach, covered with litter and salt-stained branches.

'Come on . . . There's nothing here,' shouted Anna.

Astor jumped over the wall at the side of the car park and disappeared from her view.

'Astor! I'm going . . .' she said, with a snort of exasperation.

But Astor shouted: 'Anna! Anna! Come here. Quick!'

★

Its name was *Tonino II* and it wasn't exactly a boat, it was a pedalo: red and white, with a tiller, plastic seats and a slide in the middle with a ladder that ended beyond the stern. Astor had found it under a tarpaulin.

It was perfect. You didn't have to row, only pedal. Anna knew how to do that. And her brother could help her too.

At last, a stroke of luck.

They'd have to push it into the water, but that wouldn't be hard; they could put some branches underneath it and roll it down.

She planted a kiss on Astor's forehead; he wiped it off in disgust, gazing at the sea. 'How long will it take us?'

'A long time.'

*

What did they need for the crossing?

Water-wings for Astor. No, lifebelts would be better. Life jackets would be better still. Water. Food. They'd be cold – so warmer garments. A change of clothes. And those yellow jackets for the rain. In short, a lot of things.

The shops on the sea front all had their shutters down and the ones that had been broken open were empty. In a bathing establishment they found some orange lifebelts and some towels behind a cabin. They broke a window of the Squill Restaurant and, searching in the larder, found three tins of sea urchin meat and two bottles of Chardonnay. They couldn't find any oilskins, but they took two trolley cases full of pullovers and trousers from a car boot, and some transparent plastic macs from a lorry.

They finished kitting themselves out with the sun still high in the sky, and put the luggage in the bows.

Moving the pedalo down to the shoreline was more complicated than expected; it was heavy and the branches wouldn't roll on the big stones. By the time they got the bow into the water they were exhausted.

The sea was calm but the wind blew cold spray in their faces.

They put on two cardigans and two pairs of trousers each, and the plastic macs on top. They looked like a pair of puppets wrapped in cellophane.

Ready?

Ready.

Astor had sat down in his seat and was blowing raspberries, imitating the sound of an engine.

'Say goodbye to Sicily,' said Anna.

The little boy closed his hand. 'Ciao.'

At least he wouldn't miss anything.

The dog was sitting at the end of the beach looking at them, his good ear pricked up.

'Come on, Fluffy. Quick.'

Fluffy didn't move.

'Go and get him, Astor.'

Astor puffed out his cheeks and ran towards the dog. 'Come on, Fluffy.' But when he tried to approach him, Fluffy dodged away to one side. 'Come here.' He tried again without success. 'Stop! Stay!' Hands on hips, he turned towards his sister. 'He won't come.'

They tried as hard as they could to catch him, in a three-way game of tag, but the dog circled round them, tail between his legs, ready to accelerate away as soon as they came anywhere near him.

'What are we going to do?' asked Astor, breathing hard.

Anna shrugged. 'I just don't know.'

She'd thought of everything, except Fluffy. She'd assumed he wouldn't have any problems getting on the boat; wasn't it really just a tiny piece of land? 'I've got an idea.' She took a tin of sea urchin meat out of the rucksack, opened it and showed it to the dog. 'Mmm . . .' she said, dipping her finger in the orange paste. 'Do you want some?' It was really revolting.

The dog took a few cautious steps towards the food and Anna, holding her breath, took one step towards him. 'Try it. It's delicious.' She poured the pulp out onto a rock and stepped back. Fluffy approached warily, sniffing the air, then put out his tongue and started licking.

As one, they both jumped on him. Astor held him down while Anna put a rope round his neck. 'Gotcha!'

They started pulling him towards the shoreline, but the dog dug his paws in and shook his head, whimpering, until with a sharp tug he broke free of the noose and ran off into the car park.

'He'll never get onto the boat.' Anna threw the rope on the ground and looked at the sky. 'I've had enough. It's getting late. We're leaving him here.'

Astor gazed at her in disbelief. 'We're not taking him with us?'

'No.'

'Let's give him some sleeping pills.'

'There's no time. We've got to go. It'll be dark soon.'

'You want to leave him here?'

'Yes.'

The little boy fell on his knees. 'No.'

Anna went over to him and stroked his head. 'Listen to me. He'll never get on that boat. Even if we managed to force him, he'd jump in the water as soon as he got a chance. And if he jumped out into deep water, he'd drown.' Anna saw that the sun had been swallowed up by clouds. 'We must go.'

Astor dug his toes in between the rocks. 'Please . . . don't leave him.'

She crouched down in front of him. 'Fluffy has come with us this far. Nobody made him; he chose to follow us. Now he's decided not to come any further. If he wants to stay here, we can't do anything about it. He's free to do what he likes.' She gave a forced smile. 'He's a Sicilian dog; he'll survive.'

Astor sniffed. 'He's not a Sicilian dog. He's our dog.'

Anna held out her hand. 'Come on.'

He lowered his head, moaning: 'I'm not coming.'

'Please . . .'

The little boy slapped his palm on the ground. 'I'm staying with Fluffy.'

'Don't be silly.' She tried to grasp his hand.

He folded his arms. 'No.'

She looked at him in silence, then very calmly said: 'Come on.'

The little boy wound a tuft of his hair round his forefinger and pulled it. 'No. No. No.'

Anna bit her lip and clenched her fists.

Why was everything so difficult? They'd found the pedalo, the lifebelts, the clothes, but that stupid dog was scared of water, and now her brother was playing up too.

'You're coming!' she murmured, eyes closed.

Astor lowered his head. 'No. I'm not coming. I'm not coming. I'm not coming.'

At the third 'I'm not coming', anger swept through Anna, stiffening the muscles of her arm. She made one last desperate attempt to contain it, whispering: 'Astor, do as I say. Go to the boat. It's for the best.' But the answer was another no. 'That's it! I've had enough!' She seized her brother by the hair and dragged him bodily towards the pedalo, shouting, kicking, wriggling and trying to cling onto the rocks. 'Now get on the damned boat.' She grabbed him by the seat of his trousers and pushed him onto the sun lounger, accidentally knocking his head against the handrail. Astor howled, eyes swollen and bloodshot, face flushed, nose running. Anna didn't hear and felt neither pity nor remorse. She wasn't going to let anyone stop her, let alone a neurotic dog.

Without looking back, she pushed the pedalo off, grazing her knees on the pebbles as she did so, and jumped in. She climbed over Astor like he was a sack of potatoes, sat down and started pedalling.

Fluffy's yelps were lost in the wind.

★

Anna pushed on the pedals while Astor cried. The pedalo advanced slowly through a maze of buoys.

After a few experiments she understood that if she pulled

the tiller to the left the boat went to the right, and vice versa.

Astor had stopped crying, but was still sobbing and sniffing. *He'll get over it.*

Once they reached the mainland he'd forget about Fluffy. We forget about everything. Everything passes. Mama. The house with the mulberry tree. Pietro. Now there was only her and him.

And if he doesn't get over it, who cares.

The current was carrying the boat out to sea. Anna had no way of knowing how long it would take them to get to the other side. She took another swig of wine and concentrated on the pedals.

'Anna! Anna!' Her brother squeezed her shoulder hard and started jumping up and down. 'Anna! Look!'

She jumped to her feet and turned round. A little white dot was appearing and disappearing among the waves.

At first she thought it was a buoy, then a floating seagull, then she saw her dog's head.

'It's not possible,' she whispered. 'How did he do it? We're too far out.' A wave of heat spread over her throat. 'What a bitch I am.'

Astor sat down beside her and started pedalling. 'Come on, quick.'

Anna pulled the tiller and the pedalo went into a slow curve, leaving a white wake behind it. They pedalled away with gritted teeth, clutching the armrests, trying not to lose sight of him. He was there, but a moment later he wasn't.

'Where is he?'

'I don't know . . .'

'There he is! There he is!' Astor pointed at the dog's head, which had re-emerged.

They started pedalling again, even harder than before, though their legs were stiff with the effort.

'Hold on, hold on. Please, Fluffy, hold on,' begged Anna.

But the boat, going against the current, was advancing too slowly. The Maremma was drowning in front of them, flapping his legs in the spray.

'Fluffy! Fluffy!' they shouted.

They were close. For a moment they saw the dog's muzzle: he was gasping, eyes popping out of his head, then the sea sucked him down.

'Don't stop,' Anna shouted to her brother. 'Keep pedalling.' And she jumped onto the bow, leaning out with her chest and arms. A white mass was coming fast towards her, sliding along below the surface like a ghost. She reached out and grabbed his coat with both hands, but the current drove him under the boat. Searching for some hole to plant her foot in, but not finding one, she overbalanced and fell into the sea. She passed under the pedalo, swallowing water, banging her head against the hull, but didn't let go. Holding the dog with one hand, she managed to grab hold of the ladder with the other. Half-drowned and stretched as taut as a hawser between Fluffy and the boat, she held on until the impetus eased. Astor, in trying to help her, slipped on the wet sun lounger and nearly fell into the sea himself. He got up again and grabbed his sister by the wrist.

They tried to hoist the dog onto the slide at the bow, Anna pushing from below, Astor pulling him by the legs from above. He seemed to be made of lead.

'Hold him, hold him,' said Anna and climbed up to her brother's side, gasping. Together, by pushing against the handrail with their feet, they managed to pull Fluffy onto the boat.

Anna was exhausted, shivering with cold, and could hardly breathe. She brought up seawater and Chardonnay. Astor's chest was heaving.

They shook the dog, trying to revive him, but the head, with its open, glassy eyes, bounced limply on the fibreglass surface.

'Is he dead?' stammered Astor.

Anna started thumping the dog on the chest, shouting: 'No, he's not dead.'

This animal was like a cat; he had nine lives. He'd survived the tortures inflicted by the scrap merchant's son, fire, fights to the death with other dogs, hunger and thirst, wounds, infections, and now he was dying like this.

Anna bent double, hiding her face in her hands. 'It's my fault. It's all my fault.'

Astor cried, his mouth buried in the Maremma's neck. The sea splashed and shook them, pulling towards the coast of Calabria.

Tock. Tock. Tock.

Fluffy's tail beat feebly on the sundeck.

He hadn't used up his seventh life yet.

★

'I'm going to marry this guy.' Anna was hugging Fluffy, who lay panting next to a puddle of drool and water. 'Is it possible to marry a dog?'

Astor spread his arms. 'I don't know.'

Trembling, she planted a kiss on the Maremma's nose and whispered in his good ear. 'Forgive me. You're my darling. And I'm a complete shit.'

'I want to marry him too,' said the little boy.

'Okay. We'll both marry him.'

Her teeth chattering, Anna took off her wet things, rubbed her skin hard with the towel and put on her spare clothes.

She poured some wine into Astor's cupped hands, but Fluffy didn't like it. A few moments later, as if nothing had happened to him, as if he hadn't just been resuscitated, he stood up of his own accord, shook himself a couple of times, staggered unsteadily forward and sat down at the bow like a figurehead.

Brother and sister started pedalling again, while the sun continued its westward descent. The current pushed them rapidly towards the land as the waves broke over the bow, splashing them with salty spray which dried on their faces like masks. Every now and again a flying fish emerged from the water and glided into the distance.

They passed a large yellow buoy with solar panels and a small tower with a beacon emitting flashes of red light.

That's what I saw from the balcony.

As they drew nearer to the coast, they could make out empty beaches, breakwaters, and silent, lifeless houses and blocks of flats.

Anna didn't speak; a weight lay on her heart. During the journey, day after day, she'd been infected with hope, and had silently started to believe that Calabria was different.

★

They left the pedalo on a beach full of small boats heaped up one on top of the other and set off towards the city.

They crossed a field of olive trees, passing the gate of a villa with a weed-filled swimming pool. They walked between rows of half-built blocks of flats with exposed brickwork and rusty reinforcement bars protruding from columns. They forded a putrid marsh streaked with coloured strips of petrol.

In the distance, supported by huge piers rammed into the mountainside, ran the autostrada. They came to a piazza where there was a little bar whose sign had fallen down, a looted mobile-phone shop and a big grey concrete church from whose pediment the mosaic had broken off. They went up a wide street full of burnt-out shops and bars. A lorry lay on its side in the middle of the road, its nose as one with the crumpled remains of a Smart car.

'Where are the Grown-ups?' Astor complained.

Anna didn't reply.

A black and white cat materialised from nowhere and crossed the road. Fluffy raced off.

The cat darted and swerved, but the dog kept after it, trying to bite its behind. With a prodigious leap the cat sprang onto the roof of an Opel. From there it flew towards a shop and slipped under its shutter, which was raised half a metre. The Maremma followed.

'Cats again.' Anna was incredulous. 'Wasn't he on his last legs?'

Faint, muffled barks came from inside.

'Fluffy! Fluffy! Come out of there,' Astor called him.

'Could you go and get him?'

Astor sat down on the pavement, rubbing his calves. 'You go.'

Raising her eyes to the sky, Anna took the torch out of the rucksack, switched it on and ducked under the shutter.

The large rectangular room had no windows. The walls were hung with surfboards, photographs of singers, T-shirts, boots and old jeans. In one corner there was a red telephone box and a pinball machine. The shelves, made of wooden planks, were empty, the clothes scattered on the floor. She could hear Fluffy barking furiously, but couldn't see him. She went over to the counter, which was decorated with rows of padlocks. The cash register lay on the floor. Behind, a steep narrow staircase led down into the storeroom.

Anna pointed the torch, went down the stairs and entered a cube-shaped room; skylights on the ceiling provided a murky light.

The Maremma was growling at the cat, now a bridge of fur looking down at him from its vantage point on a pile of boxes. Suddenly the dog leaped at it, bringing the boxes tumbling down. The cat flashed across a wall and disappeared up the stairs.

A blue box had fallen open on the floor in front of Anna. There was a pair of shoes inside it.

She picked one of them up and squeezed it between her fingers. A pleasant smell of fresh rubber and leather. Her tongue felt thick in her mouth; she moved it, catching a bitter taste. She shone the torch on the label.

Adidas Hamburg. Made in China. US 8 ½ UK 8 FR 42.

Three black stripes, yellow suede vamp, nut-brown sole.

She sat back on her bottom, leaned forward and put her head against the cold tiles.

She tried to call Astor, but had lost her voice. She breathed out the air she'd held back in her lungs. The dog, the coat rack with the jackets, the water dispenser, the red fire extinguisher, the blue boxes, were all spinning around her.

'Anna. Are you down there?'

*

They opened all the boxes, searched all over the storeroom and upstairs in the shop. But there weren't any others.

Astor turned one of the shoes over in his hand, as if it wasn't real. Then he held it out to his sister. 'Put them on. Go on.'

Anna looked at him in silence, tears in her eyes, lips pressed tightly together. Slowly she took off her walking boots, wiped her feet with a vest, loosened the laces, pulled up the tongue of the shoe and put in her foot. Then she tied a double bow.

Her brother passed her the other one.

She tucked a lock of hair behind her ear. 'One each.'

*

They ducked out under the shutter, each wearing one over-sized Adidas and one of their old boots, and shuffled off, with Fluffy trotting beside them.

The sun had gone down behind the grey buildings, but the lower part of the sky still had its red glow.

A butterfly rose up from a carob tree, floating in the air against the wind. A gust carried it towards them. It brushed against Anna's hair and was pushed towards Astor, who reached out his hand; it paused for a moment on his palm, then resumed its uncertain flight. Then another appeared, and yet another, until they were surrounded by hundreds of wings, which filled the street in a black and yellow snowstorm.

Leaving the houses behind them, they started up the slip road towards the autostrada, which ran along a hillside stepped with vineyard terraces.

When they came to the tollbooth, Astor stopped, straightened his leg and looked at the shoe. 'What if it doesn't work if you only have one?'

Anna took hold of his hand and said: 'It doesn't matter.'

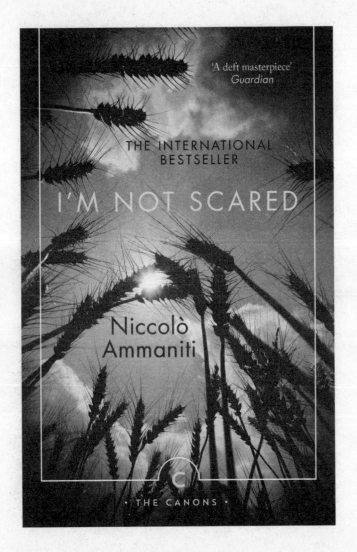

'A deft masterpiece'
Guardian

THE INTERNATIONAL
BESTSELLER

I'M NOT SCARED

Niccolò
Ammaniti

C

· THE CANONS ·

'The new Italian word for talent is Ammaniti'
The Times

CANON▍▍GATE

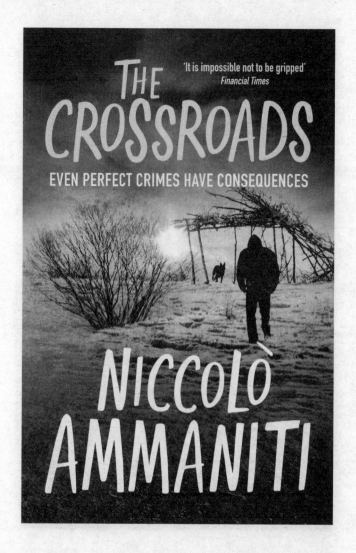

'It is impossible not to be gripped'
Financial Times

THE
CROSSROADS

EVEN PERFECT CRIMES HAVE CONSEQUENCES

NICCOLÒ
AMMANITI

'Energy and danger spray off it like water from a
choppy sea . . . Very hard to put down'
Guardian

CANON❙❙GATE

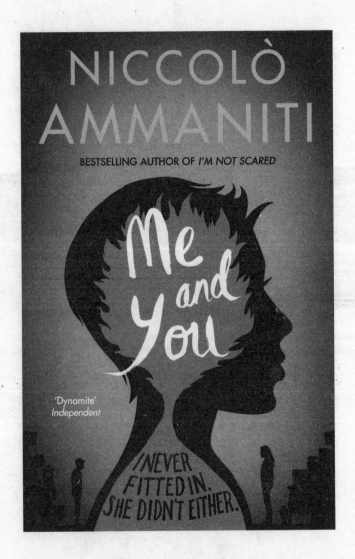

NICCOLÒ
AMMANITI

BESTSELLING AUTHOR OF *I'M NOT SCARED*

Me
and
You

'Dynamite'
Independent

I NEVER
FITTED IN.
SHE DIDN'T EITHER.

'Exuberant and audacious'
Observer

CANON‖GATE